I0772586

Reviews of
Don Johnston Novels

The Dar Lumbre Chronicles

"A clever extrapolation of today's sociopolitical pathologies to the next century . . . Ingenious narrative . . ."

— *Kirkus Reviews*

The Alamogordo Connection

"First contact is an intriguing hook, made more effective through believable details of carrying out scientific research and rain-forest trekking, bolstered by Johnston's background in biology, chemistry, and jungle survival."

— *Kirkus Reviews*

THE
ALAMOGORDO
CONNECTION

Don Johnston

Dedication and Special Thanks

This novel is dedicated to my family and friends.

My special thanks to Janice Stewart
for her proofreading and editing help.

PROLOGUE

At 4:00 a.m. on July 16, 2045, a sonic boom sounded over Alamogordo, New Mexico, and a shockwave rocked the city.

Jolted from a deep sleep, Dustin Rhodes threw back the cover and sat upright in bed. He stretched his arms and yawned. A moment later, still groggy, he swung his feet to the floor.

April turned toward him. "What is it, Dusty?"

"Did you feel the house shake?"

"Uh-huh. Was it an earthquake?"

"I heard a rumbling noise," Dusty said. "Must have been an aircraft. Maybe NatGov is testing another secret model."

April rolled over and sat on the edge of the bed beside Dusty. "It'll be hard to keep it secret if they wake the whole town while conducting a test."

Dusty glanced at the clock on the nightstand and stretched his arms again.

"It's too early to get up," April said.

"And too late to go back to sleep," Dusty added.

April leaned her head on Dusty's shoulder and said, "I smell roses."

"Strange," Dusty said, putting his arms around April. "We don't have a single rose in the house or yard."

Thirty-five miles south of Alamogordo, in a trailer house in Orogrande, Darien Segura got up at 6:00 a.m. and dragged into the kitchen. Still in rumpled pajamas, with disheveled hair and needing a shave, he opened his refrigerator and removed a coffee cartridge from the bag. He dropped the cartridge into the coffee maker. The machine gurgled and produced a cup of hot black liquid. Darien picked up the cup and sat down at the tiny breakfast table in the living-dining area.

With the third sip of black coffee, Darien returned to full consciousness and remembered the sonic boom which shook his trailer. He picked up the remote and pointed it toward the wall-mounted TV. The screen came to life and showed a line of olive drab Jeeps and Humvees forming a perimeter around the Trinity Site Monument. A black helicopter, with its spotlight sweeping the scene, circled overhead. Men and women in military fatigues stood at parade rest with their backs to the vehicles as they faced a small crowd gathering outside of a yellow *Do Not Cross* ribbon. Two ambulances, a fire truck, and a minivan from a TV station were parked single file along the road. Reporters and photographers milled around talking into recorders and filming videos, while first responders waited in readiness.

Darien watched intently as a news banner scrolled across the bottom of the TV screen:

METEORITE STRIKES NEAR TRINITY SITE

At the upper right of the screen, in a picture-in-picture square, an excited young Mescalero woman was reading the news. Darien clicked on the small square and it expanded to fill the screen as the woman read the news:

"Today is July 16, 2045, exactly 100 years after the first atomic bomb test. Two hours ago, a large meteorite landed near the Trinity Test Site obelisk marking Ground Zero. The impact kicked up a cloud of dust and sent shockwaves detectable for several hundred miles. Aided by a northwest wind, the dust cloud reached Alamogordo a short time ago. Those with allergies or other breathing difficulties are urged to stay inside. Initial chemical tests show no toxic compounds in the dust, although it has been reported to carry a faint floral aroma.

"Military personnel from Holloman Air Force Base and Fort Bliss have cordoned off the area until further notice. Residents are urged not to attempt to visit the site as all access roads have been barricaded, and private vehicles will not be allowed to pass. Stay tuned for further reports."

CHAPTER 1

Still mulling over the meteorite strike, Darien finished his coffee and placed the cup in the kitchen sink, which already contained most of his meager supply of mismatched and chipped dishes. His dishwasher had fizzled out three months ago, and he couldn't afford to get it repaired. Darien hated washing dishes by hand and was thinking about eating all of his meals at the nearby McDonald's. He passed the restaurant every day and thought he could survive indefinitely on selections from the All-Day Breakfast menu. He planned to stop by for a couple of sausage biscuits this morning on his way to work. Since it was Sunday, the McDonald's wouldn't be crowded this early.

The trailer house in the New Mexico desert was the only home that Darien could remember, but it wasn't actually his first home. Moreover, he hadn't always been Darien Noah Segura. For the first few weeks of his life, he'd been somebody of unknown origin without a name. As a newborn baby, he had been abandoned in the Darien Province of Panama. Missionaries found him beside a dim footpath leading into the jungle. He was lying in a hand-woven basket, dirty, naked, and covered with a ragged piece of cheese cloth to protect him from mosquitos. At the time, the couple who would become his adoptive parents, Lamech and Eve Segura, were seeking to adopt another baby to grow up with Rachel, their newly-adopted daughter. After completing a mountain of digital red tape, the missionaries brought him to the United States and the Seguras adopted him. They named him Darien Noah—Darien after the place he was discovered and Noah after the Biblical figure. He'd always believed that he had a sibling living in the jungles of Panama, and exploring his birthplace was at the top of his bucket list.

Darien's iTab sounded Dustin Rhodes' ringtone. Dusty was a fellow member of the local Amateur Astronomy Group, and Darien knew that he was calling to discuss the meteorite strike and would likely connect it to *Planet X* in some way. The two friends discussed astronomy frequently, but each had his own distinct viewpoint. Darien, an astronomy student, tried to focus on provable facts; however, Dusty's conversation always involved space aliens, ufology, lost planets, Hanger 51 legends, and the like. Dusty could work Planet X into any discussion. The tenth planet hypothesis had gained considerable interest lately, thanks to the newly-elected President, Rex Horn, admitting that he was a tenth planet junkie. In addition, a recent YouTube posting claimed that Chinese billionaires were secretly constructing a space ship to make an expedition to locate the hidden planet. Several Planet X societies had cropped up lately, and a couple of them were planning to incorporate as nonprofit religious institutions.

Darien touched the screen of his iTab. "Hey, Dusty. What's up."

"Did you see the news this morning?"

"I saw the broadcast from Trinity Site."

"There's more to the story than they're telling."

"Tell me quickly. I've got to leave for work in a couple of minutes."

"Did you get a good look at the meteorite?"

"Not really. It was almost completely buried, and the military vehicles were blocking the view."

"I enlarged the image," Dusty said. "The surface looks strange."

Darien shrugged. "It looked like ordinary iron to me."

"Not to me," Dusty said with conviction. "The surface was sort of . . . *faceted*."

"Like a stealth aircraft?"

"Uh-huh. Maybe it was designed to be invisible to radar."

"*Designed?*"

"I'm convinced that it was made by intelligent beings. Possibly it came from Planet X right here in our solar system," Dusty said.

Darien wasn't shocked by Dusty's bizarre statement. It was everyday conversation for his life-long friend.

"A similar thing happened over twenty years ago," Dusty continued. "I've read that eye witnesses back then said the meteorite looked manmade, but NatGov scoffed at the idea, so nothing came of it. "

"The strike twenty years ago wasn't near the Trinity Monument."

"I know, but it kicked up a dust cloud which reached Alamogordo, just like the meteorite did early this morning."

Darien glanced at his iTab clock and realized he didn't have time to go into a drawn-out discussion. "This is a great topic for our meeting Saturday night," he said. "I hope everybody comes."

"The guest speaker is Dr. Edward Pauling. He always draws a crowd."

"I have to go," Darien said. He had no doubt the meteorite strike would invigorate the tenth planet advocates, whether Dr. Pauling mentioned the subject or not. It didn't take a major event to get them worked up.

Astronomy had been Darien's first love as long as he could remember. His initial encounter with the subject occurred shortly before he was five years old. It was a near-religious experience. The day after his parents relocated the family trailer to La Luz, Darien was exploring the barren yard and found a fifth-grade science book half-buried in the desert sand. The first ten pages were torn out, but page eleven was a stunner, a brightly colored diagram of the solar system complete with circular dials to show each planet's orbit. At Darien's repeated requests, his mother read the names of the planets several times that day. By bedtime, he could name them in order.

A few years later, after spending numerous nights under the New Mexico sky with binoculars and a telescope, he could identify all of the major constellations, most minor ones, and hundreds of stars. At the age of twelve, Darien became interested in SETI, the *search for extraterrestrial intelligence,* and he downloaded the SETI@home app on the family computer. The app linked the computer and millions of other home computers to a SETI experiment based at UC Berkley. To date, the program had failed to produce concrete evidence that any extraterrestrial message had ever been received, but Darien, along with millions of other aficionados, remained hopeful. Maybe he would make SETI his career choice.

Darien's family had moved repeatedly, but never more than twenty-five or thirty miles from Alamogordo. His earliest memories were of living near Tularosa at the edge of the Eagle Ranch Pistachio Groves, a location still close to his heart. Workers in the groves befriended Darien as a toddler and provided him with a never-ending supply of free pistachios. After living in Tularosa, Darien's family moved several times before settling down in Orogrande. The old trailer was too rickety for another move, so Darien didn't envision another address change any time soon.

Quickly donning his security guard uniform, Darien left the trailer and got into his Volkswagen Beetle parked in the gravel driveway. Darien, twenty-two years old, and the VW nearly that age, resembled each other. Due to spending so much time in the sun, his complexion matched the car's faded tan paint. His khaki uniform completed the illusion that he and the vehicle had melded into a cyborg.

The worn-out VW and dilapidated trailer had fallen into Darien's hands when his parents made a hasty departure from the country two years ago. Since it was unlikely that they'd return to the U.S. any time soon, Darien had availed himself to the car and house as if he were the sole owner, which wasn't really the case. His sister by adoption, Rachel, had an equal right to both properties, but so far, she hadn't demanded that he sell them and split the proceeds. He hoped she wouldn't do so any time soon; he was strapped for cash.

Darien and Rachel had grown up in good sibling harmony. Over the years, many people had told them they looked alike and both enthusiastically embraced the resemblance. But Rachel had an outstanding feature that Darien couldn't match—one blue eye and one brown eye, a genetic aberration known as *heterochromia*. While in elementary school, Rachel had worn contact lenses to mask the feature, but upon entering junior-high, she'd boldly tossed the lenses aside and claimed the oddity as her trademark. Since then, she'd collected more than a dozen pictures of famous people who shared her unique characteristic.

As small children, Darien and Rachel never fought and seldom argued, but when they became teenagers, Darien morphed into a conspiracy theorist, a situation which triggered numerous lively discussions and an occasional argument, as well. Rachel couldn't accept Darien's theory that NatGov was trying to turn the entire populace into lemmings, but to him, it was obvious that they were.

When the two major political parties united to form the *Republican and Democratic Society*—immediately dubbed *the RADS*—Darien realized NatGov had begun to operate as a one-party system, even if Rachel didn't see it that way. Political arguments with his sister sometimes ended in exasperation, but never anger. The bond between them was far too strong to be affected by politics.

Another difference of opinion related to the place they grew up. Darien loved the New Mexico desert, but Rachel had always planned to look for some other place to live. As fate would have it, a major sociopolitical change set the stage for Rachel's departure. Six months before her eighteenth birthday, California seceded from the Union and offered a neoteric lifestyle to those swearing allegiance to the new republic, and when she turned eighteen, Rachel was quick to do so.

The newly-formed government offered every citizen a guaranteed annual income via their crypto currency, BitCal, which replaced the U.S. dollar within the borders of the Republic. Government-assisted housing was available to all citizens, regardless of income. CalGov had banned all firearms, except those issued to police officers. In addition, they passed a bill forbidding the new republic to go to war and adopted a neutrality mantra, *Peace Through Equality*. California's Legislature, elected in proportion to the racial makeup, established the duties of the justice system before any Supreme Court Justices were appointed. One of the main duties of the Court was a biennial review of

The Empowerment Mandate in the Constitution. Clearly, California was determined to make everybody equal, whether they liked it or not.

Darien suspected that California's sudden break-away had been incited by a *deep state* operation like the *Illuminati*—or maybe a doppelganger of the Illuminati, such as the *Trilateral Commission*, the so-called non-partisan discussion group started by David Rockefeller in 1973. Whatever the case—Illuminati, Trilateral, or somebody else—Darien was totally convinced that an underground political organization was concentrating on establishing a *new world order* by getting their puppets elected to high offices in major countries, as well as in the UN. Apparently, they'd convinced NatGov that California could serve as a stepping stone to a *one-world-government*, and many RADS approved of the Golden State's secession. Every time they talked, Rachel touted California's innovative plan of governance. Darien saw it as a totally foolhardy scheme.

When Rachel moved to California four years ago, she'd hoped to become a fashion designer—maybe even a model—in Los Angeles or San Francisco. Darien wasn't surprised that she wanted to design and model clothing. As a child, she liked to *dress up* and always took meticulous care of her clothes, most of which came from Goodwill. The modeling opportunity had yet to materialize, but while working from home as a freelance graphic artist, Rachel had done a few small gigs for a fashion designer in New York. Darien knew her hopes of hitting it big were still alive.

In spite of their vastly different sociopolitical opinions, Rachel visited Darien at least twice a year, and although she'd begged him to do so, he'd never visited her. During her last visit three months ago, he'd promised to visit her over the Thanksgiving holidays. He intended to keep his promise and was beginning to look forward to visiting Hermosa, the community where Rachel lived.

Dodging a portable basketball goal that he'd left in the driveway the day before, Darien backed out and touched the *AutoPilot* icon on the instrument panel. The old VW turned north on U.S. 54 toward the Mayflower Project.

CHAPTER 2

Carly Hansen drove north on U.S. 54, still finding it hard to believe she was outside of Texas for the first time in her life and was driving from El Paso to Alamogordo by herself. She was making the trip alone because her mother was suffering from a severely upset stomach—*turista*, apparently—and was in no condition to take a seventy-mile round trip. They'd talked about the robo-bus as a possibility, but the bus stop was too far from Carly's destination for her to lug her suitcases and other belongings. Since she had an appointment with her faculty advisor early Monday morning, driving alone seemed to be the logical choice. She was enjoying it, and so far, it was going well.

As the car hummed along on autopilot, she studied the terrain and its sparse vegetation. One similarity between New Mexico and Texas caught her eye immediately. The desert and the gulf coast were both extremely flat. Other than this one likeness, she found little else to remind her of her home state, not that she'd expected to. Her life was undergoing a quantum shift, one she'd anticipated for several years, and she was ready to meet any challenge which came her way. The differences between Texas and New Mexico weren't a major concern to her. She planned to turn the move into a learning experience, not only in geography, but in demographics and psychology as well.

Two weeks earlier, Carly had been checking her email every five minutes and pacing the floor of a tiny apartment in Gulfgate, the Houston subdivision where she'd lived all of her life. At twenty-two years old, she was still living with her mother whom she called by her given name, Hope. Carly had just completed her bachelor's degree summa cum laude at the University of Houston. To continue her studies, she would have to move to another university. Carly had applied for academic scholarships, fellowships, or grants at a dozen universities, ten of which responded promptly, but negatively. She'd begun to think about trying the student loan route, something she hated to do because she didn't want to graduate from college with a massive debt facing her like so many people her age were doing. Besides, getting a student loan wouldn't have been a cinch. NatGov was granting fewer loans every year because defaults were at a record high, and currently, there was a new student-loan bill in congress with RADS on one side of the issue and Independents on the other.

No university admissions office seemed to care that she'd graduated as valedictorian of her high school and finished her bachelor's degree with a GPA of 4.0. Her academic record couldn't have been better. Academics weren't the problem. The problem was her major, and she knew it. Carly's undergraduate degree was in psychology, and she wanted to continue in the field, but with special emphasis on *parapsychology*, the study of unexplainable mental phenomena. Parapsychology was so disdained by most academics that few universities would touch it. Still, she believed that she'd seen evidence of its existence.

Living near the NASA complex, Johnson Space Center, Carly had developed a keen interest in the psychological changes affecting astronauts as a result of extended exposure to space. NASA had done an excellent job in the field of aerospace psychology and psychiatry. Their major effort was directed toward maintaining the mental health of astronauts, as would be expected, but Carly wanted to go beyond the normal and delve into the paranormal. She'd seen a modicum of data—inconclusive, to be sure—which seemed to indicate that some of the astronauts on the first Mars mission had demonstrated rudimentary ESP ability during a crisis. These unique powers disappeared shortly after the space travelers returned to Earth, if they'd actually occurred in the first place. Carly wanted to study unusual space-related phenomena and had set her heart on a PhD in that field. Since her alma mater didn't offer a doctorate program in the controversial course of study, she'd expanded her search, but so far, to no avail.

Her first hope had been Rice University, but Rice didn't offer paranormal studies related to space. The Director of Admissions had responded to Carly's application for admission with a long email commending her for her sterling academic record and encouraging her to obtain an advanced degree at some other university and then apply to

Rice to pursue a post-doctorate program. She planned to keep the director's advice in mind, and maybe she'd contact Rice again in a few years if future career moves brought her back to the Houston area.

After her closest friend at the University of Houston had received financial aid to continue her education at the graduate level, Carly entertained high hopes for herself, but they were fading with each passing day. The friend was planning to pursue an advanced degree in a subject which seemed totally whimsical to Carly, *Political Correctness in the Modern World*. It piqued her that such a subject could trump psychology. If the last two universities on her list failed to come through, Carly feared she'd turn into a cynic, and she didn't like cynics.

Staying in the Houston area would have been convenient for Carly. She'd been dating Garth Howard since her senior year in high school, and they'd known each other since elementary school, so long that Garth sometimes seemed like a brother or merely a good friend. Garth considered them to be going steady, even though it was by tacit agreement rather than by spoken words. Currently, Garth was working as a summer intern for Alpha Offshore Logistics and was scheduled to graduate from Texas A & M University in Galveston at the end of the fall semester. His major was maritime engineering. With that degree, he could easily find a job in the Houston/Galveston area, where he wanted to continue living. On the other hand,

Carly knew that if she left Houston, it would be several years before she returned, if ever.

From the day she entered college, Carly suspected she would have to leave Houston to pursue her education beyond the bachelor's level. Consequently, she'd laid all of her cards on the table and told Garth that she intended to pursue parapsychology, no matter where she had to go. Garth was still chafing over the fact that Carly had put her chosen field of study ahead of their relationship, but as she saw it, he'd made a similar choice by maintaining such a strong attachment to the area where he'd grown up. Now that she'd moved to New Mexico, Carly wondered if she and Garth could maintain a long-distance relationship. They'd agreed to try, realizing it would be difficult.

Carly, an only child, hadn't had an easy life. Her father, a veteran of the perpetual Afghanistan war, suffered from PTSD—*post-traumatic stress disorder*—and couldn't hold a job. They lived in housing subsidized by the NatGov branch known as HUD, *Housing and Urban Development*, and her mother eked out a meager living as a barista at Amazon-Starbucks and other high-end coffee shops. When Carly was six years old, her father was killed in a one-car crash while driving drunk. She didn't blame either of her parents for the troubles which befell them; both had been dealt a poor hand in the game of life. Maybe they could have played their cards better, maybe not. Whatever the case, she wouldn't judge their eccentricities. She had plenty of her own to deal with, and unlike many others, she knew it.

When she was twelve years old, Carly had developed anorexia by eating less and less over a period of time. She didn't do it because of a desire to lose weight; she simply lost her appetite. Hope would say, "Honey, you can't go to school without breakfast. Eat a little of your oatmeal or a bite of toast with some milk." She remembered the repetitive days—getting up and dressing, the breakfast charade, going to school, coming home, doing homework, the dinner farce, watching a little TV with Hope, and going to bed with Minnie, her Rat Terrier, curled up at her feet. This monotonous routine continued for three years and Carly became skeletal. Hope took her to various doctors, including psychiatrists. Nothing helped.

At fifteen years of age, Carly had an *ah-ha moment* which changed her life. The moment came during a school day-trip to the Johnson Space Center. After seeing the array of space capsules, pressure suits, rocket boosters, rocks from the moon and Mars, the students watched a video entitled *The Psychology of Space Exploration*. Carly stared at the monitor with unblinking eyes. The video answered questions about general space psychology and NASA's programs to deal with the rigors of space, but it avoided any hint of paranormal phenomena, an approach that left several questions unanswered. When it ended, Carly knew what she wanted to do with her life. From that moment on, it was *parapsychology-or-bust*. She wanted to tackle unusual psychological phenomena, particularly ESP and was determined not to let anything or anyone stop her from doing it.

When she came home that evening, she requested pizza for dinner. After checking her billfold, Hope called Amazon-NY Pizza and ordered a large thin-crust pizza with pepperoni, Italian sausage, black olives and mushrooms. Amazon's drone delivered the order fifteen minutes later, and Carly wolfed down four slices and drank a 16-ounce Dr. Pepper, despite Hope's warnings that she was eating too much and would throw up. Other than a couple of tremendous burps, Carly suffered no ill effects from the pizza and Dr. Pepper binge.

The anorexia disappeared immediately and never returned. Both Carly and Hope were amazed, as were all the doctors who'd treated her without success. Merely choosing the field of psychology as her future vocation had rid Carly of a psychological problem of her own. She could hardly wait to find out what would happen when she began to study its more advanced applications.

During the two years following Carly's miraculous recovery, she grew three inches taller, put twenty pounds on her lanky frame and started setting the curve in every class she took. Moreover, she and Hope grew beyond the typical mother-daughter relationship and became close friends. Carly was inspired by her mother's resiliency. Somehow, Hope was able to close the door on a difficult past and set her sights on the future. They still had money problems, though, a constant feature of life as far back as Carly could remember.

Two weeks ago, a life-changing event occurred. Carly replayed it in her mind…

She was checking her email for the hundredth time when the front door opened, and Hope entered the apartment. They embraced briefly and Carly said, "I'm hungry and was thinking of making scrambled egg sandwiches for dinner. Would you like that?"

"That sounds good. I'll help you."

As they started toward the tiny kitchen, their linked iTabs chimed simultaneously, signaling that both of them were receiving the same text message.

Carly stared at her screen. "It's New Mexico State," she said, her voice rising. "They're offering me a full scholarship to attend their Alamogordo campus."

"Thank God," Hope said, breathing a sigh.

Carly pointed to the screen. "Look! They're offering me a part time job too."

"Doing what?"

Carly stared at the screen for several seconds. "It just says *graduate research assistant*."

They hugged again, laughing and crying at the same time. With heads together, they read the email again. It was from the Dean of Admissions and included more than they'd hoped for—full tuition, a meal plan, a dorm room, and a part-time job. It was beyond Carly's wildest dreams.

"We have to make plans," Hope said. "I'll call Anna and see if she still wants us to move in with her."

"Are you sure you want to move to El Paso?"

Hope nodded. "With you gone, there's no reason for me to stay here."

CHAPTER 3

Darien drove north under a cloudless sky. It had already rained two inches in July, well above average, and the orange desert on both sides of Highway 54 was garnished with clumps of plants—ubiquitous mesquite, various species of cacti, yucca, needle grass, and even a few sprays of red penstemon and blue salvia. Unlike his sister, he saw no reason to leave this part of the world. Its quiet beauty was unique and subtle.

Soon after Rachel moved to California, their parents, Lamech and Eve Segura, left New Mexico as well. Their dad had been a part-time televangelist and a full-time croupier at the Inn of The Mountain Gods in Ruidoso. This blending of divergent professions had seemed odd to Darien as far back as he could remember. He still harbored memories of clinging to his mother's skirts as a small child while his flamboyant dad worked the crowds, either in the casino or at a tent meeting in the Mescalero-Apache Reservation.

Two years ago, the game of charades fell apart. During the early stages of an investigation into the comingling of evangelism donations with casino funds, their parents fled the United States and wandered through Costa Rica, Panama, Columbia, and other countries without clear-cut extradition policies. Darien suspected his father was attempting to reestablish himself in some profession that handled loosely-documented funds. Eve left New Mexico with her husband, even though she wasn't a target of the investigation. Darien missed his mother terribly, and although he was somewhat reluctant to admit it, he missed his father too. They were family, albeit rather idiosyncratic and dysfunctional. He hoped they would reunite someday, but at the moment, it didn't seem likely. The last time he heard from them, they were on their way to Rio de Janeiro.

As he passed the Post Office, he glanced at the public news screen mounted atop its roof. The huge monitor was replaying the same scene he'd seen on local TV earlier, but with editorial comment provided by the Alphabet News Network. Headlines scrolled along the bottom of the screen in bold letters:

WAS METEORITE AN ALIEN SPACECRAFT?
RADS PUSH TO IMPEACH REX HORN
RADS INVESTIGATING PARABELLUM.ORG

Ten years ago, the government had passed the *Public Information Mandate* requiring news screens to be displayed on buildings which housed organizations affiliated with NatGov. The Alphabet News Network worked closely with Washington—primarily the RADS—to provide a 24/7 stream of political commentary presented in the form of headlines repeated ad infinitum. While the news screens were ubiquitous in larger cities, this was the only one near Orogrande. Darien never paid any attention to it unless an unusual headline popped up.

When he passed the souvenir shop, Rocks & Stuff, Darien switched off the autopilot and swung the VW into the McDonald's at the intersection of U.S. 54 and Highway 506. Glancing at the dashboard clock, he decided to go inside and eat the Big Breakfast Special, scrambled eggs, sausage biscuit, pancakes, and coffee. This was one of his favorite meals. Occasionally, he ate it for lunch, too, but with a Diet Coke instead of coffee.

After devouring the big breakfast, Darien changed out the VW's battery pack at the Exxon station next to McDonald's and headed east on Highway 506. The road was not magnetized to support autopilot functions, but Darien had driven it so many times that he'd become the autopilot. An impressive chain-link fence, ten feet tall and topped with razor wire, ran along the south side of the highway to his right. This was the site of the Mayflower Project, the largest space ship ever to be built. The project employed hundreds of people, most of them living in Alamogordo about twenty-five miles to the north. Darien was a security guard trainee working part time at the main entrance of the project. His flexible work schedule allowed him to take a full load of classes at New Mexico State's Alamogordo Campus where he would earn his bachelor's degree in astronomy at the end of the summer semester.

Project Mayflower—the world's first attempt to terraform Mars—was scheduled to be completed in a few months. The ship was the first to be equipped with an anti-gravity propulsion drive which, when fully charged, could travel in space for years without needing to recharge. Moreover, due to the new drive's speed, Mayflower could travel to Mars in well under three months. Even so, no human astronauts were scheduled to make its maiden voyage; all tasks would be performed by robotic machinery with AI. The machines were programmed to erect massive electromagnetic domes and extract oxygen and water from Martian rocks to create an Earth-like atmosphere within the domes, after which they would plant numerous types of seeds. If the project succeeded, the Martian atmosphere would be self-sustaining at some point in the future, hopefully no more than a hundred years. When the atmosphere contained sufficient oxygen, the new frontier would be opened to permanent residents, and *Homo sapiens* would inhabit a planet other than Earth.

NASA had an extraordinary plan for Mayflower after the Mars expedition. The terraforming machinery would be removed and replaced with algae tanks and tissue culture equipment capable of producing food to sustain around 100 astronauts indefinitely. With its water and waste recycling system, the ship would be a self-contained eco-system suitable for exploring other planets. Journeys to the far reaches of the solar system were already in the planning stages. Mayflower was President Rex Horn's pet project and one of his major campaign promises prior to being elected last year. Most Americans, including many of those voting for Horn, doubted that he could get it funded. During the campaign, the RADS vehemently opposed the project and claimed that Horn would spend the *Entitlement Reserve* building a spaceship to use in searching for Planet X. Consequently, Project Mayflower turned out to be a major talking point used against Horn.

In spite of the RADS' *no-holds-barred* effort, voters dealt them a major setback by electing billionaire Rex Horn, an import-export mogul from Florida, who had spent fifty million dollars of his own money to launch his campaign. At that point, to the surprise of many, some big money appeared in Horn's coffers as if by magic. The President's opponents hadn't yet figured out who the major donors were, but all indications pointed to a clandestine organization called *Parabellum.org* which had made several large donations from an offshore bank, an action which the RADS considered to be a slam-dunk impeachable offence.

Darien believed the Republicans and Democrats, still maintaining that they were two separate parties, had colluded to rig the election well before the primaries began; consequently, the election results were a major shock to them. Democrats were especially peeved because it was their turn to claim the presidency. Now, they were licking their wounds. With the help of the Alphabet News Network, they were plotting revenge against President Horn and beginning to investigate Parabellum.org, which—according to Alphabet—was a shadowy junta which Had propelled Rex Horn into the presidential office illegally. The RADS claimed they would complete the dossier on the underground organization early next year, and as a result, there was no doubt that Rex Horn would be impeached and removed from office.

Mr. Horn had ignored his critics and kick-started Mayflower. The new President, who seemed to have a bit of serendipity, allied with an unlikely group, the CCC, the *Climate Change Coalition*. The CCC believed that climate change would make the Earth totally uninhabitable in two or three centuries, thus terraformed Mars could save mankind from extinction. The CCC was a powerful organization which had supporters among Republicans, Democrats, Independents, Socialists, and several nascent parties. With support from political organizations which generally opposed each other on every issue except climate change, President Horn launched the Mayflower Project immediately upon taking office. Since then, the fury against the project had diminished slightly, but several high-ranking RADS claimed they would block Mayflower funding if they regained control of the House at the next mid-term election, which polls showed they had a good chance to do.

To further complicate matters, China had recently joined the CCC, thereby making Darien leery of the way Mayflower financing was put together. China was contributing some resources to the project, but NatGov was picking up most of the tab with money borrowed from China. So, one way or another, China was holding the purse strings of the project, a shaky situation which was growing shakier with Rex Horn threatening a tariff war with Asia. So far, he hadn't levied any tariffs, but the threat was affecting the stock market—not a big concern for Darien, since he had no money to invest and wasn't expecting to have any in the near future.

Moments after leaving the Exxon station, Darien pulled into the graveled parking lot across the highway from the main gate of the Mayflower Project. He got out of his car and walked toward a cluster of dull brown temporary buildings which housed the Mayflower security detail. Breezeways made of corrugated sheet metal linked the buildings, and a constant trickle of foot-traffic moved along the paths. Nearly everyone that Darien met was wearing a khaki uniform like his, and they exchanged greetings as they hurried to their assignments.

He went into the main building and approached the check-in counter where his supervisor, Rico Piedra, sat at a desk staring at his iTab screen.

Rico looked up. "Hi, Darien. I need you to drive today."

"Good. Who am I driving?"

"That windbag, Congressman Charles Sullivan," Juan said. "Two armed guards will accompany you."

"Where will I be taking him?"

"He wants to ride around the perimeter fence to get a better view of the construction in progress. Get a Jeep from the motor pool and bring it back here. Just wait out front until the congressman shows up."

Darien was glad to have something semi-productive to do. Even though he was twenty-two, he was not allowed to carry a weapon because he was still a trainee—actually, pretty much a *flunky*. The weapon rule seemed bizarre to Darien who, as a teenager, had plugged quite a few sidewinders and other snakes with a 22-caliber rifle while exploring the desert between Orogrande and McGregor range.

He checked out a Jeep and waited while reviewing Astronomy 310. His final test for the summer semester was scheduled for next week. Thankfully, it would be his last test as an undergraduate. When the fall semester started, he would enter graduate school. Lately, he'd spent considerable time pondering career choices available to those with advanced degrees in astronomy.

At the moment, SETI remained high on his list. He began to replay its short history in his mind.

The search for extraterrestrial intelligence began in 1959 at the National Radio Astronomy Observatory in Green Bank, West Virginia. The first SETI researcher, Frank Drake, used an 85-foot radio telescope to search for radio signals from two stars, Tau Ceti and Epsilon Eridani. The observatory's equipment was primitive by today's standards. Early researchers focused on the detection of FRBs, *fast radio bursts*, having a frequency of 1420-megahertz, the frequency of the hydrogen atom, the most plentiful element in the universe. This approach was based on the assumption that extraterrestrials who were trying to contact Earth would see this frequency as the logical choice for contact.

Modern SETI-centric telescopes utilized multiple small radio antennas rather than a large single-dish telescope. Currently, more than 100 radio telescopes throughout the world participated, including The SETI Institute located in the Cascade Mountains of California. The Institute had continued to be heavily involved, even after California's exit from the union.

Many things had changed since the beginning of SETI, but one thing hadn't—no one had deciphered a single message from outer space. In fact, no one had proved any incoming signal to be from an extraterrestrial being. Still, after seeing SETI's future possibilities, Darien was convinced that it would be a logical career choice. Since he planned to pursue a PhD in astronomy, he didn't need to make his final decision today. He had several more years to think about it.

Just before noon, Rico came out of the main security building. "The congressman cancelled," he said, as he approached Darien. "Return the Jeep and sign out. I'll see you tomorrow."

"I'm off tomorrow."

"Okay . . . whenever."

After signing out, Darien retrieved his VW and decided to take the long route home. He headed east on Highway 506 and turned south on Mayflower Drive along the eastern edge of the fenced area. This was the tour Congressman Sullivan had intended to take. There was no other location on the property or near it which afforded such a good view of the space ship nearing completion. To Darien's right, a quarter of a mile away, the gleaming fuselage of the Mayflower was silhouetted against the cloudless sky. The structure was surrounded by several gigantic cranes and extensive scaffolding. Two cranes working in unison swung a plate into position as the noonday sun danced on the glistening metal like St. Elmo's Fire.

Darien mentally compared the Mayflower with the Airbus 1000, the biggest airplane flying today. The A-1000 could seat 900 people when configured in coach mode, or a third as many when configured in luxury mode, but the spaceship was considerably bigger. Construction of the gigantic spaceship had triggered considerable dialogue among Planet X advocates, and many of them believed that Mayflower was linked to the tenth planet in some way. Darien wished he could believe the hidden planet scenario; however, all of the astronomy he'd studied so far prevented him from doing so. Still, it was an intriguing thought, and he enjoyed talking about it with his friends.

Once past the Mayflower complex, Darien turned west onto a winding gravel road, Castner Drive, keeping the imposing fence to his right and a tumbleweed-decorated ditch to his left. The seldom-used road intersected U.S. 54 a mile south of Orogrande. The scenic route, as Darien referred to it, would add thirty minutes to his drive time, but since he'd prepped to the max for his astronomy exam, he could dawdle the afternoon away with no regrets.

As he drove, his thoughts drifted back to Madison. For nearly four years, they'd taken this drive together occasionally, sometimes just the two of them, and at other times, with friends. Although he'd had a couple of *puppy love* incidents in junior high, Madison Ellison captured his heart the first time he saw her when both were seventeen. She'd just moved to Alamogordo from New York with her mother, who'd been hired as a drama professor at NM State. While she was in high school, Madison had acted in several school plays and local theater productions. Upon graduating from high school, she enrolled in NM State and continued to delight local audiences with her unique thespian talents for two additional years. Just when Darien thought his relationship with Madison was idyllic, it ended abruptly. The Big Apple called her back home in an extraordinary fashion. She landed the part of Katherine in *The Taming of the Shrew*, which was making a come-back in a theater off-Broadway. As suddenly as she'd arrived in New Mexico, Madison had departed, seemingly with no regrets. Her last words were, "Look me up if you come to New York." A chilly goodbye, to say the least.

For the most part, he'd recovered from the sudden breakup. At least, that's what he told himself, but occasionally, memories of Madison resurfaced when least expected, as was the case today. A few months after Madison's abrupt departure, Darien began to date again, usually women from the Alamogordo area. So far, no one had come close to filling the void in his heart. Lately, his dates had grown fewer and farther between, and his social life consisted primarily of pick-up basketball at the YMCA and occasional get-togethers with his best friends.

Pushing aside the thoughts of Madison, Darien coasted to a stop at the intersection of Castner and U.S. 54. To his left, a lone car approached, and Darien waited for it to pass. When the vehicle was directly in front of him, a thunderous explosion sounded, generating shockwaves which rocked Darien's Volkswagen. Rubber strips peeled off the car's right front tire as it fishtailed and hit the shoulder at an oblique angle, spraying gravel onto the highway. As Darien watched in awe, the car spun around and slammed backwards into a historical marker, stopping abruptly with a resounding thud. The trunk popped open, revealing several suitcases.

Darien analyzed the situation quickly. A traveler had barely escaped a rollover and needed help. He jumped out of his car and ran to the driver's side of the green Toyota.

A woman was slumped over the steering wheel.

He tapped the window. The woman stirred but didn't look up.

He tapped again, harder. The woman raised her head and looked toward him with jaw agape and fear showing in her blue eyes. "Are you okay?" he asked, motioning for her to lower the window.

The woman stared at Darien.

"Lower the window."

The woman's lips moved, but no sound came out.

"Lower the window, please," Darien repeated.

Blankly, the woman continued to stare.

CHAPTER 4

When the car fishtailed and the autopilot shrieked an emergency signal, Carly's life flashed before her eyes. The flashback ended when the car stopped abruptly, and Carly realized that she'd narrowly escaped a rollover. She remembered her head slamming against the headrest as the car skidded backwards and hit a solid object. She was woozy from the impact but didn't think she was seriously injured.

As her mind began to clear, she realized that a man was standing outside of her window. He was speaking, but the ringing in her ears prevented her from understanding a word he said. Fearfully, she stared at him wondering if he'd caused the accident on purpose. She'd heard of such things happening in isolated areas like this. The man was wearing some sort of uniform, but it could be a disguise. Anybody could buy a uniform from Amazon. This was the stuff of bad dreams.

The man stood there looking at her. Was he waiting for her to respond? Or was he thinking about breaking the window and dragging her out? Nothing about him revealed his intentions. She fought down the panic, and decided she had nothing to lose by saying something.

She tried to speak, but no words came out.

The man spoke again, sounding far away, but this time, Carly could make out the words, "Lower the window, please."

She touched the button, but paused before depressing it, still wondering if she should open the window or not. Carly considered bolting out of the passenger door and making a break for it, but even if she could outrun the man, there was no place close enough to run for help. She reweighed the situation. One thing was certain—she needed help, and no one was in sight except the stranger outside her window. It was either him or nobody. Maybe he was her guardian angel or a Good Samaritan. Whatever the case, her fate was in his hands. She pressed the button slightly, lowering the window an inch.

In a quivering voice, she asked, "Are you a police officer?"

The man pointed to the emblem on his shirt. "No, I work at the Mayflower Project."

She was still suspicious. "How did you get here so quickly?"

"I was right over there," the man said, motioning toward his car. "Your tire blew out when you were directly in front of me. You nearly hit me."

His demeanor was convincing, and Carly decided to go for it. She lowered the window completely and said, "I'm Carly Hansen."

"Darien Segura at your service."

"Can you help me?"

"Yes. Are you hurt?"

"I don't think so," Carly said. She unlocked the door and pulled the handle. The latch didn't release.

Darien tugged on the outside handle and the door opened.

Carly was fully committed at that point. "Could you help me check the car for damage?" she said, as she slid out and faced Darien.

Carly was five eleven, wearing black shorts with a Houston Rockets jersey and cap. Her auburn ponytail protruded through the back of the cap. Darien stared at her, which didn't surprise her at all. Nearly every man she'd met since turning sixteen had done so. She'd learned to ignore it.

"Uh . . . do you have ARS—Amazon Roadside Service?" Darien asked.

Carly shook her head. "I have the service for Texas but haven't extended it to New Mexico yet. Guess there's nothing to do but call a repair shop, if I can find my iTab." She got back into the car and started rummaging through books and papers which had accumulated on the passenger-side floorboard while the car was skidding.

"Don't call any roadside service outfit," Darien said. "They'll charge an arm and a leg to come out here. We can handle this ourselves. First, let's see if the car is alright. Then, I'll change the tire for you if you'll tell me why you left Texas and started driving around in the New Mexico desert by yourself."

"Okay, you've got a deal."

They walked to the rear of the car and examined it carefully.

"Just a dent in the bumper," Darien said. "That's all I see. The sheet metal and plastic seem to be okay. At least, nothing is pressing against the rear wheels."

Carly breathed a long sigh. "Guess I was lucky, after all."

"Pull the car away from the marker a little. I need more room to work."

Carly got in the car, started the engine, and eased forward about six feet. Darien took two well-worn pink suitcases out of the trunk and sat them on the ground next to the marker. After some momentary fumbling, he got out the spare tire and jack but couldn't find the lug wrench.

"Do you know where the lug wrench is stashed?" he asked while rolling the spare toward the front of the car.

"I don't know if there is one," Carly said. "I've never changed a tire in my life."

"I've got one of those cross-shaped lug wrenches in my car," Darien said. "It'll fit anything."

Three minutes later, he had the car jacked up. Before tackling the lug bolts, he looked over his shoulder at Carly and said, "You agreed to tell me how you ended up in New Mexico. Remember?"

"Okay, here goes," Carly said. She told her story, including a condensed version of her anorexia and her father's tragic death. She ended with the recent acceptance notification from New Mexico State and her mother's decision to move in with her sister in El Paso while Carly lived in Alamogordo.

By the time she finished her short biographical sketch, Darien had installed the spare tire and was lowering the car.

"You're all set," Darien said as he stood and faced Carly. "But you need to get the flat fixed and put back on ASAP. The spare is one of those stupid donuts—not meant for permanent use, and you shouldn't drive over fifty miles an hour as long as it's on the car."

"Thanks for rescuing me," Carly said. "If not for you, I'd have called for roadside service, and I don't have money to spare."

"Welcome to the club."

Darien motioned toward Carly's cap and said, "I take it you're a basketball fan."

"Yes—the Houston Rockets," Carly said with a vigorous nod. "And I play the game, as well. What about you?"

"I play quite a bit at the YMCA."

"I read that New Mexico State is building a new sports complex on the main campus."

"It's called the Pistol Pete Sports Complex," Darien said. "It was named after a famous western gunfighter and lawman named Frank 'Pistol Pete' Eaton."

"I know," Carly said, "but before I read the article, I thought it was named after Pete Maravich, the basketball legend."

"So . . . how do you think the Rockets will do this fall?"

"With Harden as their new coach, I think they have a good chance to win it all."

"People out here say Golden State will win again."

"No way."

"We'll see," Darien said. "Now, let me give you some advice about desert survival. The State Troopers patrol this highway regularly. If something like this happens again before you add New Mexico to your roadside assistance policy, call them or just wait for them to come by on patrol. They'll change the tire for you."

"That's good to know. And now I have a request."

"Go ahead."

"Tell me about yourself."

"What do you want to know?"

"Everything. You've extracted a lengthy autobiography from me but told me nothing about yourself."

Intending to keep it brief, Darien began, "I was born in Panama, and . . . "

"Panama?" Carly interrupted. "I have a Panama connection too."

"What is it?"

"My middle name is Morgan. I'm related to Henry Morgan, the pirate who sacked Panama in 1671."

"Wow! I'm speechless."

"Sorry I interrupted your story," Carly said. "Please continue."

Darien told his life story in less than five minutes and closed with, "I'm about to start my master's program in astronomy at NM State's Alamogordo campus."

Carly pointed to the emblem on Darien's uniform. "I thought you were working on the Mayflower Project."

Darien shook his head. "It's a part-time security job and will end soon. I have a job as a graduate assistant this fall."

"Doing what?"

"Various things, including teaching the lab for Astronomy 101."

"I need to take some science courses," Carly said. "Maybe, I'll take astronomy." She realized that she and Darien might be linked through their studies, whether intentionally or not. He was interested in space. She was interested in the unusual effects of space on astronauts. The subjects fit together very well.

While they were talking about the upcoming fall semester, a Highway Patrol vehicle coasted to a stop on the shoulder. A State Trooper got out and walked toward Carly's car. Even before the officer spoke, Carly sensed that he and Darien knew each other.

"Hey, Darien," the trooper said. "Is everything okay?"

"Everything's fine now," Darien said. "I changed the lady's tire."

The officer looked toward Carly. "Ma'am, I'm Sergeant Dustin Rhodes with New Mexico State's Highway Patrol. Would you like for me to arrest this *bandido*?"

Carly's chin dropped as Darien and Sergeant Rhodes burst out laughing.

Darien motioned toward Carly. "Dusty, this is Carly Hansen. She just moved here from Texas."

Dusty touched the bill of his cap. "Welcome to New Mexico, Miss Hansen."

CHAPTER 5

Darien picked his way through light traffic to the university campus and pulled into the parking lot adjacent to the Townsend Library. The lot was half full of vehicles, an unusual situation for Saturday evening. Apparently, the meteorite strike had renewed the interest of some barely-active members of the Amateur Astronomy Group. Darien hoped it had. There was plenty to talk about, and they'd engaged a good speaker to lead the discussion.

Last year, the university had built a pavilion adjacent to the parking lot and dubbed it *The Vista*. The new addition featured covered walkways around four sides of a tiled common area. Several marble columns, suggesting the Parthenon, stood at one end of The Vista, and a sundial surrounded by sturdy tables and chairs occupied the center of the tiled area. The Vista was a nice place to study, hang out with friends, or relax and read a good book.

Students milled about. The evening was hot, but a light breeze made it bearable, as did the predominant clothing style, shorts and scanty tops. A trickle of students carrying backpacks left the Vista and went toward the library. Others were getting ready to leave at sundown and move their activities to bars and restaurants as far as possible from the campus. When Darien was a freshman, he'd wished he had enough money to join the college *in crowd*. Now he realized that not having discretionary funds was a blessing in disguise, forcing him to focus on his studies.

Darien walked through the library, which was used primarily as a study hall. The few books on display were locked in glass cases and seldom checked out. The real library was on the internet and ubiquitous e-books were eliminating paper books from modern society. Soon, they would have little use except as decorations or museum displays. The thought made Darien sad. He loved paper books and still owned a collection of science fiction novels written by old masters like Philip K. Dick, Ray Bradbury, and Kurt Vonnegut. He even had a couple of novels by the little-known writer, Don Johnston, who published his first paperback novel, *The Dar Lumbre Chronicles*, when he was eighty years old. Johnston was somewhat old school, but at least, his sci-fi novels seemed possible.

At one end of the room, a small group of students studied together, talking softly and pointing toward their iTab screens. The screens displayed material from *STEM* classes—*science, technology, engineering and math*. At the opposite end of the room, outnumbering those who were studying, others were playing video games. Their iTab screens told their story as well. They were competing online in a hot new game, *Global Cooling on Mercury*. Darien suspected the online gamers would make up the lower quartile of the curve when grades were posted, and the STEM students would grab the As and Bs. It nearly always worked that way.

Darien greeted fellow students as he walked through the library. Excluding the incoming freshmen, he knew everybody on campus by sight, although he didn't know all of their names. It was the same situation in the city of Alamogordo and surrounding areas. Except for military personnel assigned to Holloman Air Force Base, he knew almost everyone within a thirty-mile radius of the college campus.

Bypassing the Starbucks adjoining the library, Darien bought a Diet Coke and a package of cheese crackers from a vending machine on the walkway and went into the newly-constructed conference room/study hall between the library and the university science building. A massive ersatz pecan table surrounded by straight-backed chairs occupied the center of the room, and small tables with folding chairs provided additional seating at the rear of the room. Early arrivals jockeyed for position around the main table but left the head position open for the speaker, who had yet to arrive.

Darien looked around and spotted Dusty and April Rhodes seated at a small table with Roger and Ashley Carson. Each of the four was about the same age as Darien, and he'd known them as long as he could remember. While they were growing up, Darien, Dusty, and Roger spent a lot of time together. When the trio of friends reached their late teens, another trio came into the group, two of which were April and Ashley. The other . . . Madison.

The Rhodes and the Carsons had gotten married six months ago, not a surprise to Darien since they'd dated for several years. At first, he feared the newlyweds might leave him as *odd man out*, but it didn't happen. They still stayed in contact regularly through text messages, social media, and facetime—sometimes even by old-fashioned telephone calls. Lately, April had assumed the role of matchmaker, apparently thinking it was time for Darien to find a new love interest. He'd ignored her so far, but she was beginning to get persistent.

Signaling for Darien to join them, Dusty dragged a chair from an adjoining table.

Everyone said their *hellos*, and Darien squeezed in between Dusty and Roger. He could feel all eyes on him and knew that Dusty had told the others about Carly Hansen. An inquisition by April was in the offing; it started immediately.

"We saved a place for the tall blonde you rescued," she said.

"Her hair is red or maybe auburn—but not blonde."

"We hoped you'd bring her tonight."

"She has a boyfriend."

"In Texas or here?"

"Texas."

"Then you fumbled the ball."

Darien shrugged. "She had to go back to El Paso."

"For how long?"

"Until the fall semester starts."

"That's not too bad," April said. "Only a couple of weeks."

Determined to change the subject, Darien asked, "How's your hydroponics garden doing?"

"I've already started a fall garden," April said, "although it's probably a little too early. Yesterday, I set out some squash plants. When they produce, we'll have you over for a fried squash and hamburger cookout, followed by a poker game. We haven't played in a while."

"Sounds great, "Darien said. "I'll show up with an empty stomach and a sock full of pennies."

Darien had a special interest in the garden, having helped assemble the hydroponics equipment which Dusty ordered from Amazon. April was one of the few home gardeners in Alamogordo, and the only one Darien knew who grew vegetables in July and August. Her spring garden had been outstanding, and she claimed her summer crop was just as good, in spite of the fact that several nay-sayers had said it wouldn't survive the heat. It seemed ironic that people in Alamogordo believed that NatGov could terraform Mars, but didn't think anyone could grow a summer garden in the New Mexico desert. What a paradox.

Ashley leaned toward Darien and said, "Rachel texted me yesterday. She said you're planning to visit her at Thanksgiving."

"At long last, I'm going to The Republic of California, and I'm excited about it."

The quintet of friends made small talk until a murmur went through the room indicating the guest speaker was arriving. Everyone looked toward the entrance as an elderly man wearing a rumpled white suit appeared in the doorway. The man's drooping moustache and unruly white hair were Einsteinian, a fitting trademark for the well-known theoretical physicist, Dr. Edward Pauling. The physicist was accompanied by Eric Jordan, another of Darien's friends, who was currently serving as president of the local astronomy club.

A hush fell over the room as the two men walked to the head of the table.

Twenty years earlier, Dr. Pauling had retired from CalTech to devote his time to the promotion of astronomy clubs, especially local clubs like the one in Alamogordo. While at the university, his specialty had been the detection and analysis of radio waves from outer space, particularly fast radio bursts which he thought were engineered signals, although most of his colleagues disagreed with him. Recently, he'd stated that he was beginning to accept the idea that a tenth planet might be found in the solar system someday, a statement which exasperated the academics and delighted amateur astronomy clubs and President Horn.

Eric called the meeting to order. "Good evening, ladies and gentlemen. Thank you for coming. We have a special guest speaker tonight, Dr. Edward Pauling. He will comment on the meteorite strike and other current events, perhaps including his take on recent reports of Planet X sightings. After his opening address, he will take questions from the floor. Without further delay, please welcome our guest, Dr. Edward Pauling."

Everyone jumped up and cheered. Dr. Pauling stood at the head of the table and waved to the crowd. After a brief ovation, he held up a hand for silence. Quiet fell over the conference room, and everyone sat down.

Before the guest speaker could say a word, Darien's iTab vibrated, and a piercing *general alert* ringtone sounded over the university PA system. The alert was part of the *Public Information Mandate*. In his four years of college, Darien could remember less than a half-dozen times when the system had been activated, but in each case, an important announcement followed the alarm.

"Attention please," a smooth computer voice said. "Please stand by for a message from the President of the United States. Attention . . . please stand by . . . "

Everyone froze and turned their eyes toward the front of the room where a gigantic monitor was coming to life.

Three circles of light—red, white, and blue—appeared on the screen and exploded into bright splinters. As *The Star-Spangled Banner* played in the background, the tri-colored fragments morphed into a live view of the American flag hanging in the Oval Office beside a picture of George Washington. The President was seated at a mahogany desk with Washington's picture at his back.

President Horn was wearing the traditional blue suit and red tie. He was a large man in his sixties, with dark eyes and prominent brow ridges—a *Neanderthal man in a custom suit*, according to his enemies. Still, in spite of his vaguely primordial features, Rex Horn projected a commanding and powerful image. Now, when he spoke, the RADS listened, something they'd failed to do during the presidential debates, much to their chagrin. The camera zoomed in on the President. He glanced briefly at an iTab on his desk and then looked into the camera and began speaking:

"Good evening, my fellow Americans. Thank you for tuning in. I called this news conference to update you on a NASA project which I launched recently. But first, a little background information.

"For many years astronomical installations all over the world have occasionally picked up radio bursts from outer space. Most of these signals were celestial noise or terrestrial interference. However, about twenty years ago, fast radio bursts—FRBs—began to arrive at frequent intervals from a star cluster known as Messier 13, or simply M13. A number of well-known astronomers pointed out that the signals showed the characteristics of manufactured signals, and a few of them believed that they were messages from extraterrestrials.

"A few months after receipt of the first strong M13 signals, the United Nations formed a committee to investigate them, and after a year-long study, recommended that the signals be treated as coded messages from possible enemies. As a result, governments all over the world restricted access to the M13 signals, and some classified them as top secret. That was ridiculous since the earliest signals were already in the hands of anybody who wanted them. All this restriction did was hinder further study of the unique FRBs. Now, after twenty years, the consensus of opinion has swung back. Most of today's astronomers no longer support the concept that these radio signals are extraterrestrial messages. However, I'm convinced that they are."

President Horn paused, allowing his last sentence to sink in.

At the pause, a murmur rippled through the room, but stopped immediately when the President continued, "Let me repeat—extraterrestrials are trying to contact us. Someone, or something, out there is transmitting signals our direction. It is time for us to take our heads out of the sand and find out what these messages say and who is sending them.

"Astronomers and other researchers have studied these radio waves for years in an attempt to make some sense of them but to no avail. Many scientists are writing them off as nothing more than space noise, but a few continue to believe that they are extraterrestrial. As I stated, I believe so too.

"Several top astronomers recently told me they don't think our current approach will ever solve this mystery. In the past, we've relied exclusively on those trained in science, technology, engineering, and math. Obviously, these STEM disciplines will always be involved in the study, but it's time to include other disciplines in the study as well. In order promote a novel approach, I've authorized funding for a project called the M13 Contact Study. These funds will be available to outstanding students in psychology, anthropology, linguistics, and sociology. Perhaps other subjects will be added in the future. I'll even consider funding interdisciplinary studies, if they can be fitted together in some logical way. The M13 funds will be administered by DARPA—the Defense Advanced Research Projects Agency. It's my intention to develop a new generation of SETI researchers—bright young people who can think outside the box. We've been doing the same thing repeatedly for years and expecting to get different results. It's time to try a different approach.

"Recently, subtle changes have been detected in the pattern of the incoming radio waves, changes which indicate that the United Nations might have been right twenty years ago. The pattern resembles distress signals such as SOS or MAYDAY, according to some observers. Others say the patterns are more like CEASE AND DESIST warnings. Someone is trying to get our attention.

"I believe that extraterrestrials have visited the Earth several times in the past. One such visit resulted in the UFO crash near Roswell in 1947, but the facts were suppressed by the government. I'm putting a stop to handling space-related information that way and will keep you informed as we move forward. My goal is to get more young people, especially high school and college students, involved in disciplines related to transmitting and receiving information over vast interstellar distances. I intend to emphasize an innovation-driven approach on this new

SETI effort. By doing so, I believe we have a good chance to contact life beyond our solar system."

President Horn paused and stared at the main camera. The conference room was pin-drop quiet, and all eyes remained focused on the Oval Office scene. After a dramatic pause, the President concluded, "Ladies and gentlemen, please trust me on this effort. I have America's best interests at heart. Thank you for your attention. God bless you, and God bless America. Good night."

The President's image faded away like a Cheshire Cat, and pandemonium hit the conference room.

***

The following afternoon, Darien was watching the Sunday news on a desktop computer in his trailer. He seldom watched broadcast news, but today's offerings had drawn him in for frequent updates. All of Alphabet News' Sunday programs had come out against President Horn's unusual approach to investigating the possibility of extraterrestrial contact. The headline scrolled by again and again:

CITIZENS REJECT HORN'S M13 CONTACT STUDY

Darien didn't see how President Horn's opponents could have responded so quickly following his Saturday evening broadcast from the White House, but somehow, prominent RADS senators and representatives appeared Sunday morning on all programs produced by Alphabet News. Every guest denounced Mr. Horn's new program as ridiculous and a waste of taxpayer money. Several suggested a special investigation into Mr. Horn's authority to put DARPA in charge of the funding. Horn's enemies in Washington had worked with Alphabet News all day to keep the frenzy alive and would continue to do so as long as their audience would listen. Darien clicked on the first headline and the story appeared:

Washington, D.C. Several prominent senators and representatives promised to make a concentrated effort to cut funding or otherwise block President Horn's outlandish proposal for studying radio waves. Congressman Sullivan from New York described the President's plan as "pie in the sky" and a waste of tax-payer's money. He said he will attempt to redirect the funds to programs that address immigration equality and other social programs. Stay tuned to Alphabet News for updates.

Darien read snippets from several other anti-Horn news bulletins. One article referenced a YouTube video in which Horn had used the words *astronomy* and *astrology* interchangeably several times, apparently unaware of the difference. Another claimed the President had consulted a mentalist and horoscopic advisor before running for office, and still another tagged him as a proponent of psi phenomena, especially ESP. The list was virtually endless. Darien was amazed at the supply of anti-Horn publicity that constantly flowed through the RADS *breaking news* pipeline. A few months ago, it was Project Mayflower, but now that the anti-Mayflower campaign had lost its traction, Parabellum. org was on center stage. Apparently, the M13 Contact Study would follow. And, after that . . . who knows?

CHAPTER 6

Carly awoke from a deep sleep, groggy and momentarily uncertain where she was. She yawned and looked around a few seconds before recalling that she was on a sofa bed in Anna's El Paso apartment. The unit was a ubiquitous HUD efficiency apartment with living, dining, and kitchen areas in one room and with a smaller room divided into a bedroom and a bathroom. Anna's living-area furniture was simple and functional, consisting of the lime green sofa bed on which Carly lay, along with matching chairs, end tables, and a tiny dinette suite. The entire apartment was neatly arranged and uncluttered, suggestive of military quarters.

Still yawning, Carly remembered dreaming about riding a train, although she'd never been on one, other than the kiddie ride at Houston's Hermann Park Zoo. While she was mulling over the dream, she heard a train whistle in the distance and realized that the sounds of a real train had triggered her dream. She looked at the clock on the end table. It read 6:01 a.m.

Trying not to make any noise, she swung her feet to the floor and stretched her arms. Even after a week, her neck was stiff from the car accident, but otherwise, she was okay. After slipping on her robe, she went into the kitchenette and opened the refrigerator. As she took out the orange juice, she heard a soft voice say, "Good morning," and looked around to see Anna coming out of the bedroom.

"Hey, Anna," Carly said. "Hope I didn't wake you."

"You didn't—it was the six o'clock train. It's my alarm clock. The only problem is, I can't shut it off on the days I don't work."

"I was about to get a glass of orange juice," Carly said.

"How about coffee instead?" Anna asked, moving to the refrigerator where Carly was holding the door open.

"That sounds better than OJ."

"Let's drink it on my mini-balcony. There's a cloud bank forming in the east, so we'll get the chance to enjoy the morning before the temperature skyrockets."

Moments later, with coffee in hand, they moved to the tiny balcony and sat down in chairs so close together that their knees touched. El Paso was coming alive with a cacophony of sounds—the rumble of a train in the distance, intermittent whistle blasts, the whine of electric vehicles in the street below, car horns honking, and dogs barking.

Carly took a sip of coffee and asked, "Do the trains wake you at night?"

Anna shook her head. "No. I've learned to tune out the night trains."

Anna Phillips, Carly's aunt, was thirty-two years old, only ten years older than Carly. They could have passed for sisters, in spite of the differences in their height and hair. Anna was about four inches shorter than Carly and wore her blonde hair close-cropped, as she'd worn it in the Army.

Anna had lived with Hope and Carly in Houston from the time she was sixteen years old until she graduated from high school. During that time, she'd occasionally called Carly *little sister*, usually when trying to extract information or give advice. The bond they developed remained strong, even though they lived in different parts of the country. Upon graduating from high school, Anna joined the Army and went to dental hygienist school. The Army transferred her to Fort Bliss in El Paso, but unlike many transplants from the gulf coast, Anna liked the area and remained in El Paso after her discharge from the army. She still worked as a dental hygienist.

Anna looked at Carly. "The move out here is a big change in your life. What does your boyfriend think about it?"

"Garth—he doesn't like it."

"Are you going steady?"

"Uh-huh."

"*Uh-huh?*" Anna repeated. "You don't sound very enthusiastic about it. What gives?"

"Sometimes, it's hard to tell," Carly said, shaking her head slowly. "As you know, Garth and I grew up together. Without talking about it specifically, he assumed that we were going steady, and I guess I did too."

Anna shook her head slowly. "Let me tell you a cold hard fact, little sister. You can't build a relationship on assumptions."

"You sound like you're speaking from experience."

"I am."

"Tell me about it," Carly said, leaning toward Anna.

"Remember Justin, the sergeant from Fort Bliss who came to Houston with me that time."

Carly nodded. "He seemed nice."

"He wasn't—he was a jerk."

"I can't believe it. What happened?"

"We worked in the same office complex on the base, and saw each other every day for a couple of months before he asked me out," Anna said. "We didn't have much in common except our military service, but that seemed like a good place to start. After a few weeks, I fell for him and *assumed* he felt the same way . . . "

"Go on."

Anna continued, "We dated regularly for over a year, but never really talked much about our future—a lot like you and Garth. After a while, I realized that he was interested in a license to my bedroom but not a marriage license. I tried to convince myself that everything would work out, but I was naive. When I began to press him on the future, he split, and I haven't seen him since. So . . . don't assume, little sister."

"That's pretty strong advice."

"I think it's good advice," Anna said. "And now I'll tell you a secret. I checked out your rescuer, Darien Segura, on Facebook."

"Anna!"

They laughed, and Anna said, "I'll bet I know something about him that you don't know."

Carly's eyebrows shot up. "Well . . . tell me."

"When Darien was a senior in high school, he won an asteroid naming contest sponsored by NASA."

"What name did he pick?"

"Orogrande."

"I should have known."

They sipped coffee in silence for a few minutes as the rising sun painted a gold border around a clump of dark clouds gathering in the east. Carly pondered Anna's advice about men and decided that it was incomplete without an update on Anna's current social life. "So," she said, "how long was it after you broke up with Justin before you started dating again?"

"Oh . . . a couple of months, I guess."

"What about now? Do you have a steady?"

"Not exactly a steady, assumed or otherwise," Anna said, "but I'm dating a nice guy—a dentist named Carlton Jacobs. We go out fairly often and enjoy each other's company. He was engaged once, but it didn't work out. He knows what happened between Justin and me, so we're both cautious. Neither of us wants to rush into another commitment until we're sure it's the right thing to do."

"Are you happy with that arrangement?"

Anna nodded. "Yes—for the time being at any rate."

"I wish I could say the same thing about Garth and me."

Anna put her hand on Carly's arm. "It'll work out one way or the other."

Without answering, Carly smiled faintly, thinking that Anna's *one way or the other* remark might be a back-door reference to Darien. If so, Anna was really jumping to conclusions. Carly had told her almost nothing about her first impressions of Darien, impressions that she'd now assimilated into an extensive psyche profile. Although his good looks and charming manner might belie it, Darien seemed to be nursing an old wound, maybe a relationship that had gone bad not very long ago.

Interrupting Carly's introspection, Anna asked, "Are you going to study animals, as well as people, in your pursuit of ESP?"

"Probably both. Whatever the university will let me do. Now that President Horn is funding the M13 Contact Study, who knows what might happen next? Apparently, he's interested in psi phenomena—especially ESP—as a tool for analyzing the messages. It may sound crazy to many people, but I love the approach he's pushing."

"NM State must have been impressed by your grades."

"Maybe so, but a lot of other universities weren't," Carly said, reflecting on the recent turn of events in her life. It was hard for her to believe that NM State was venturing into the study of space parapsychology, a discipline which only a few universities gave any credence. Carly was anxious for the semester to start. She'd waited a long time for this opportunity.

Anna stood and said, "I wish we had more time to talk, but I've got to get dressed and go to work. If you want to, you can relax out here until it gets too hot."

"I need to send a couple of text messages," Carly said, rising to follow Anna into the apartment. As Anna disappeared in the bedroom, Carly sat down on the sofa bed and retrieved her iTab from a nearby end table. In her mind, she composed a brief message to Garth, but before she touched the keypad, the iTab sounded Garth's ringtone, and his picture appeared onscreen—a complete surprise since it wasn't like him to call this early.

"Garth! What's going on?"

"Hi, Carly. How're things out west?"

"Okay, I guess," Carly said, feeling apprehensive. "Why are you calling so early?"

"Alpha Offshore wants to extend my internship through another semester," Garth said. "In return, they'll guarantee me a job when I graduate."

Surprised, Carly asked, "You're okay with delaying your graduation?" All Garth had talked about lately was graduating and getting a job in the Houston area.

"I don't mind delaying it for one semester," Garth said. "What do you think about my change of plans?"

"I don't know what to say."

CHAPTER 7

On Saturday morning, Darien retrieved his dusty Volkswagen from the parking lot beside the library and headed toward the White Sands National Park. He planned to meet Roger and Ashley at the Roswell UFO Festival's portable exhibit, a traveling roadshow featuring items similar to those displayed in permanent exhibits in Roswell. Roger's father, Keith—or *Kit* as he preferred to be called—had persuaded the festival manager to schedule the show near Alamogordo immediately following the annual show in Roswell. Darien had seen the exhibit several times but was looking forward to seeing it in a new light since—in the eyes of many—the President's recent speech had authenticated the events described in the displays.

U.S. Highway 70 was busy in front of Holloman Air Force Base where a line of cars waited at the traffic signal controlling access to the highway. While sitting at the red light, Darien glanced at the news screen atop the Amazon-Capital One Building. Several new headlines were scrolling by:

HORN EMBRACES ESP
PLANET X ADVOCATES FORM NON-PROFIT CORP
RADS CONTINUE INVESTIGATING PARABELLUM

After a brief glance at the headlines, Darien redirected his thoughts back to the UFO exhibit. He wondered if the exhibit would actually draw the crowds Kit Carson claimed it would. Even if it did, the concept of increased tourism was a *yin and yang* situation among Alamogordo's city council members. Some wanted to maintain the status quo forever, while others wanted the city to grow.

Just past Holloman Air Force Base, Darien pulled into the Visitor's Center and found an empty parking space near the complex of adobe buildings. A soft breeze lifted the American flag atop the main building, billowing it like a spinnaker. NatGov was talking about redesigning the flag, and Darien thought they should. He was fine with fifteen stripes, but fifty-two stars didn't seem appropriate, now that California was no longer a part of the nation.

The parking lot was nearly full, and a trickle of pedestrians picked their way through the parked cars and walked toward the Visitor's Center. Behind the main building, a tall chain-link fence enclosed a group of brightly colored portable buildings which housed the exhibits. Darien bought a Diet Coke from a vending machine and took a long sip.

A voice from behind him called, "Hey, Darien."

He turned to see Carly approaching through the milling crowd. She was wearing faded cut-off jeans and a red Houston Rockets jersey like the one she'd worn at their initial encounter. Instead of a baseball cap, a floppy-brimmed straw hat rested atop her auburn hair. Oversized sunshades and gold hoop earrings completed her attire.

"Hi, Carly. What are you doing here?"

Carly closed the gap between them. "I was on the bus to El Paso and decided to detour by the park."

"You came the right day. Admission is free to students every Saturday during the summer."

The first room of the Visitors Center was a souvenir shop selling a hodgepodge of toys and other space-related paraphernalia—ersatz moon rocks, UFO replicas, space-station construction kits, geology sets, telescopes, binoculars, and the like. Throughout the shop, children were begging parents or other guardians to buy the eye-catching gadgetry. Near the exit door leading into the park, a counter displayed hats, sunshades, sunscreen lotion, and bottled water, all items in high demand this time of the year.

"By the way," Carly said, as they picked their way through the gathering crowd, "I signed up for Astronomy 101."

"Great! I'll be your lab instructor."

"What experiments will we do?"

"It's an entry-level class, so the lab projects will be pretty simple," Darien said. "We'll start off with some common household items—pins and needles, thread, popsicle sticks, rulers . . . stuff like that. We'll use those things to build a sextant to track the movement of the moon and estimate the distance to nearby stars. How does that sound?"

Carly frowned. "I thought we'd try to decode some radio waves."

"Not right away. First, we have to build some simple astronomy equipment."

"I'm not very good at arts and crafts."

"Don't worry," Darien said. "It'll be easy. And later in the semester, we'll analyze some images from telescopes around the world, including space-based telescopes like Hubble."

"That'll be more fun than building lab instruments. I'm looking forward to it."

"Me too," Darien said, pleased that he and Carly would get to spend some time together, albeit in a laboratory.

They left the Visitor's Center and went into the main exhibit area where a plastic boardwalk stretched across snow-white sand from one building to the next. The exhibit buildings and open-air displays formed an irregular circle inside the perimeter fence, and a clump of concession stands occupied the center of the circle. Umbrella-covered picnic tables completed the family-friendly layout.

A crowd was forming in the picnic area. Many women and girls wore shirts parodying the rainbow-hued buildings, an advertising gimmick dreamed up by the promoters of the festival. Casually-dressed men mingled with the women and children. Teenage boys lounged in the doorways of the exhibit buildings and checked out the girls strolling along the walkway. Young children ran amok, shrieking as they darted from one building to another playing hide-and-seek, catch-me-if-you-can, or some other game that involved running and yelling.

"Nice," Carly said, sipping her water. "The Festival organizers thought of everything."

"They've done this many times," Darien said. "It's a travelling circus without the animals." He and Carly turned right on the boardwalk, joining a clump of people taking the counterclockwise route through the displays.

"Darien! Hold up," a voice behind them called out as they approached the first exhibit. Darien recognized the voice immediately. It was Kit Carson.

"We're being summoned," Darien said, as he and Carly stopped and looked toward the man approaching them. Kit, moving with frantic vigor, wore tropical khaki shorts with matching shirt and a pith helmet. The noonday heat had reddened his slightly plump cheeks.

"Who's that?" Carly asked.

"It's Kit Carson, a friend's dad. He's the mayor's right-hand man."

"Why's he calling you?"

"He likes to talk," Darien said. "I've known him forever." He watched in amusement as Kit tried to get past a small crowd of people blocking his path. Darien knew everyone in the group. All of them were residents of Alamogordo, and they were not about to let the mayor's assistant get past them without an appropriate amount of conversation.

Darien and Carly watched as Kit conducted a mini town-hall meeting on the boardwalk. The lively conversation was punctuated with hand gestures and an occasional laugh. As quickly as it started, the meeting ended. Kit gave a friendly, but dismissive, wave of his hand, stepped off the boardwalk onto the sand and made his way around the group. Several well-wishers waved at him as he walked toward Darien and Carly.

Kit stepped back onto the boardwalk and extended his hand toward Darien. "I was just leaving," he said. "I'm glad we bumped into each other."

Darien grasped the outstretched hand and they shook vigorously.

Kit looked at Carly. "I've been wanting to meet you."

Darien, thinking that Carly might be put off by Kit's blunt approach, made a minimalistic introduction. "Kit Carson . . . Carly Hansen."

To Darien's relief, Carly thrust out her hand. "Nice to meet you, Mr. Carson."

"Call me Kit," Carson said, grasping Carly's hand. "Everybody does."

"Roger and Ashley will be here in a few minutes," Darien said. "This is the last weekend before school starts, so we don't want to waste it."

"Have you visited New Mexico before?" Kit asked in Carly's direction.

Carly shook her head. "All I know is that it's called the *Land of Enchantment*."

Darien's iTab chimed and he glanced at the screen. "It's Roger," he said. "They'll be here in about ten minutes."

"I can't wait for them," Kit said. "I've got to meet someone at the office, but I'll treat you to lunch here in the park."

"Thanks," Darien said. "What do we do to claim it?"

"I keep a tab open at one of the concession stands," Kit said. "Stand No. 3—the yellow one with pictures of Saturn on it. Get whatever you want and charge it to me."

"That's very generous of you," Carly said.

"I've got to go," Kit said. "Enjoy your visit." He turned toward the exit.

A few minutes later, Roger and Ashley ambled into the park, and Darien introduced them to Carly. Everyone exchanged hugs and hellos, and they went into the building housing the first exhibit, *UFO Remnants*. Just inside the front door, a glass case displayed a replica of the *Roswell Daily Record* dated July 8, 1947. The featured headline, *RAAF Captures Flying Saucer on Ranch in Roswell Region*, was highlighted in yellow. A half-dozen early-teens jockeyed for position in front of the display, while Darien and his friends waited behind them.

"What was the Royal Air Force doing in Roswell?" one of the boys asked.

"Read the article, stupid," another boy retorted. "RAAF means Roswell Army Air Force."

"No, it doesn't," a girl countered. "It's Air *Field*, not Air *Force*."

"Now who's stupid?" the first boy said.

"Both of you," the girl said.

After some minor jostling, the youngsters laughed and moved on, as the thirty-something woman escorting them delivered a sharp whispered warning about *behaving or leaving*.

Darien motioned for Carly to come closer to the display. "We've seen this before, but now, I think it'll take on a new meaning."

Together, they read the article:

On June 14, 1947, William Brazel, a foreman working on the Foster homestead, noticed clumps of debris scattered across ranchland approximately 30 miles north of Roswell, New Mexico. Brazel reported his find to the Roswell Army Air Field (RAAF), and later told the Roswell Daily Record that he and his son saw a large area of bright wreckage made of rubber strips, tinfoil, sticks and something that appeared to be tough paper. According to reports, Brazel—along with his wife, son, and daughter—returned to the site and gathered part of the material and stashed it under some brush. On July 7, Brazel saw Sheriff Wilcox and reported his find. Shortly after the Daily Record article appeared, U.S. Government agencies, primarily the FBI and the military, took over the investigation and attempted to debunk the UFO claim. Thirty years later, hundreds of documents were obtained under the Freedom of Information Act by UFO researchers who concluded that at least one alien spacecraft had crashed near Roswell, alien bodies had been recovered, and a government cover-up of the incident had taken place.

In addition to the featured *Roswell Daily Record* article, several other newspaper columns were displayed in glass cases near the front entrance of the building. The chronological arrangement of the articles emphasized the government's debunking efforts. Most of the early reports tended to accept the concept of an alien spacecraft crash, while later articles walked back the original story. Moreover, virtually everyone who was connected to the government recanted, suggesting that high-level pressure had been exerted on the witnesses.

Carly looked toward Darien. "So . . . some of the original claims about alien contact were really true."

"It looks like that might be the case, but a lot of people still don't think so, regardless of what the President says," Darien said.

Ashley pointed toward Darien and Roger. "These guys have discussed the Roswell UFO incident ever since I can remember," she said. "Roger believes it was an alien spacecraft, but hasn't convinced Darien."

They moved on to the *UFO Remnants* housed in a long counter with a glass top. Beneath the glass, several items were on display—strips of black rubber, crumpled tinfoil, a pencil-sized telescoping rod, and a wooden cross resembling a kite frame. A small plaque identified each item.

"None of this is original, is it?" Carly said.

"No," Darien said. "Somewhere in the fine print, there's a statement which says everything here is a copy or a replica."

"The UFO Festival organizers went to a lot of trouble," Carly said. "I was expecting videos."

"We'll see some videos too," Darien said, "but where they could, they used replicas to make the display items look as much like the originals as possible."

"Sort of like a certificate of authenticity," Roger said, "But with an obvious problem—if the original is a fake, then a duplicate of the original is also a fake. That was part of the government's debunking argument."

"It's a pretty good argument," Darien said, "and they presented it well. Now, it looks like they might have been covering up something."

The quartet worked their way through the *UFO Remnant* building with the teens trailing close on their heels and moved to the next exhibit building, *Alien Autopsies*. The interior lighting of the autopsy display room was subdued, enhancing the low-quality videos displayed along the walls. The first screen showed a monochrome movie of a white-coated man with his back turned to the camera. The man picked up a scalpel from a nearby instrument tray and approached an operating table bearing a supine figure. Turning slightly sideways—but not enough to reveal his face—the white-clad man touched the scalpel to the thigh of a nude figure on the table. For a split second, the corpse was clearly visible. It resembled a pre-teen child with a bulbous head, the prototypical *alien figure* which had been depicted countless times in sci-fi movies. As Darien and his friends watched, the brief video ended and started to replay. They watched it four times.

"As you would expect, the government claimed this film is a hoax," Roger said. "They released two statements which conflicted with each other. One statement claimed the body was an *anthropomorphic* dummy used to study airplane or car crashes. The other statement claimed the body was a mummified Native American child discovered in the late 1900s."

"Sort of a multiple-choice debunking approach," Darien said.

A few minutes later, they exited the alien autopsy exhibit and Roger said, "Why don't we eat now? I'm starving."

"Good idea," Darien said. "We can see the rest of the exhibits after lunch."

They headed for the food court where every cart was painted a primary color and decorated with clip art pictures of stars, moons, and planets. As per Kit Carson's instructions, they selected the yellow cart decorated with pictures of Saturn. The attendant, a young Mescalero woman, wore a smock depicting the same theme as the cart. She stood by as Darien and his friends looked over the hand-lettered menu above the service window.

The food cart presentation was a 100-year jaunt into the past. A soft-drink dispenser mimed a soda fountain in an old movie theater, and a rectangular tray on the counter held sweetener packets, stirring sticks, and straws. Beside the tray, squeeze bottles of mayonnaise, mustard, and ketchup were lined up like toy soldiers. Long skinny hot dogs sizzled and popped on a grease-spattered rotisserie, and the aroma of smoked meat hung in the air. From an unseen speaker, a piano plinked out a honky-tonk rendition of *The House of Blue Lights*, completing the *backward-in-time* pantomime down to the last detail.

The attendant shooed a fly away with a wet dish towel and said, "Foot-long hot dogs are on special today—two for the price of one."

After a brief discussion, they ordered six foot-longs with potato chips and lemonade. The server placed two trays on the counter and asked, "What condiments would you like?"

"What do you have?" Ashley asked.

The woman pointed toward the squeeze bottles and said, "All that . . . plus onions, cheese, and chili."

"Load mine up," Ashley said.

"Mine too," the others said in unison.

When the order was ready, Roger placed his iTab on the counter and touched his right thumb to an icon labeled *Kit Carson*, thereby charging the purchase to his father's account. Darien and Roger each picked up a tray and went to a nearby picnic table.

Before they could sit down, Darien's iTab chimed.

"It's Dr. McLennan," he said. "I wonder what he wants."

As his friends sat down and began to divide the hot dogs, Darien touched his iTab screen to retrieve the message:

Darien,

Since President Horn's message, I've had to juggle the fall schedule for several graduate assistants, including you. I'm reassigning you to the Astronomy 201 lab. If you have any questions, check with me Monday. Otherwise, I'll see you in the lab on Thursday after-noon for the first session.

Dr. Craig McLennan, PhD.

Darien muttered an expletive under his breath.

"What is it?" Carly asked.

He placed his iTab on the table and pointed to the text.

"That's a bummer," Carly said. "Maybe I should drop the class."

"Stay with it," Darien said, as he sat down. "You need the science course, and I'm sure we'll get other chances to take classes together, thanks to President Horn."

"Why don't you sign up for Psychology 301?"

"I don't have the prerequisites."

"We're going to test monkeys for ESP early in the semester," Carly said. "Maybe you could enroll as an observer."

Darien rubbed his chin thoughtfully. "Possibly, but I have a better idea."

Carly's eyebrows shot up. "What is it?"

"Have you turned in a proposal for your thesis?"

"No, I'm still working on it."

"I'm not finished with mine either," Darien said. "Let's combine them and propose a study of extraterrestrial contact via two completely different disciplines—astronomy and psychology. The President mentioned this type of study. Let's see if he's serious."

"It's certainly an example of thinking *outside the box.*"

"It's that, alright," Darien said, "or else one of the most ridiculous idea ever thought up."

Darien and Carly tossed ideas back and forth between bites, as Roger and Ashley listened. Darien was so caught up in the conversation with Carly that he paid scant attention to his life-long friends. He was pleased that she'd bought into his proposal for working on the M13 Contact Study together.

Upon finishing the meal, Ashley stood and said, "We need to go. We promised April and Dusty we'd watch a movie with them this afternoon—maybe the old classic, *Pirates of the Caribbean.*" She gave Roger a quick poke in his ribs, prompting him to get up. It was obvious that Roger hadn't heard anything about a movie, and Ashley was joining April as one of Cupid's helpers.

Everyone exchanged goodbyes. Roger and Ashley headed toward the exit.

"Tell me the truth," Darien said, "do you really think monkeys might have ESP?"

"I don't know about monkeys, but some dogs do."

"What makes you think so?"

"Once I had a rat terrier named Minnie," Carly said. "She was the smartest dog I ever saw. She was white with one black ear—her right one. There was another female in the same litter whose left ear was black. They looked just alike, except for their ears."

"Was the other dog as smart as Minnie?"

"No, Minnie was smarter. I think she had ESP."

"Really?"

"Something strange happened the day my dad died in a car wreck," Carly said. "It was so bizarre that I've never told anyone. I was seven years old when it happened. I'd probably never heard of ESP. Anyway, that afternoon I felt something terrible was about to happen. Minnie, was acting strange—as if she felt the same thing. I was reading *Green Eggs and Ham* while Hope made dinner, but I couldn't concentrate. Minnie curled up on my feet and started whining, something she'd never done before. Hope turned on the TV to watch the six o'clock news. Just as the news came on, Minnie jumped up and howled; then she lay down at my feet and whimpered for several minutes. Later that evening, a Houston police officer called and told Hope about the fatal accident. It happened at six o'clock."

Carly trailed off, and Darien said, "So, that event convinced you that paranormal experiences really do happen?"

"It certainly helped," Carly said with a nod. "I think Minnie sensed a tragedy was about to happen and tried to tell me, but I couldn't understand."

"Where did you get Minnie?"

"From a family which had just moved into our neighborhood," Carly said, "and believe it or not, they came from New Mexico."

"What was their name?"

"Smithers."

"*Smithers!*" Darien exclaimed. "I knew two families by that name. Both left the area when I was three or four years old. As I recall, one family moved to Houston and the other to Ruidoso."

"Now that's a *small-world* story."

Darien nodded. "If you read it in a novel, you wouldn't believe it."

As the conversation continued, Darien was amazed at how well Carly fit in with his lifelong friends. It seemed like she'd always been a member of the group, but there was an *elephant in the room*—Carly's boyfriend, Garth.

Still . . . Garth was in Texas.

CHAPTER 8

Carly stepped into the nearly-empty hallway and joined a small clump of students headed toward the exit. Everyone in the group greeted her, and several of them called her by name. Though a newcomer, Carly felt a sense of belonging. She paused as she passed the Astronomy Lab, and Darien popped out.

"Hello, Stargazer," Carly said. "I was looking for you."

Darien fell in step with Carly. "How did you know I was in the building?"

"Where else would you be?"

"Are you staying on campus this weekend?"

"Yes, I have to. Hope was planning to come get me, but her car broke down, and she can't get it repaired until Monday. I didn't want to waste money on Uber, so I'm staying."

"Do you have anything scheduled for this afternoon?"

"I'm thinking about watching the Astros at three."

"Are they still in first place in the West?"

"Yes, but only two games ahead of the Oakland A's, the team they play today."

As they approached the front door of the building, they joined a line of students processing through an exit turnstile. A retina scanner above the door noted their exit from the building, and they stepped out onto the sidewalk.

"Have you had lunch?" Darien asked.

"No. I was about to get a snack from the vending machine when Dr. Graves called me to her office."

"Let me propose something better than that."

"What?"

"Let's go to Orogrande and eat at McDonald's. Then, we'll tour some of the abandoned gold mines. How does that sound?"

Carly pursed her lips thoughtfully. "Are you asking me for a date?"

"I wasn't thinking of it that way," Darien said with a shrug. "Should I?"

"Don't," Carly said, shaking her head, "because I'd have to say *no*. But if we go Dutch on lunch, I guess it wouldn't be a date."

"I'll take that deal. Let's go."

A few minutes later, they were in Darien's faded VW heading south. Carly was looking forward to spending the afternoon with Darien, even though she was somewhat out of her comfort zone. Soon, she would have to tell Garth that her research partner was a man. Now that she'd spent a little time with Darien, she couldn't help but wonder how things might have developed between them if they'd grown up together. The thought was intriguing, but after dwelling on it a moment, she brushed it aside as a fantasy from another universe. She refocused her concentration on the real universe as they headed toward Orogrande.

"My Spanish is good enough to know that Orogrande means *big gold,*" Carly said.

"A misleading name, if there ever was one."

"How so?"

"It had a different name until the early 1900s when someone found a nugget the size of a man's finger in the mountains. At that point, it became known as big gold—*Oro Grande*, which later became one word."

"And the gold rush was on."

"Exactly," Darien said, with a nod. "According to folklore, shortly after the discovery, the little town blossomed into a population of more than 3000, and numerous con games were pulled on the newcomers, the main one involved taking them into the hills to discover planted gold."

"Were any other big nuggets found."

Darien shook his head. "Never. A better name would have been *Oro Poco*—Little Gold."

Carly smiled. "But you like the name, Orogrande. You gave it to an asteroid."

"How'd you know that?"

"My aunt saw it on Facebook."

Darien shrugged, but didn't follow up.

"How many people live in Orogrande?" Carly asked.

"Exactly one hundred, according to the last census."

"Will we pass your trailer on the way to the gold mines?"

"No, it's a couple of miles further on, but we could circle by it when we leave, if you would like to see how a poor boy lives in New Mexico."

"Probably similar to the way a poor girl lives in Texas."

"There's not much to see between here and Orogrande," Darien said, "but I think you'll enjoy visiting a couple of abandoned gold mines when we get there."

"Maybe we'll find a nugget."

Darien chuckled. "Not likely. I've combed every square inch of this area a thousand times and never found a nugget bigger than the head of a pin."

"Is there a roadside park near Orogrande?"

"No. Why do you ask?"

"I was thinking we could pick up something at McDonald's and eat lunch in a park."

"There are a couple of abandoned buildings which might serve the purpose," Darien said. "One old assay building has a long porch facing Highway 54. It's on the west side of the highway, so the porch will be shaded. Would you like to eat lunch there?"

"Sure, let's do it."

Moments later, they pulled into the McDonald's drive-through window and ordered four sausage biscuits, a large order of fries, and two Diet Cokes. Carly retrieved her iTab from her backpack behind the seat, transferred fifty percent of the total to Darien's iTab, and with a smile, said, "I took care of the extra penny."

When the order came, Darien handed it to Carly. She placed the Cokes in the holder between the front seats and put the bag of food between her feet.

"Are there any roads leading to the gold mines?" Carly asked, as Darien eased the VW out onto the highway. The whimsical idea of finding a nugget was still in her mind.

"There aren't any roads safe to travel for more than a short distance. Most of them are blocked by piles of dirt, or have washed out."

"I didn't think it rained that much out here."

"We get about twelve inches of rainfall per year," Darien said, "but it rained more than usual in July. Some of it was hard enough to wash away dirt roads or even graveled ones."

As they drove beneath the cloudless sky, Darien reeled off the names of the shrubs and cacti lining both sides of the highway and pointed out several tumbled-down shacks which had housed souvenir shops or restaurants for a brief time. Carly listened attentively as Darien described the desert. Though the area was desolate, it possessed an unspoiled natural beauty that appealed to her.

Darien slowed the car and pointed to his right. "That's the old assay building I was talking about," he said. "We can eat on the porch and explore the area behind it. There are a couple of mines close by."

"Look!" Carly said. "There's a picnic table on the porch."

"Somebody else had the same idea we did."

"The table has benches too. We're in luck."

The car bounced as Darien guided it across the rutted terrain and stopped near the porch. "Grab the food," he said, "and I'll bring the drinks."

They stepped on the porch and put the food on the green plastic table which had benches attached to it.

"The table and benches are clean," Carly said. "It looks like somebody ate here a few minutes ago."

They sat down opposite each other, divided the sausage biscuits, and placed the box of lukewarm French fries in the middle of the table. Conversation flowed freely as they ate. Carly found it easy to talk to Darien, particularly about similar growing-up experiences they'd both had, even though worlds apart. She was amazed to have so much in common with a man she'd known for less than a month.

After they devoured everything, Carly said, "I could have eaten one more sausage biscuit."

"Me too—they're habit forming. Maybe we'll get some more on the way back."

They stood, and Darien pointed to several faded posters thumbtacked to the wall. "Do you want to buy a gold mine?"

They crossed the porch and examined the posters. "Are they really trying to sell mines which have never produced any gold?" Carly asked.

Darien nodded. "They are. Some of these mines have been sold and resold several times."

Carly read aloud from the posters, "By-Chance Mine, Grizzly Bear Mine, Lucky Mine, Missing Link . . . rather inventive names."

"Let's take a look at a couple of them."

They got into Darien's car, circled behind the building, and drove along a dirt path leading toward the mines. Less than a half-mile from the assay building, the road ended abruptly at a massive pile of orange dirt.

"End of the line," Darien said. He pointed to a dim footpath. "That trail leads to some nearby mines." A short walk later, they came to a small mine shaft with metal grating covering the opening.

"Why does this mine have a door?" Carly asked.

"It's not really a door," Darien said. "It's grating to keep large animals out and provide entry and exit for bats."

Carly backed away. "Bats?"

"Don't worry. They don't come out until sundown."

"Are you sure?"

"Pretty sure."

Cautiously, Carly approached the grating and peered inside. Sunlight illuminated the mineshaft until it made a horizontal turn about ten feet below the surface. A wooden ladder with several broken rungs leaned against the side of the shaft. Scaly brown lizards crept along the ladder. As Carly watched, one of them flicked out its tongue and caught an unsuspecting fly. She glanced back at Darien, who had an amused gleam in his eye, obviously getting a kick out of introducing her to the desert.

"I smell ammonia," Carly said.

"It's bat guano."

"Ugh! Let's find another mine."

"There's one this way," Darien said, pointing toward another trail.

They fell in step and walked along the dim path lined with tumbleweeds and other desert flora. Carly pointed at several plants and repeated the names Darien had mentioned earlier. When they'd covered about fifty yards, the road turned sharply and dead-ended at another mound of dirt. Carly was mystified. "Why so many dirt piles?" she asked.

"The dirt is tailings from old mining operations. The Bureau of Mines uses it to block the access roads."

"Why are they trying to keep people from exploring this area?"

"Nobody cares if you explore on foot," Darien said, "but would-be explorers kept getting stuck and stranded while trying to drive to the mines. So the Bureau blocked the access roads to protect city-slickers vacationing in the desert."

Carly frowned. "City-slickers like me?"

"Not you. You've already learned the names of the plants around here."

"Impressed?"

"Definitely."

As they circled the mound, they came upon a green plastic bucket full of orange dirt. A yellow shovel and rake lay near the bucket, and the ground was cross-hatched with lines where it had been raked.

"Somebody's been looking for gold," Darien said.

"These are beach toys," Carly said. "Somebody brought kids out here to play. It looks like they left in a hurry. Maybe they found a big nugget."

"I doubt it."

Carly dumped the dirt from the bucket and placed the shovel and rake inside it. "These toys match the table and bench set," she said. "We ought to put them on the porch."

When they arrived back at the assay building, Carly surveyed the surroundings thoroughly. A shallow ditch ran along the dim road leading from the mines to the highway right-of-way. A recent shower had deposited a small sandbar on highway property at the end of the ditch. An unreflective urge hit Carly, and still carrying the bucket, she headed toward the sandbar at a fast pace.

"What are you doing?" Darien asked.

"Prospecting for gold."

"Good luck," Darien said. He followed Carly toward the highway and watched as she dropped to her knees and began to rake the dry reddish soil. After raking frantically for a moment, Carly looked up and said, "I have a feeling there's something here."

"Dig on," Darien said with an amused smile.

Carly tossed the rake aside and picked up the shovel. Methodically, she began to turn over the soil, clump by clump, running her fingers through each shovel full of sand that she turned over. Several times, her fingers touched a hard object which felt like it might be a nugget but turned out to be gravel instead. Time and again, nothing but gravel. Just as she was beginning to think that she must look like a dumb cluck to Darien, she felt something different—something smooth and heavy. Could this be the real thing? She grasped the sand-coated object between her thumb and index finger. With great care, she blew the dust away, and a flash of gold-colored sunlight reflected off the object.

"Eureka!" Carly shrieked. "A nugget."

Darien dropped to his knees beside Carly. "Let me see it."

Carly held the nugget in the palm of her hand and extended it toward Darien. "I hope it's not fool's gold," she said. "Can you tell the difference?"

Darien picked up the nugget and studied it carefully.

"It's real gold," he said, "but this is the strangest nugget I've ever seen."

"How so?"

"It's like twin BBs fused together."

***

On Monday afternoon, while Carly sat in the library studying, her thoughts drifted back to her recent Orogrande adventure. Though she'd made it clear to Darien that shared McDonald's sausage biscuits didn't constitute a date, in retrospect, it seemed like one, and the thought was somewhat disconcerting. After thinking about it for a while, something else bothered her too—the way she'd talked so much, telling Darien everything about her life as far back as she could remember. Carly had never thought of herself as a garrulous person, but now, Darien would think she was. Analyzing her actions, as she always did, it was easy to see how it happened. Darien was someone new who didn't already know everything about her. That made him easy to talk to. Darien hadn't pried; he didn't need to. She'd laid out her life story of her own free will and enjoyed doing it. What harm could there be in that?

Her iTab pinged, and Carly picked it up to see an avatar of Dr. Miriam Graves, her faculty advisor.

She touched the screen and said, "Hello, Dr. Graves."

"Good afternoon, Carly," Graves said. "Hope I'm not interrupting something important."

"You're not. I'm lollygagging in the library."

"I'd like to talk to you about your research proposal this afternoon, if possible."

"How about right now?"

"That would be great. Come to my office."

Carly stuffed her iTab into its carrying case, slung it over her shoulder and left the library. Although she'd talked with Dr. Graves only a few times, Carly felt like they were on the same wavelength. The professor had invited Carly to call her *Miriam* if she liked, but she hadn't done so yet. Dr. Graves had been in the Air force twenty years before becoming a college professor, and a *chain-of-command* approach seemed more appropriate. Graves was about the same age as Carly's mother, but looked much younger and reminded Carly of Anna, her aunt who was only thirty-two. Like Anna, Dr. Graves reflected her military background in everything she did.

Carly entered the outer office. Graves' administrative assistant, Janice Smith, motioned toward the inner office and said, "She's expecting you. Go on in."

At Graves instruction, Carly sat down.

"Congratulations, Carly," Graves said. "The research proposal that you and Mr. Segura submitted has been tentatively approved by DARPA."

"What do they mean by *tentative?*" Carly asked, trying to remain calm.

"DARPA requested more details about how you plan to test for ESP."

"We'll get on it right away."

"Approval went up the chain of command to our college president, Dr. Sheldon Leonard," Graves said. "He spoke with a DARPA agent. The agent assured him that this research fell into the category of projects which Mr. Horn advocates, blending two distinctly differing disciplines. Incidentally, in his recent speech, some of Mr. Horn's phraseology about *thinking outside the box* reminded me of the research paper you wrote during your senior year at the University of Houston."

"I doubt the President read my paper," Carly said.

"It was this paper which brought you to my attention," Graves said. "Not the fact that you were an *A-student*. Everyone awarded a scholarship in psychology this year was an *A-student*."

"Were astronomy scholarships awarded on the same basis?"

"Yes, including Mr. Segura," Graves said. "I saw him go into Craig's office a few minutes ago, and they're discussing this project, as well. Thanks to President Horn, we will actually study ESP as a possible tool to decipher extraterrestrial contacts. We may get laughed off of planet Earth or we may solve a perplexing riddle. In either case, this should be an exciting adventure. Aside from your classroom work, this is the primary study you'll be doing as a graduate student."

"Fantastic!"

"I'll drop my professional façade for a moment," Graves said, leaning toward Carly and smiling faintly. "Mr. Segura is a handsome young man."

Carly suppressed a smile. "Yes, he is," she said, nodding slowly. "But I have a boyfriend in Houston." She was surprised at how quickly a serious conversation had turned to *girl-talk* at the mention of Darien Segura.

As quickly as it started, the girl-talk ended. Graves leaned back in her chair, reconstructed her professor's demeanor, and said, "Let's get back to the subject at hand. Later this week, Craig and I will meet with you and Mr. Segura to discuss more details of your research proposal."

"Will I continue to report to you?"

"Yes, and Mr. Segura will report to Craig," Graves said. "By mutual agreement, and with the consent of the dean, I'll coordinate the overall project. Obviously, Craig and I will make a concentrated effort to provide you with unified leadership."

"Will DARPA have any control over the research?"

"I've asked my department head that same question," Graves said. "He assured me that we'll have academic freedom. Yet, whoever controls the purse strings controls the project to some degree, so we'd be naive not to think DARPA will be tracking our results closely in order to keep the President informed. And Mr. Horn may expect results faster than we can produce them. Hopefully, we'll make enough progress to keep the funding."

Carly nodded. "We'll do our best."

Graves stood. "Okay, have a good evening, and I'll see you tomorrow."

Carly left the office elated but well aware that the upcoming project would challenge her like she'd never been challenged before. She visualized President Horn looking over their shoulders holding a stopwatch, the old-fashioned wind-up type going *tick-tock, tick-tock, tick tock…*

CHAPTER 9

Darien arrived at the science building annex as the temperature approached 90 degrees, warm for a mid-September day. In front of the main entrance, a half-dozen people carrying signs marched back and forth on the sidewalk. A steady stream of students passed by the demonstrators, some accepting leaflets from the sign-carriers and others ignoring them completely. Several students stopped to talk briefly with the protestors before moving on, and two uniformed guards watched the proceedings from a Campus Security golf cart parked at the curb. Such protests had increased after Rex Horn's election and again after his M13 Contact speech. Darien wondered if the President would take a stand against the protesters, or if he would side with them regarding animal rights. With Horn's idiosyncratic personality, it was anybody's guess.

The protesters were orderly, and Darien was certain that security had checked their permit. He didn't observe any overt hostility and guessed that college students who supported the demonstration and those who opposed it were split about fifty-fifty, as would be the case on virtually any topic in America today. Darien believed the RADS had intentionally fragmented the country along multiple lines— sex, age, nationality, religion, income, education, rural/

urban, north/south, east/west and probably other ways he hadn't thought of yet. He saw the system as a political jig-saw puzzle with the two controlling parties attempting to assemble enough pieces before major elections to elect candidates that they could control. This system had worked well for years, but at the last election, Rex Horn threw a monkey wrench into the *divide-and-conquer* political machinery.

One of the signs identified the protestors as members of the SPCA, the Society for the Prevention of Cruelty to Animals, and other signs proclaimed the society's current messages along with some anti-Rex Horn messages:

MONKEYS HAVE CONSTITUTIONAL RIGHTS TOO
FREE ALL NON-HUMAN PRIMATES
PARABELLUM DOSSIER NEARS COMPLETION

One thing leaped out at Darien—he'd never seen a single one of the protestors before. They certainly weren't students at NM State. He surmised that they'd been bussed in, maybe from California, although it would have been a long bus ride. Still, that possibility made sense because San Diego and Alamogordo had been in a *monkey war* for some time. Several years before California seceded from the union, the San Diego Zoo loaned four rhesus monkeys to the Alamogordo Zoo. When California became a separate nation and asked for the animals to be returned, the Governor of New Mexico reported that the monkeys had died after producing several offspring. At that point, CalGov insisted that the Alamogordo Zoo still owed the San Diego Zoo four monkeys, if not the originals, then their offspring.

Another thing was obvious from the signs. The anti-Horn faction would take any opportunity to state their case against the President, and lately, this faction seemed to be increasing in number.

One of the protesters offered Darien a leaflet, but he declined and entered the annex. He was in agreement with the society's stance against cruelty to animals, but giving monkeys constitutional rights was another matter entirely, a concept he'd never support.

He went up the stairs to the second floor and joined a clump of students trudging down the hallway. At first glance, everyone looked alike. Many wore threadbare jeans and colorful tops, most wore backpacks, and nearly all thumbed their ITabs as they walked along. Darien glanced around and located Carly just ahead, not a difficult task, even with her back toward him. She was the tallest woman in the group, and the only one with an auburn ponytail. He quickened his pace and fell in step with her.

"Hi, Carly," Darien said. "What gives with the protesters outside?"

"I don't know," Carly said. "According to Dr. Graves, we've met SPCA guidelines and have a valid permit from NatGov."

"Well, whatever happens, this is the day I've been waiting for. Dr. McLennan gave his okay for me to observe any psychology class or lab that I wanted to."

"He seems like a nice guy," Carly said, "and looks so Scottish that I expected him to talk with a brogue."

"He's from Kansas."

"Are he and Dr. Graves an item?"

"Not that I know of," Darien said, "but they might become one. His wife died of cancer a couple of years ago, and she's divorced."

They walked along the hallway with their fellow students, most of whom were going to a lab of some type. The crowd was chatty. Darien overheard snippets of a half-dozen or more conversations, all of them discussing after-class plans. The mood was light and jovial.

Darien saw a thin gold chain around Carly's neck, and dangling from the chain was a sparkling object—the nugget from Orogrande, Carly's one-in-a-million find.

He pointed toward the pendant. "How'd you get that done so quickly?"

"Hope and Anna did it for me," Carly said.

"It's spectacular."

"The chain belonged to Hope, and Anna knows a jewelry repairman in El Paso who put a loop on the nugget at cost. That's the only way I could have afforded it."

"That's probably the biggest nugget found in Orogrande since the gold rush," Darien said. "Maybe it's your good luck charm."

"I see it as an omen, instead of a good luck charm."

"Because it's twin BBs?"

"Absolutely," Carly said, smiling. "We're going to test twin monkeys for ESP, and I just found twin gold BBs in a spot where others had searched for years. See how I'm connecting the dots?"

Darien and Carly entered the glassed-in balcony above the laboratory. Early-arriving students had already claimed the seats along the front window and others were streaming into the room. The electricity of expectancy filled the air.

Darien pointed. "Let's grab those seats along the aisle. We're going to have a full house today. Most are probably observers like me."

"We're all observers today," Carly said. "Our assignment is to watch the experiment and write a report on our observations."

"Why didn't Dr. Graves let you help?"

"I'm not certified to work with non-human primates."

Darien frowned. "Oh . . . that."

"At any rate, this *monkey-see-monkey-do* experiment is great advertising for the university."

"I read the paper you sent me," Darien said.

The paper was from the turn of the century when researchers transmitted brain waves from monkeys at Duke University to a computer at MIT. Upon receiving the waves, the computer activated a robotic arm in the MIT lab. In preparation for the experiment, electrodes were implanted in the cerebral cortexes of the monkeys. This technique worked, but the implants deteriorated rapidly and other methods of transmitting brain waves had been sought for years. A recently-developed bipolar antenna ended the need to implant electrodes in the subject's brain.

The antenna was worn as a skullcap, and scientists had expected it to end the animal-testing controversy, which didn't happen. Psychologists and others involved in animal testing were still tip-toeing a tightrope.

Darien was not surprised that psychology—or even parapsychology—had reached *hot topic* status around Alamogordo. What was surprising to many, however, was that NatGov was funding the studies at a venue as small as NM State's Alamogordo Campus. When President Horn broke the news of this new ESP study, Alphabet News commentators went into an editorializing dither. *Why not MIT or Duke? Why not Johns Hopkins? Why not CalTech?* Why not *my favorite university?* Both President Horn and his Press Secretary had brushed the topic aside during several news conferences. It was obvious that Mr. Horn had very little concern for what his opponents thought.

Darien believed he understood the situation, even if Alphabet News didn't. New Mexico displayed unique locations and had witnessed one-of-a-kind events. He ran through the list—Los Alamos Atomic Laboratory, the first nuclear blast at Trinity Site, secret aircraft flights, rocket tests over White Sands, the Roswell UFO incident, other UFO sightings, meteorite strikes, and Project Mayflower. He saw plenty of reasons to study space psychology in the Land of Enchantment.

Darien's introspection was interrupted by the pneumatic hiss of hallway doors swinging open as a bustle of activity unfolded in the laboratory below the balcony.

Circuits hummed and lights brightened as two animal handlers wearing green hospital scrubs entered the room. Each pulled a bright metal cage housing two rhesus monkeys. The cages had imitation thatched roofs, and were equipped with swings, climbing trees, balls, and a variety of multi-colored plastic toys. Two women wearing white lab coats walked behind the cages.

"Who is the other woman with Dr. Graves?" Darien asked. "I've never seen her before."

Graves went to the center of the room and turned toward the audience. "Good afternoon," she said. "I'm Dr. Miriam Graves, and this is Sandra Harrison, an SPCA representative. As required by federal law, she's here to insure that these primates are handled in accordance with our permit. In addition, there are cameras in the room which will broadcast this experiment to the appropriate authorities for review. We are following NatGov protocols to the letter, yet as you know, animal experimentation is controversial, even in tests like ours where the animals aren't harmed in any way. Several lower courts are hearing animal rights cases as we speak. However, amid the controversy, and following the proper guidelines, we will continue as planned.

"Our four subjects have participated in similar tests before. They know they will get treats if they perform their tasks properly. Are there any questions before we start?"

When there were none, Graves continued, "Monkeys normally give birth to a single offspring, just like humans.

However, multiple births are not uncommon, and our subjects this morning are two sets of male twins named Art and Bart, and Cale and Dale—or just A, B, C, and D. Most psychologists believe that ESP, if it's found at all, will likely be found in twins communicating with each other; however, we'll test these monkeys two ways, as non-twin pairs and as twin pairs."

Graves motioned toward the handlers. The green-clad trainers sprang into action, sliding a clear plastic partition into each cage, thereby dividing it into two identical sections with one monkey in each section. The monkeys went to the divider and made faces at one another until a handler motioned for them to approach the front of the cage. All four of them responded immediately, and the handlers passed out treats. The handlers then gave each monkey a helmet antenna which looked like a white plastic baseball cap. In unison, the well-trained monkeys donned the antennas and stood at parade rest, waiting for another chocolate-covered marshmallow.

Darien glanced at Carly. "Who's running this show? The monkeys or their handlers?"

"These monkeys know what they have to do in order to earn treats."

Graves resumed her lecture. "In each cage, one monkey has ten flashcards and his twin has a box containing ten balls duplicating the colors of the cards. When the handler gives the signal, the first monkey will select one of the cards and hold it up. The second monkey will hold up the corresponding ball. They've participated in this type of test numerous times, but today, we will add a new test—one they've never seen before."

The first test began at Graves' signal. Both non-twin pairs of monkeys made a perfect score on the first round, and repeated the score when paired together as twins. After each set of tests, the handlers gave out treats. The monkeys gulped them down and began jumping around and chattering, begging for more.

"Obviously, this first test has nothing to do with ESP," Graves said. "It's a learned reaction, important training because it reinforces the monkeys' desire to perform well in order to get a reward. The next study looks nearly the same but is completely different. The subjects would require ESP in order to score 100%."

The handlers replaced the clear divider with a partition of plywood, making it impossible for any monkey to see his counterpart. The monkeys chattered in plaintive tones making it obvious they didn't like the new direction the test was headed. Graves stood where all of the monkeys could see her and signaled for the test to begin. When the test ended, the monkeys in one cage had matched the colored balls and flash cards only once in ten tries, and the monkeys in the other cage had matched the items three out of ten.

"Combined results, a total of four correct matches in twenty attempts," Graves said. "This small number of attempts is not a statistically significant sample; however, both tests gave a combined score of 20%, the average we would get by running the test thousands of times."

The handlers rearranged the monkeys by putting one set of twins in each cage. With the divider in place, no monkey could see his twin, but each of them appeared calmer, seeming to realize that his brother was on the other side of the plywood barrier. The thought of ESP crossed Darien's mind briefly, but he dismissed it, certain that the monkeys recognized each other by smell and by the constant chatter they kept up.

"This next test will tell us if the monkeys perform better when matched as twins," Graves said. "If they do, this would suggest the possibility of ESP. Please note, I said *suggest the possibility*. That's all it would be. The tests would have to be repeated many times before any conclusion could be reached."

As the test began, Darien looked back and forth between the cages and realized immediately that the two sets of twins were performing at a dramatically different level. The monkeys in one cage were fumbling around in an uncertain manner, while those in the adjoining cage were so well-synchronized it appeared that they could see one another. One pair of monkeys got only one match, while the other pair got eight matches.

Darien studied Miriam Graves reaction and read surprise on her face. She cleared her throat and said, "Students, these results are so extraordinary that we need to repeat them immediately. What I would like to do is . . . "

Before Graves finished her sentence, four armed NatGov Special Agents dressed in black uniforms burst out of the hallway. They ran to the monkey cages and positioned themselves between the handlers and the cages. Showing fright on their faces, the handlers backed away.

An agent wearing captain's bars approached Graves and asked, "Are you in charge of this laboratory?"

"Yes. I am," Graves said evenly, "and we have a NatGov/SPCA permit to run today's experiment. I'll pull it up on my iTab."

"Don't bother," the captain said, waiving Graves' iTab aside and extending his own tablet toward her. "This is an order signed by President Horn. It invalidates your permit and orders the release of these primates immediately."

"On what grounds?" Graves asked, returning the officer's gaze with an icy stare.

"This morning, California granted personhood status to several kinds of non-human primates, including rhesus monkeys," the officer said. "NatGov has a treaty with California which bans unlawful detention of their citizens, so in a surprise move, the President ordered their return immediately."

While a staredown continued in the lab below the balcony, Darien felt his iTab vibrating with a cluster of incoming messages. He lay it in his lap, observing that practically everyone in the room was doing so as well. The dancing icons on his screen showed that the social media was ablaze with messages. He touched the Twitter icon, and a message stream began to scroll down at an unreadable pace. He double-tapped the icon, and the initial tweet materialized onscreen.

The tweet was from President Rex Horn: *I decided to let California have the monkeys. Maybe they'll vote Independent in the next election.*

A roar erupted throughout the room. It was about a fifty-fifty mix of cheers and jeers.

***

That afternoon, Darien sat alone in the library, reviewing his astronomy notes. Tomorrow would be Friday, the day Dr. McLennan often gave pop quizzes. After an hour of study, he was about to retrieve his Volkswagen and return to Orogrande when his iTab chimed. Dusty Rhodes' avatar appeared on the monitor.

Darien touched the icon and said, "Hey, Dusty. What's up?"

"Hello, Uncle Darien."

"What are you talking about?"

"Get alert, man," Dusty said with a broad smile. "April's pregnant."

"Wow! Congratulations."

"We want you to be godfather, surrogate uncle, or something like that."

"My pleasure. When is the baby due?"

"About the middle of April."

"I saw April and Ashley driving past the campus this morning as I was going to class," Darien said. "I wondered why they were out so early."

"They were going to the doctor."

"Both of them?"

"Well . . . uh . . . "

Darien's iTab chimed again, and Roger Carson's avatar popped onscreen. Even before answering, he knew what Roger was calling about. Ashley was pregnant too. He was about to become *double-uncle Darien*.

CHAPTER 10

Starbucks was half full when Carly entered early Monday morning. The tantalizing aroma of fresh-brewed coffee greeted her as she picked her way through the tables. The coffee shop was the regular pre-class meeting place for a gaggle of students with discretionary funds available, a group which didn't include her or Darien, although they had friends in the group. Today, regardless of financial status, they'd decided to treat themselves to a continental breakfast as a reward for getting tentative approval of their research proposal. Since neither of them had a class until 10:00 a.m., they could relax a bit before plunging into their busy schedules. She salivated at the thought of latte accompanied by a pastry yet to be decided.

Carly greeted someone at nearly every table as she walked toward the *Place Order Here* sign. Before she reached the counter, Darien entered through the door connecting the coffee shop to the library. She waved at him. He joined her and they stepped to the counter.

The short barista in his early twenties looked at Carly and said, "Hello. Would you like to go to a party tonight?"

Carly met the barista's gaze and said, "Not with you."

The barista turned toward Darien and said, "How about introducing me to your new friend."

"Greg, this is Carly Hansen," Darien said. "Carly—Greg Newman."

"Pleased to meet you," Carly said.

"Likewise," Greg said. "Sorry I was obnoxious."

"No problem," Carly said.

"Carly is studying parapsychology," Darien said. "She knows how to deal with people like you."

"*Para?*" Greg said. "What's that mean?"

"She can read your mind," Darien said.

"Really?" Greg said, redirecting his gaze toward Carly. "Can you tell what I'm thinking right now?"

"Yes, and you may as well forget about it."

The three of them laughed, and Darien said, "She has a boyfriend, and he's bigger than you."

"It's always that way," Greg said, shaking his head. "What can I serve you?"

They ordered tall lattes and Darien requested a splash of vanilla in his. To accompany the drinks, Carly chose a blueberry scone and Darien an apple Danish. As per their earlier agreement to go Dutch, Greg rang up their purchases separately, and they took out their iTabs and touched the *Pay-Now* app. A mini-screen atop the pastry display case blinked green to indicate acceptance of the payments. They moved to the end of the bar and watched Greg prepare the drinks the old-fashioned barista way. A few years earlier, Starbucks and other coffee shops had tested robot baristas to prepare drinks, but customers complained that the robotic service was cold and impersonal. Moreover, some claimed the coffee they brewed didn't taste the same as coffee made by people. Apparently, barista jobs were secure well into the future, even though many other professions were succumbing to robots with artificial intelligence.

A minute later, Greg placed two hot lattes on the counter beside the pastries which Darien and Carly had selected.

Darien motioned toward an empty table in the far corner of the room. "Let's go over there," he said, as they picked up their orders.

Once they were seated at the table, Carly said, "Did you look at the articles on brainwaves that I sent you?"

Darien nodded. "I did. They're very low bandwidths compared to what I'm used to."

"It's best to think of them as a mixed spectrum of waves, sort of like a musical concert," Carly said. "Most of our activity will be focused on beta waves which are produced during problem solving, decision making, or other highly focused mental activity."

"Beta waves," Darien said. "Let me see . . . that's approximately 12–40 hertz."

"What did you think about the Duke/MIT study?" Carly asked.

"Psychologists didn't call it telekinesis, did they?"

"Oh, no," Carly said, shaking her head. "Brainwaves didn't move the arm. They activated a computer which moved it. But I hope we can find people able to transmit brain waves directly to each other, without using a computer."

"Why do you want to eliminate computers?"

"The researchers at Duke and MIT worked together on everything," Carly said, "including the computer set-up. We don't have that luxury. If someone out there is trying to contact us, we don't have a clue as to what equipment they're using."

"I'm sure they'll be using some type of computer."

"We may have to do so, as well," Carly said. "Still, I hope we can find *person to person* ESP without using accessory equipment."

"I'm comfortable with brain waves," Darien said. "What about your SETI assignment?"

"I did it," Carly said, with a nod. "The first thing I noticed was the inventive names the SETI pioneers used—Ozma, Pheonix, and Cyclops. I read everything you suggested and am ready to start studying FRBs, rather than reading about other people studying them."

"There's one thing we've glossed over so far," Darien said. "Even if we discover ESP, the incoming radio waves will have to be converted into some form compatible with brain waves before ESP could possibly be of use."

"We can see, hear, feel, taste, and smell. That's the five senses," Carly said, "and now, we're looking for the sixth—ESP." She was 100% convinced that it existed and almost as certain that she and Darien would prove it, hopefully in the not-too-distant future.

"Still, those with the sixth sense will need to receive the signals in some form they can process," Darien said.

"We'll figure out a way to do it," Carly said, her jaw firm with resolve. "I'm convinced we'll play a role in solving this long-standing riddle."

"We'll give it our best shot," Darien said.

"Several years ago, I read an article about the observatory in Puerto Rico sending a message into space during the mid-seventies," Carly said. "Is it possible the recent surge of incoming signals is related to the message we sent? Maybe someone is answering."

Darien shook his head. "Not possible. The Arecibo Observatory sent their message to the star cluster M13, the object of current attention. That cluster is about 25,000 light years away."

Carly did a quick calculation. "So, if they answer immediately upon receipt of our message, we'll get their reply around 52,000 AD."

Darien nodded. "Something like that, give or take a couple of centuries."

"What about the President's claims that Earth is receiving urgent messages like SOS, MAYDAY, or CEASE AND DESIST?"

"That seems rather unlikely," Darien said. "Mr. Horn might have been putting extra frosting on the cake. The time required to respond is so long that asking for help or sending a warning from the M13 region would be meaningless. Any crisis a distant world is facing would be ancient history long before their message reached Earth."

Carly pursed her lips thoughtfully and asked, "What message did we send to M13?"

"It was a bitmap that included the numbers from 1 to 10, several chemical formulas, the image of a telescope, a diagram of the solar system, and a stick figure depicting a human."

Carly's eyes widened. "A stick figure?"

"Uh-huh."

Carly bumped her forehead with the heel of her hand. "A sobering thought just hit me," she said. "What if we decode the radio waves and they turn out to be a stick figure family like the ones you see on the rear window of cars? You know—a mother and father, some children, a dog . . . maybe a cat."

Darien shrugged. "As I see it, we should concentrate on deciphering the messages, rather than worrying about their content."

"Regarding M13 being 25,000 light years away, do you think it's possible to travel faster than light?"

"I think 186,000 miles per second is the speed limit of the universe," Darien said.

"What about teleportation?"

"You don't believe teleportation is actually possible, do you?"

Carly was puzzled. "You think we have a chance to locate people with ESP. Why cross teleportation off the list of possible psi phenomena?"

"ESP is considerably different from teleportation," Darien said, with strong conviction lacing his voice. "Brainwaves are electrical impulses. To me, that makes ESP theoretically possible; however, I don't see any scientific basis for teleportation."

"One of these days, you're going discover something that can't be explained by the laws of science," Carly said. "And when you do, you'll look at the world in a new light."

"Maybe it will happen soon."

"I noticed that all the early signals were recorded on paper charts for further analysis. How are signals commonly processed today?"

"Modern radio telescope arrays collect a whole range of radio frequencies, and use computers to divide the waves into narrow-band channels, billions of them in some instances. The signals are stored on computers, of course, not on graph paper."

"I see something encouraging," Carly said. "Both brain waves and radio waves have known frequencies which can be recorded and studied in a variety of ways. We have a chance to succeed if we can find some people with ESP."

"Your fellow psychologists say twins are our best chance," Darien said, "especially identical twins. After thinking about the monkey tests, I'm wondering if Art and Bart are fraternal twins, and Cale and Dale are identical."

Carly shrugged. "The monkeys looked pretty much the same to me."

"Let's put together a plan for rounding up a few identical twins for a small pilot study."

"What's the population of Alamogordo?" Carly asked.

"About 51,000, according to the 2040 census."

Carly's brow furrowed as she made a quick calculation. "Twins make up around 3% of the population," she said. "So over 1500 twins should be living here, some in every age group. We'll have to decide which age group to study."

"I suggest we concentrate on high school juniors and seniors at first," Darien said, as he thumbed his iTab. "They'd probably be the easiest to recruit."

They began scrolling through the U.S. Census Bureau data on their iTabs. After tapping furiously at her screen for a moment, Carly said, "Adding the numbers for ages 16 through 18 indicates there should be about 60 twins living in Alamogordo who are juniors or seniors in high school."

"That would be 30 sets," Darien said. "I have no idea how many of them are identical, but I know several sets who are. Surely we can entice some of them to come in for testing."

"What would be the best way to do it?"

"The university maintains close ties with the surrounding community," Darien said. "If our advisors can get DARPA to approve the plan, the Publicity Office can get the word out quickly."

"The participants will expect rewards," Carly said. "Just like the monkeys."

"Maybe we can give a three-day pass to Disneyland for everyone who takes the test?"

"I like that idea," Carly said, her voice rising with excitement, "and it shouldn't be cost prohibitive. Our advisors would probably approve it and submit it to DARPA."

"If we find people with ESP, we'll have to offer them something to make them want to link up with the M13 Contact Study."

"How about college scholarships?"

"That would be expensive," Darien said, "but Mr. Horn emphasized thinking outside the box. Maybe he'll put his money where his mouth is."

"We may be selecting our replacements when we bring high school seniors into this study," Carly said. "If we don't solve the problem, it'll fall into their hands."

"Let's give it our best shot and see what happens."

"I'll draft up an amendment to our proposal and text it to you," Carly said. "Edit it and send it back. When we agree on everything, I'll present it to Dr. Graves. Hopefully, we can get past the tentative status."

"Be sure to emphasize this first round will be a pilot test," Darien said. "We don't want anyone to think we're claiming that we can solve this riddle by testing a handful of people living in Alamogordo. We need to develop some test protocols. That's about all we can expect from a small test."

"I agree completely."

"Will we use flash cards like the ones used in the monkey test?"

"No," Carly said, shaking her head, "although cards, called *Zener Cards*, have been used to test for ESP. Nobody trusts such tests because cards are easy to manipulate and produce pre-determined results. We'll probably use a new test developed by DARPA."

"DARPA seems to be controlling every aspect of this project," Darien said. "It worries me a little to have them looking over our shoulders."

"Me too. But we wouldn't have gotten this chance without their involvement."

***

Two days later, as Carly entered her room at the end of a busy day, her iTab pinged and the words, *Text from Miriam Graves* appeared.

She touched the screen and a message materialized:

Carly,

Great news! The amended proposal that you and Mr. Segura presented for pilot testing twins for ESP has been approved by DARPA, and we will proceed shortly. I'll inform Mr. Segura by text this evening and would appreciate both of you coming by my office at 7:30 on Friday morning.

Dr. Miriam Graves, PhD.

"Yes!" Carly said, clenching a fist and waving it in the air.

CHAPTER 11

Anticipating a special evening, Darien parked in front of the Rhode's house on San Simon Circle in Mesa Heights. A few hours earlier, April and Ashley's doctor had informed them that they both were carrying twins who would be delivered about the middle of April. Since Darien and Carly had just gotten approval to search for ESP in twins, the timing of the news made it seem like fiction. Darien's godfather role had expanded exponentially since its inception.

Mesa Heights was still under construction. The new subdivision was HUD's answer to the housing shortage caused by the Mayflower Project. The beige stucco houses all had the same open floor plan with two bedrooms and a small study. The tan exteriors were identical, except half of the garages were on the left end of the house and half on the right, making them mirror images of each other. The effect was a little too cookie-cutter for Darien's taste. He preferred the wide-open spaces.

He rang the doorbell. April opened the door with Dusty close behind her. "Come in," she said. "Roger and Ashley are running late as usual, but we aren't going to wait for them."

"We want you to taste the fried squash while it's still hot," Dusty said.

"When can you bring Carly to one of our get-togethers?" April said.

Darien shrugged. "Probably not any time soon. She's busy with school work most of the time, and that guy from Houston texts her about a dozen times a day."

"You need to be a little pushier," April said.

Ignoring April's match-making efforts, Darien asked, "Are Eric and Lynn coming?"

Dusty shook his head. "They went to Ruidoso for a long weekend."

"How could they miss a party like this?" Darien said.

"On the spur of the moment, Lynn's parents decided to make a quick trip to the *Inn of the Mountain Gods*," April said. "They begged Eric and Lynn to join them. You know how it is. Lynn has a hard time saying no to her mother."

April motioned toward the sofa. "Sit down, and I'll get you something to drink. We have iced tea and lemonade, so I can make an Arnold Palmer, if you'd like one. We also have beer and soft drinks."

"That's the Rhodes' standard drink menu," Dusty said, "but we're trying to broaden our horizons. April bought a couple of bottles of wine today. We can try one of them if you like."

"I'll take a Diet Coke for now," Darien said. "If you open the wine later, I'll sample it."

"We've been studying California wines," Dusty said. "The one April bought is called *Ménage a Trois*. It's an inexpensive Napa Valley wine, but that may change soon. President Horn is going to put a tariff on everything coming from California."

"Unless the RADS impeach him before he gets the chance," April said.

"They don't have the votes to do it," Darien said. "Besides, Horn loves to bicker with his enemies on social media in order to get free publicity."

"They're coming up with new accusations every day," Dusty said. "Some of them are pretty inventive—like this Parabellum thing."

"Do you think the congressional investigation into that organization will actually come up with an impeachable offense?" April said.

Darien shook his head. "Probably not, but that doesn't mean the RADS won't use it to impeach him if they can get the votes."

"I don't think Parabellum.org really exists," Dusty said.

"It must," April said. "It's in the news all the time."

"That doesn't mean much nowadays," Dusty said.

"It exists alright," Darien said. "At least on paper. It was incorporated in Florida three or four years ago."

"I never heard of it until Rex Horn took office," Dusty said.

"Me either," Darien said. "When it first began to be mentioned in the news, I googled the name, and a simple website popped up. It didn't mention anything about contributing to Rex Horn's election campaign, or anything about political affiliations. In fact, the site seemed to be under construction."

"If they're an underground organization, why would they put up a website?" April asked.

"That's what I wondered," Darien said. "The first time I heard the term *parabellum*, I wasn't sure what it meant, so I looked it up. In Latin, it means, *prepare for war*. The whole phrase is *si vis pacem, para bellum*, which is *if you want peace, prepare for war*."

"I seem to remember that phrase from Police Academy," Dusty said. "Did the United States ever use it as a slogan?"

"Not that I know of," Darien said. "But a long time ago, President Ronald Reagan had a similar motto, *Peace Through Strength*. Parabellum's website mentioned the motto."

"I knew I'd heard it before," Dusty said.

"I believe Horn is using Parabellum to threaten his opponents," April said.

"That's what the RADS claim," Darien said. "They've spent a lot of time investigating it."

April motioned toward the sofa again. "Sit down, *please*," she said emphatically. "The fried squash is getting cold while we're talking politics. Darien, I'll bring your Coke. Would you like another beer, Dusty?"

"No, thanks. I'm good."

"I hope the squash is still crisp," April said, heading toward the kitchen.

A moment later, she came back into the room carrying a serving tray above her head in a manner that concealed its contents from the seated men. With a flourish, she placed the platter on the cocktail table in front of the sofa and said, "Help yourselves, gentlemen."

Darien looked at the squash and his jaw dropped. "They're heart-shaped," he said. "Is this some kind of special occasion?"

"They grew that way," Dusty said. "Every neck has two bodies."

Dumbfounded, Darien stared at the squash.

"We didn't tell you about this when we first noticed it," Dusty said. "We wanted to surprise you in person."

"Does anybody else know?" Darien asked.

"Just Roger and Ashley," April said. "We planned to surprise them, too, but they wandered into our back yard while we were working in the garden yesterday."

The doorbell rang announcing the arrival of the Carsons. Darien got up and followed Dusty and April to the front door. The five friends exchanged hellos and hugs and returned to the living area.

"Sit down," Dusty said. "April will get you something to drink. We have the same things we always have."

"I'll take a beer," Roger said. He sat down and reached for the squash.

"Let me help you," Ashley said, moving toward the kitchen to join April.

Roger looked toward Darien. "What's your take on these weird-shaped vegetables?"

"I don't know what to make of them," Darien said, "but I'm sure that you and Dusty think the meteor caused this to happen."

"The idea makes sense," Roger said. "Just think—April and Ashley are having twins, and now twin squash are growing in our garden. Something weird is going on."

Dusty nodded vigorously and said, "Maybe the meteorite was hollow and contained some kind of chemical."

"The Space Force could be running a test," Roger said.

Darien pondered the situation. His friends maintained that the Space Force occupied stealth satellites orbiting the Earth, the old *eye in the sky* concept with satellites conducting surveillance on everyone, friend and foe alike. The idea that this complex system could be put into operation without anyone knowing about it didn't make sense. On the other hand, many things had gone on—and were still going on—in the New Mexico desert that didn't make sense.

After a lively discussion about the meteor strike's relationship to twins, the quintet of friends moved to the backyard, and Dusty put hamburgers on a preheated grill. Flames flared up, a cloud of gray smoke appeared, and the aroma of charcoaled beef filled the air. The sun hung low in the orange-colored sky, and the temperature hovered near 72 degrees, making the late September evening perfect for a hamburger cookout.

While sipping his beer, Dusty flipped the burgers with a long-handled spatula, and the conversation jumped from one topic to another, as it had done over the years. At this point in their lives, *starting a family* was one of the few topics which could compete with Planet X discussions and conspiracy theories.

"The burgers are ready," Dusty announced, as he deftly removed the sizzling patties from the grill and placed them on a warm platter.

"I'm looking forward to the poker game after we eat," Roger said. "My luck was terrible last time. I lost a hundred pennies."

"It didn't have anything to do with luck," Darien said. "It was your playing that was terrible."

"You should go back to playing for matches," Dusty said.

The life-long friends had a laugh at Roger's expense and began to assemble their burgers. Darien didn't see himself as the fifth wheel in the group, yet he couldn't help but reflect on how well Carly had fit in during the tour of the Roswell Exhibits and what a great addition she'd be to the party going on right now.

CHAPTER 12

"It was a little disappointing that only eight sets of twins volunteered," Carly said, as she and Darien approached the science building annex. "I was afraid Dr. Graves would postpone it until we could find some more."

"She wouldn't postpone anything that has a snowball's chance to uncover ESP," Darien said. "If this project is successful, she'll be able to write her own ticket."

They entered the building. Miriam Graves stood inside the hallway thumbing her iTab. "Darien," she said, "you know everybody who signed up. Wait outside and direct them to Room 101. Carly and I will double-check the test equipment."

Darien stepped back outside just in time to see the first family approaching. In the next ten minutes, he directed seven more families into the lab, all of whom arrived nearly the same time. When everybody was accounted for, Darien went to the lab to join the volunteers. A long table ran the length of the lab. Eight game consoles were lined up along one side of the table designated the *Receivers* side. A screen running the length of the table prevented the receivers from seeing their counterparts—the *Transmitters*—on the opposite side of the table.

For the last two days, Carly and Darien had studied the ESP test equipment manufactured by Simulacrum Inc. Carly was familiar with several of the company's products, including the popular internet game *Global Cooling on Mercury*. Simulacrum claimed to be the most avant-garde computer company in the world. Recently, she'd heard they were developing artificial intelligence communities for running polls and surveys. Rumors claimed that the company was developing AI citizens who could actually be polled like real people. That rumor was rather difficult to believe, even though Simulacrum manufactured some great products. She felt comfortable with the test equipment on the table before her.

"May I have your attention, please," Dr. Graves said in a loud voice.

When the chatter subsided, Graves continued. "Thank you for volunteering to participate in this ESP test. As promised, each family will receive a three-day pass to Disneyland, no matter how the test turns out. Now, at this point, I'd like for all parents and guardians to go across the hall to the faculty break room. There are several vending machines in the room for those who would like a snack. The tests will take about an hour and a half, after which an Amazon drone will deliver pizza, and we'll have a party in the faculty break room."

The parents followed Graves instructions. She turned toward the teenagers and continued, "Let me have your attention, please. You'll be tested as both ESP *Transmitters* and *Receivers*. The graduate students and I will be *Operators*. Now, I want one sibling from each pair of twins to sit in front of one of the consoles on the receivers' side of the table. The remaining sibling will sit on the transmitters' side. Both sides are clearly marked. Transmitters will concentrate on all moves the operator makes and attempt to transmit the information by ESP to their siblings seated opposite them. So . . . if there are no questions, please take your seats."

The teen-agers jockeyed for position until all were seated according to Graves' instructions. She snapped a picture of the arrangement and made notes on her iTab as Carly took up her position in front of the operator's console with Darien standing behind her.

"Miss Hansen will explain the rules and conduct the first round of tests," Graves said, placing a hand on Carly's shoulder. "Mr. Segura will conduct the second round, and I'll take over for the final round."

"Okay, twins. Listen up," Carly said. "First, I want each of you to get a plastic baseball cap from the table in front of you and put it on. This cap is a helmet antenna with a receiver, transmitter, and amplifier." She paused, and the teenagers on each side of the table put on the helmets. Carly continued, "The ESP test we're about to run might remind you of the old board game, Monopoly—in fact, it's called *Interplanetary Monopoly*. In this case, instead of trying to get Boardwalk and Park Place, your objective is to colonize one of the planets, the same one the operator colonizes. When I make a move, each sibling on my side of the table will observe the move and attempt to relay it by ESP to his/her sibling on the other side of the table. That sibling will attempt to duplicate my move. To start the game, I'll go to one of the spaceports and choose a rocket ship displaying a banner in one of the colors of the rainbow. Next, I'll journey to one of the planets. The developer cites 100 as a perfect score and 50 as the average score. Any questions so far?"

"Why aren't you wearing a helmet?" one of the Steele girls asked.

"We believe identical twins have a better chance to demonstrate ESP with each other than with non-twins like me."

"Is Pluto still considered a planet?" a Leonard boy asked.

"For the sake of this game, it is," Carly said.

"Can we pick Earth to colonize?" a Naranjo girl asked.

"Yes, it's one of the nine choices."

"What about the bonus squares?" a Phillips girl asked.

"They're just a diversion," Carly said. "They simulate the *Chance* and *Community Chest* cards on the Monopoly board but don't affect the final score. Neither do detours through the asteroid belt, or the space debris hazards. These features add to the looks of the game and lengthen playing time, but that's all they do."

"My math says that if you test 1000 sets of twins, four sets might get a perfect score without any ESP whatsoever," a Zane boy said. "What would you do then?"

"Excellent question," Carly said, with an approving smile. "We'd run the test again. The chance of the same team duplicating the operator's journey two times in a row is about one in 63 thousand. Three times in a row, about one in 16 million. Obviously, we're hoping this happens. It would mean that we've located twins with ESP."

When there were no more questions, Carly said, "Okay space travelers—get ready . . . get set . . . go." She touched the screen to move her token to the South Spaceport.

As she made her move, Carly watched each player's corresponding move register on the main monitor. Two teams chose the South Spaceport immediately, creating the possibility of a perfect score on the first test. That possibility remained intact when the Brooks twins chose a spaceship with an indigo banner, the same color that Carly had chosen. Now, the chance was one in nine that the Brooks twins would score 100 on the test. That would be a hoped-for start, although the test would have to be repeated several times for verification. Carly worked her way through a group of hurtling asteroids and selected the planet Neptune to colonize. She held her breath, waiting for the Brooks twins to make their final move of the first round.

They selected Venus. So much for a perfect score.

The average score for the first round was 49.9, a score indicating the complete absence of ESP. Carly looked at Darien. He returned her gaze, but she couldn't read his expression. Although she'd known him for only a short time, Carly was sure an initial failure wouldn't discourage him to a great extent. Strong resolve was one of their shared attributes.

Carly switched chairs with Darien and he led the second round of Intergalactic Monopoly. The average score was 51.

"A very slight improvement," Carly said. "I wonder if it's possible that the improvement could be based on information the twins learned during the first round."

"Maybe I have a tell," Darien said.

"*A tell.* What's that?"

"It's subconscious behavior which reveals a poker player's strategy to an observant opponent."

"If the twins keep getting higher scores every time you conduct the test, we'll have to consider that possibility."

After the second round of testing, Darien stood, and Miriam Graves sat down in front of the operator's console and conducted the third round of tests. The average score was 49.2, a number which disproved the idea of learning to play better by repeating the test.

Graves tapped at her iTab briefly and then looked up. "Combining the three tests gives an average score very close to 50," she said. "Exactly what you'd expect from testing subjects completely devoid of ESP; therefore, we have to conclude that no one in this group has it."

"Our sample wasn't big enough," Carly said. "We'll have to expand our search."

"Even though we didn't find ESP," Graves said, "we didn't mislead anybody. In your proposal, you referred to today's test as a *pilot test.*"

"I hope Mr. Horn sees it that way," Carly said, reflecting on the way the President had issued an executive order to abort the monkey tests while they were still in progress. Such a thing could happen again. If so, nothing could be done about it until after the Thanksgiving holidays.

"I think the pizza's here," Graves said. "Let's go to the break room down the hall."

All of the twins jumped up simultaneously and headed for the exit.

"When are you leaving for California?" Carly said, as she and Darien walked down the hall to join the pizza party.

"Early Saturday morning?"

"Have a good time."

"Thanks."

CHAPTER 13

"**A**ttention—the California border is one-half mile ahead," Darien's iTab chimed in a cheery computer voice which belied the tedium of the trip. "Reduce your speed and select a lane."

Darien rubbed his weary eyes and focused on a cluster of green signs perched above Interstate 8 in the distance. He'd just passed Yuma, Arizona, and at long last, he was about to enter The Republic of California. Darien had left Orogrande at 6:00 a.m. Other than two brief stops at McDonald's, he'd relentlessly pressed westward. The trip was tiring, made more so when the old VW's autopilot conked out just short of Las Cruces, forcing him to drive manually from that point on, practically the whole way. He was destined to rely on his own driving skills until he could save the money to get the autopilot repaired.

The scenery had been repetitive throughout the journey except for one brief instance. Near Saguaro National Park, he'd spotted a clump of cacti at least forty feet high. So far, that lone botanical oddity was the highlight reel of the day as far as topography and flora were concerned. With nothing but a straight interstate and unvarying scenery for mile after mile, his GPS app, *BestRoute*, had little to say most of the trip. He'd asked the app a question from time to time to make sure it wasn't napping or that he wasn't.

Fortunately, the public news screens provided a diversion. The RADS had just completed the dossier on Parabellum.org last week, and two days ago, amid the usual cacophony concerning executive privilege, they'd subpoenaed President Horn. This morning, less than forty-eight hours after the subpoena was issued, Alphabet News had begun to criticize the President for ignoring it.

As the day went on, Darien began to detect a shift in the narrative flow. It became obvious that, even though it was Saturday, a war was being waged behind the scenes. Every news screen that Darien approached told a slightly different story than the previous one. News screens in Las Cruces, read:

HORN IGNORES SUBPOENA FROM CONGRESS
IMPEACHMENT CERTAIN

Sixty miles later, near Deming, the screens read:

HORN'S ATTORNEY TO RELEASE STATEMENT
HORN ACKNOWLEDGES RECEIPT OF SUBPOENA

Just past Tucson, Darien swung off I-10 onto I-8 and passed the last news screen east of the California border:

HORN MAY APPEAR BEFORE CONGRESS
IMPEACHMENT REMAINS PROBABLE

Darien pondered the day's news. Early in the morning, impeachment was *certain*; whereas, by the end of the day, it was *probable*—a considerable shift in less than eight hours. Maybe the dossier had a few holes in it. He hoped the President agreed to appear before congress. The hearing would be quite entertaining.

At 8:00 a.m. Pacific Time, Darien had texted Rachel to let her know he was on the way. Since then, she'd texted him regularly to find out where he was. It reminded him of their childhood days with Rachel constantly asking *are we there yet?* when the family was making a short day-trip near Alamogordo. By an odd continuity, those memories were made in the VW Darien was currently driving along Interstate 8.

About a quarter mile from the California border, the smooth highway gave way to grooved pavement, causing the VW's tires to generate a high-pitched *wake-up call.* The light traffic slowed as the travelers prepared for the customs stop ahead. Darien coasted to a stop behind a short line of vehicles, his *traveling companions,* as he'd dubbed them after hours of driving across the desert together. The car in front of him, a red Ford Expedition, completely blocked his view of the traffic signals and barriers which controlled vehicular flow into California. He lowered his window and leaned out to get a better view of the Customs Office, a white portable building, just off the shoulder of the highway. Several tan-uniformed Customs Agents with iTabs in hand stood casually in front the building, each waiting to take his turn with an approaching vehicle. The short line moved quickly, and after five minutes of inching forward, it was Darien's turn. He stopped beside an X-shaped signal equipped with flashing red lights.

As a Customs Officer approached, Darien held his iTab in position for the agent to scan his driver's license, a picture ID being the only documentation required by the California Republic. CalGov had made it easy to gain entrance to the New Republic, and many citizens of The United States, Canada, and Mexico had done so. Alphabet News constantly described California's economy as *booming* or *vibrant*, although a contrarian report by Independent.news.com claimed *busted* was a more accurate term. In the next few days, Darien would find out for himself which viewpoint was correct—probably about halfway between the two extremes, he suspected. That was nearly always the case.

The customs officer went through a checklist of banned items—vegetables, fruit, tobacco products, firearms or facsimiles of firearms, and insecticides or other toxic chemicals. After completing the checklist, the officer said, "Please open your trunk."

Darien touched the *Hood* icon, and the front storage compartment popped open revealing his battered tan suitcase with a cord tied around it. The officer gave it a precursory glance and said, "You can close the hood. I'll upload your visa to your iTab, and you can go."

"Thank you," Darien said. He heard a pinging sound, and the image of a rainbow-colored card appeared on his iTab screen. Just as he'd heard, crossing the California border was incredibly simple. The customs agent hadn't even bothered to look inside his suitcase.

"One other thing," the officer added. "I suggest that you stop at a currency exchange office and exchange some U.S. dollars for BitCal which is the only currency authorized by the California government. There's an office up ahead that's easy to get to. Just take the first exit to the right and stay on the service road."

"Okay . . . thanks," Darien said, gently pressing the accelerator.

Following the officer's advice, he went to the currency exchange office, which had a series of drive-through windows. He took his place in the shortest line, impressed that California had made exchanging currency as easy as ordering sausage biscuits at McDonald's. So far, the new nation was making him feel welcome, just like Rachel had said it would. He wondered if he'd been overly critical of the avant-garde government and relished the opportunity to find out for himself.

Darien pulled the VW back onto the interstate and fell in behind a bright yellow BMW convertible with the top down, a new one according to its paper license plate. A red banner emblazoned across the back bumper read *Peace Through Equality*. Darien realized that he was witnessing an equality paradox and wondered if he would ever be *equal enough* to afford such a beautiful car. He stayed behind the BMW until it exceeded the speed limit and then dropped back into a cluster of older cars similar to his.

About thirty minutes later, BestRoute said, "You are approaching your destination. Please observe the speed limit."

Darien slowed as he began to pass row after row of trailer houses, an indication that he was in Hermosa, the community where Rachel lived. The trailers were all the same size and the same color, clones of the original FEMA pattern. According to reports, new trailers were arriving daily from the United States. Darien wondered if the FEMA units were left over from the relief effort after Hurricane Donald slammed into New Orleans last year. And if they were, how did California put together the funds to buy them? He suspected some kind of deal had been worked out between CalGov and NatGov when California succeeded from the Union. He remained convinced that NatGov had sponsored the breakaway with a promise of *under-the-table* assistance. Most likely, the FEMA trailers were part of the deal.

Darien passed a sign reading HERMOSA. *Hermosa?* The word meant *beautiful* in Spanish, but the huge trailer park was not beautiful in any sense of the word. Besides, there was a Hermosa Beach in California long before this mobile home community ever existed. Obviously, the government functionary who chose the name had a sense of humor.

The trailers had very little space between them, an arrangement which didn't make sense with so much open land available for development. Darien still thought it enigmatic that Rachel had fled the desert of New Mexico to settle in the desert of California. Maybe she was beginning to have second thoughts. Two years ago, she'd applied for a transfer to one of the nicer communities along the coastal route, Highway 101. That move would get her out of the desert, but so far, CalGov's Citizen Relocation Department hadn't responded. Darien doubted they ever would.

"Turn left on Bonita Drive one hundred yards ahead," BestRoute said.

Darien followed the app's instructions and found himself on a gravel road stretching toward the rear of the trailer park.

"1200 Bonita Drive is on your right," BestRoute said. "You have arrived at your destination."

Darien parked a few feet from Rachel's trailer. Before he could get out of the car, she burst out of the front door and ran toward him.

"Darien! I'm so glad you came."

"Me too," he said, as they threw their arms around each other. "I apologize for not coming sooner."

"No problem," Rachel said. "You're here now, and that's all that matters."

They released their embrace and took a step back, still holding hands. Rachel, nearly six feet tall, was lean and tan with short-cropped brown hair. She was wearing creased navy-blue shorts and a blouse with yellow and white stripes, an outfit which made Darien's faded Jeans and tie-dyed T-shirt look like leftovers from a rag bin.

"You look fabulous," Darien said. "Do you have a date?"

"Yes—with my brother."

"I'm a little under-dressed to be seen with you."

Rachel shrugged. "Not really, but you know me. I like to dress up."

"I know."

"Would you like to go for a walk?"

"Sure. I'm tired of driving. Where do you want to go?"

"To the Hermosa Community Center. It's about a quarter of a mile away."

"Can we eat there? I'm starving."

"That was my plan. I didn't cook a thing."

Ten minutes later, they arrived at the strip center, a gigantic blue metal building shaped like the letter U. The Saturday afternoon crowd consisted primarily of twenty-and-thirty-somethings, most wearing faded jeans and nondescript tops—from all appearances, the *uniform of the day*. Darien fit right in, while Rachel in her neat attire, looked like a newcomer. Darien studied the crowd and could tell by their constant interaction that nearly all of them knew each other. He surmised that most of them were long-time residents of Hermosa.

"The shops in the center sell groceries, clothes, hardware—about everything a person needs to survive," Rachel said. "In addition, there's a free medical clinic at the back of the building. Hermosa is pretty much a self-sufficient community."

They entered the building through a side entrance leading into a food court furnished with plastic tables and chairs in a variety of colors. Food kiosks, each with a small serving counter and barstools, lined the perimeter of the room. As they walked along, Rachel read the names aloud, "Chocolate and Churros, Dulce Heaven, Super Subs, Juan's Taco Shop, etc., etc. They go on and on. What are you hungry for?"

"Nearly anything," Darien said. "How are Juan's tacos?"

"They're delicious. He makes fish tacos with Alaskan halibut. Not only that, but Juan and his wife live next door to me. They're wonderful neighbors."

"Then, let's stop at Juan's. I'll buy," Darien said. "I already have some BitCal."

"You do?"

"Yes, I got it at the border."

"Uh-oh," Rachel said, grimacing. "I should have told you not to do that . . . my bad."

"What did I do wrong?"

"You paid too much."

"How so?

"CalGov and NatGov have an agreement to maintain the official exchange rate at one to one," Rachel said. "However, here in Hermosa, ten U.S dollars will buy eleven BitCal."

"Does CalGov try to stop vendors from accepting American dollars?"

"Not anymore. They tried for a while, but now they've given up. Hermosa is just across the border from Mexicali. Money-changers in Mexico prefer the U.S. dollar and are willing to pay slightly more for it. Exchanging money under the table is a cottage industry in Mexicali. You can do it on every street corner."

They sat down on the barstools in front of Juan's Taco Shop. Darien looked at the menu underneath a sheet of clear plastic overlaying the countertop. A brief glance was all he needed. Rachel had already sold him on the fish tacos. He was ready to place his order, but no one was behind the counter to take it.

"Hey, Juanito," Rachel called. "Where are you?"

A voice answered, "I'm right here," and a young man stepped from behind a snack-food rack and came to the counter.

"Hi, Rachel," Juan said. He looked toward Darien. "You must be the brother Rachel's always talking about."

"Guilty as charged," Darien said. "Nice to meet you, Juan." They shook hands.

Juan stared at Darien and said, "You guys look a lot alike."

"Except for my trademark," Rachel said with a smile, as she pointed toward her eyes.

"We're both adopted," Darien said.

"Rachel told me."

"We may look alike," Rachel said, "but we don't think alike. Not at all. In fact, Darien is totally left-brained and I'm totally right-brained."

"What's that mean?" Juan asked.

"Darien uses the left side of his brain more than the right," Rachel said, "and I do just the opposite."

Juan looked puzzled. "I'm not sure I understand."

"The main difference is that Darien is analytical and I'm impulsive," Rachel said. "But there're many other differences as well. He's logical—I'm creative. He likes math—I like art. He computes—I daydream. He listens to the words of a song—I listen to the music . . . things like that. Right, Darien?"

Darien nodded. "And one other thing—she dresses a lot better than I do."

They laughed, and Rachel said, "Juan's analyzing our answers. He must be left-brained."

Juan shrugged his shoulders. "This is way over my head, but I'm a good cook. What can I get you to eat?"

Rachel deferred to Darien. He ordered fish tacos and a Diet Coke.

"I'll take the tacos, as well," Rachel said, "and a glass of water."

"Marisol is in the kitchen getting the fish ready to cook," Juan said, tapping at the computer console on the counter. "I'll tell her to come out. She's planning a daytrip for us to take while Darien is here."

"That'll be fun," Rachel said. "What day?"

"We'll be closed tomorrow and Monday," Juan said. "So, Monday might be our best day. Marisol mentioned Thanksgiving Day as a possibility, but I don't think that's a good idea."

"I'll probably leave before Thanksgiving," Darien said.

"Monday would be fine for us," Rachel said. "Where are we going?"

"Marisol wanted it to be a surprise," Juan said, "but I've already let the cat out of the bag, so I might as well tell the rest . . ."

At that instance, a petite brunette appeared behind Juan. "You talk too much, Juanito," she said, an amused sparkle in her eyes belying mock anger. "Maybe you should take over the cooking chores and let me handle the counter."

"Hi, Marisol," Rachel said. "You arrived in the nick of time." She introduced Darien and then asked, "Where do you want to go?"

"I was planning for us to go to the San Diego Zoo," Marisol said, "but I just found out that Interstate 8's robo-bus is in the repair shop, and they're not sure if it'll be ready by Monday."

"Forget the bus," Darien chimed in, his voice rising with excitement. "I'll drive the VW, and I think we should go tomorrow, instead of waiting until Monday."

"I thought you'd be tired of driving," Rachel said.

"I'm not too tired to drive to the San Diego Zoo," Darien said, feeling adrenalin surging through his bloodstream. "I've got some friends there."

"Who do you know at the zoo?" Rachel asked.

"Art, Bart, Cale, and Dale—four Rhesus monkey twins," Darien said. He recounted the story of President Horn's abrupt order shutting down the tests on the monkeys.

Rachel looked toward Juan and Marisol. "My brother is revved up," she said. "Does going to the zoo tomorrow sound okay to you?"

"Absolutely," Juan said. "Let's go to early church, and hit the road."

"Is there a church near Hermosa?" Darien asked.

Juan nodded. "There's one at the back of the subdivision."

"Catholic or protestant?" Darien asked.

"Universal," Juan said. "That's the only kind allowed by CalGov.

CHAPTER 14

"Turn left at the next traffic light," Juan said. "That'll take us to the front gate."

The four occupants of the VW were never without some interesting topic to discuss during the hundred-mile trip from Hermosa to San Diego. The constant conversation turned the occasion into a pleasant Sunday drive—not tiring, but fun. Darien, by nature the least talkative in the group, listened most of the time as he focused on his driving. The scenery was fairly repetitive, and they generally ignored it until, just outside of San Diego, they passed a small tent city which caught their attention. The city was so recently-formed that it didn't have an official CalGov city-limit sign. Instead, a cardboard placard on a stick read PLANET X. Darien slowed the VW to a crawl and snapped several pictures. They discussed the tenth planet until they reached the zoo.

Darien guided the VW into a parking lot near the entrance/exit gate. He spotted several spaces labeled *Compact Cars Only* and eased into the nearest one. "We're in luck," he said. "I expected the zoo to be a lot more crowded on Sunday."

"It'll be plenty crowded in a little while," Marisol said as they climbed out of the car. "Most of the visitors will be arriving by bus. It's cheaper than driving. Besides, a lot of people living in small communities like Hermosa don't own cars. They always travel by bus."

"Let's take in the primate exhibit first," Rachel said. "Darien won't be able to enjoy anything else until he's located his monkey friends."

Using pre-purchased tickets on their iTabs, they passed through the entrance turnstile and walked toward the primate exhibit with Juan in the lead.

"Let's take the elevated walkway," Marisol said. "It's called *Monkey Trails* and is nearly tree-top level, rather than on the ground."

Rachel read the list of primates from her ITab, "Spot nosed, capuchin, colobus, bonobo, rhesus—the list goes on."

They went up an inclined boardwalk to the Monkey Trails walk which bordered a fenced enclosure containing jungle trees, shrubs, and vines. The enclosure was topped with meshed wire to keep the primates from escaping. Parrots, parakeets, and other brightly colored tropical birds flitted through the trees. Monkeys swung on the vines and trees, performing acrobatics which seemed to defy gravity. Just inside the fence, a group of constantly-chattering monkeys sat on a platform and interacted with the people on the walkway.

Hoping to locate Art, Bart, Cale, and Dale, Darien conducted a meticulous survey of the primate exhibit. His first visual scan yielded no results, but he remained hopeful as they wandered along. The exhibit housed a multitude of primates with many species represented. Surely, the recently-arrived twins from Alamogordo were among the inhabitants of this manmade jungle.

Darien wanted to hurry, but his companions lingered incessantly at every placard and video screen describing the primates on display. He fidgeted while they read, but determined to be a compatible guest, he stifled the urge to move ahead by himself. Fifteen minutes later, he began to worry. Rhesus monkeys were the only species on his mind, and they were nearing the end of the Monkey Trails walkway without seeing a single one. As yet, he hadn't worked out a *Plan B*, but he was determined to get a look at every rhesus in the zoo until he found the ones he was searching for.

"Look!" Rachel said, pointing. "This sign says the rhesus monkeys are in this section."

Darien scanned the area quickly. A few monkeys dawdled near the fence, but not a one of them was a rhesus. Finally, in the distance, he saw several small groups of monkeys high in the trees, but they were so far away that it was impossible to tell what kind they were. Squinting, he spotted four figures lined up on a limb. *Four?* The magic number. Maybe they were about to hit pay dirt.

"Those might be the ones we're looking for," Darien said. "We need to lure them over here and check them out."

"I assume your friends know their names," Juan said. "Would they come if you call them?"

"I think the primates on our side of the fence are making too much noise for that to work," Darien said. "However, I just thought of something to try, and it requires your help."

"What do you want us to do?" Rachel asked.

"The monkeys I'm looking for have been trained to respond to colored flashcards," Darien said. "Let's use our iTabs as flashcards. I'll set my screen to red. If you'll each select a different color, we might be able to coax them over here."

"Great idea," Rachel said. Juan and Marisol nodded and began to tap at their iTab screens. Ten seconds later, each of them had picked a color. In unison, they looked at Darien, awaiting further instructions.

"Hold your iTabs as high as possible and move them around," Darien said.

They waved their lighted iTabs above their heads, but none of the monkeys in the distance showed any immediate interest in the pseudo flashcards. After a few minutes, a crowd of onlookers gathered on the walkway, and most conversation ceased. Darien could feel inquisitive eyes staring at them, but he didn't care. He had to locate the monkeys in question, no matter what his fellow zoo-goers thought. He had a strong feeling that he was about to discover something of vital importance.

"Turn your screens on and off as fast as you can," Darien said, after realizing the first attempt wasn't working. "Maybe flashing lights will attract their attention."

Darien's companions followed his instructions and signaled the hitherto unobservant monkeys via the *off-and-on* technique. They continued frantically for several minutes, and as Darien was about to acquiesce to the possibility of failure, he detected a slight movement by one the monkeys.

"Look!" Rachel said. "The one next to the tree trunk is moving!"

"He's going to climb down," Darien said, "and the others are lining up to follow him."

"I guess he's the leader," Rachel said. "He must have seen our signals."

One after another, the monkeys scurried down the tree and ran toward the Monkey Trails walkway. The lead monkey stayed in front, and the others ran along behind him like children playing follow-the-leader. When the scurrying primates reached the scaffold that supported the elevated walkway, they broke ranks, scaled the crisscrossed structure, and hopped on the platform directly in front of Darien. Reaching one hand through the fence as far as possible, the leader looked toward Darien and began to chatter loudly.

"He recognizes you," Rachel said.

"He can't possibly recognize me," Darien said. "I wasn't anywhere near him during the ESP tests." He studied the monkeys briefly and was certain that they were the twins from the aborted lab experiment. After a moment, his meticulous examination began to reveal differences which he hadn't noticed during the lab tests. Art and Bart were bigger than Cale and Dale, and their hair was slightly darker. Otherwise, all four of them looked nearly alike.

Just as Darien had observed during the lab experiment, the siblings exhibited more interaction with each other than with their non-sibling companions. All four monkeys looked at the visitors and chattered plaintively, begging for treats. In spite of the *Do Not Feed the Monkeys* sign, several teenage boys tossed peanuts through the fence. As the monkeys jostled for the peanuts, Darien began to see additional differences. Art, Bart, and Cale grabbed the peanuts with their right hands. Dale used his left. While waiting for more treats to be tossed their way the monkeys stood with their feet aligned, except for Dale, who stood with one foot slightly ahead of the other. The longer Darien watched, the more Dale's mannerisms differed from the other three monkeys. He didn't see how he could have missed so much during the ESP tests. Still, by his observations so far, Dale looked exactly like Cale.

Knowing that any physical difference—no matter how minute—would be important, Darien studied Dale carefully from head to toe. He was convinced the primates in front of him bore an important clue and was determined to find it or stay until the zoo closed.

After several minutes of scrutiny, he saw something that he'd missed previously. Cale had a small pink birthmark shaped like a teardrop on his right cheek. The same birthmark appeared on Dale's left cheek.

"*Voila!*" he whispered to himself, realizing that Cale and Dale were not only twins, they were *mirror image* twins, a much rarer variety.

He raised his iTab and began to take pictures and videos.

CHAPTER 15

The Friday after Thanksgiving, Carly sat on Anna's balcony with her iTab balanced on her knees. Reflexively, she tapped at the screen and pulled up the pictures and videos of Cale and Dale for the umpteenth time. Her initial look at them nearly a week ago left no doubt that the two monkeys were mirror image twins. Still, she couldn't stop looking at them. Darien's discovery at the San Diego Zoo had locked in the next phase of the ESP study. They had to concentrate on mirror image twins in order for the study to have any chance of success. She hoped the high-ranking officials at NM State and NatGov would see it that way, as well. Even though their research project had been approved in general, *tentative* always seemed to be the word of the day. They hoped to get it removed next week.

After Darien's initial text message from the zoo's primate exhibit, time shifted into slow motion with one endless day after another. If Carly had possessed the ability to time-travel, she would have wished the clock forward seven days so she and Darien could resume the ESP project immediately. Carly was making a diligent effort to be a good guest while at Anna's and hoped no one had noticed how antsy she really felt.

If not for Darien's discovery, the Thanksgiving get-together in El Paso would have been a relaxing break from school. The highlight of the holidays—Anna's boyfriend, Carlton, proposed early in the week, and she accepted. Carly was happy for her surrogate big sister, but seeing the newly-engaged couple plan their future together brought home the fact to Carly that she was in a relationship dilemma. For the first time in several years, *conquering the world* wasn't the only thing on her mind. Two men were competing for her attention, and ignoring that fact hadn't made it go away.

A scraping noise interrupted Carly's introspection. She turned as the balcony door slid open, and Anna stepped outside.

"The bus for Alamogordo leaves in fifteen minutes," Anna said.

"I'm ready," Carly said, rising.

***

On Monday morning, Carly was waiting for Darien in the library. A few students wandered around in near-aimless fashion, and the aroma of fresh-roasted coffee beans wafted in from the adjoining Starbucks. Carly sipped her McDonald's coffee, knowing Darien would appear any second with a similar low-cost drink in hand. Like her, Darien was never late. In the short time she and Darien had worked together, she'd detected a few eccentricities in his behavior. Fortunately, they matched her own so closely that they were an asset, rather than a liability.

Today was an important day for Carly and Darien. They were preparing to go to the main campus in Las Cruces and attend a discussion on the M13 Contact Study. They'd been told to be prepared to discuss their work in detail. This was the required step for the removal of the word *tentative* from DARPA's approval. The discussion would be led jointly by Dr. Sheldon Leonard, President of New Mexico State University, and Dr. Michael Overton, Rex Horn's DARPA representative. Overton had already been seen on campus—*snooping around*, as some said.

Twice, Carly had seen him leaving the science building annex. After the first time, she'd googled his name, and to her surprise, his complete resume appeared instantly. It was brief and simple, but very impressive. He had two doctorates, a JD in law and a PhD in computer science from Florida State University. Shortly after graduating from college, Overton had founded a computer company, Simulacrum Inc., which developed internet games. Five years ago, Overton had resigned as CEO of Simulacrum and joined NatGov as a special agent for DARPA. If there was any red flag concerning Overton, it was that he and the President were both from Florida; moreover, the two men were distant cousins, maybe fifth or sixth, not close enough that Horn's enemies could make a very strong nepotism charge. If so, they would have done it already.

After all the conspiracy theories she'd heard from Darien, Carly had expected Overton to be some enigmatic figure with no retrievable history, but that wasn't the case. Other than being a distant relative of President Horn, the only atypical thing she noticed about Overton was that he always carried a large laptop computer in a world dominated by iTabs. Still, that was a minor anomaly.

Carly's mental gyrations were interrupted by several people entering the library simultaneously, one of which was Darien with a coffee cup in his hand. He waved and approached at a fast clip. Carly remained seated as Darien placed his cup on the table and pulled out the chair next to her.

They exchanged hellos and Darien said, "Okay, let's shift our brains into high gear. We need to make a strong sales-pitch this afternoon in order to get the word *tentative* removed from our proposal."

"We were a little naïve at first," Carly said. "This is definitely going to be a nationwide search for mirror image twins, so the cost is going up considerably."

"It's still hard to believe Mr. Horn launched a program which allows non-science students to get directly involved in SETI," Darien said.

Carly shrugged. "Rex Horn isn't afraid to swim against the tide."

For the next hour, they discussed various aspects of the M13 Contact Study, trying to anticipate questions which might be brought up during the afternoon session. They settled one topic quickly—responding to questions. The floor would be Carly's when brain waves and ESP were the topic, and it would be Darien's when radio waves were the topic. Everything seemed to fall in place, except for one problematic issue, the studying of brain waves and radio waves together. After considerable discussion, they decided the best approach was to table it for the moment and concentrate on the first step of the project, finding people with ESP. If they failed to do that, the study was doomed, and there would be no second step.

At 2:00 p.m., they were satisfied with their preparation and ready to go to the main campus in Las Cruces. Their 3:30 p.m. meeting didn't synchronize with the I-70 bus schedule, and Darien's VW had barely made it back from California, so they decided to take an Uber robo-cab.

As they left the library, a blast of cold air hit them, and Carly turned up the collar on her coat. During her five months of living in Alamogordo, she'd noticed that summer and fall temperatures were similar to Houston, but now, December was bringing snow, and her meager winter clothes weren't adequate.

Darien touched the Uber app on his iTab and selected *Next Available Cab.* Three minutes later, a robo-cab resembling a giant ladybug pulled to the curb, and they got in.

An hour later, the robo-cab coasted to a stop in front of the Administration building. During the hour-long trip, they'd evaluated the *good vs bad* aspects of the President's unusual approach to studying the radio waves from outer space. One point was obvious. If successful, the project would make NM State famous and gild the President's legacy. The counterpoint was obvious too. If the project failed, NM State would revert back to *small college* status once again, and the M13 Contact Study would morph into a dead albatross for the RADS to hang around Rex Horn's neck.

They entered the Administration building and joined a group of students heading toward the elevator. Even with hellos and high-fives being exchanged all around, the mood was serious. Several strangers spoke to Carly as they walked along, and she overheard snippets of conversation about the M13 Contact Study. Obviously, all of the students were involved in the study in some way. Also obvious was the fact they were studying something other than a blend of psychology and astronomy.

"I wonder if everybody in this group is going to ask for additional funding?" Darien said. "Or, are we the only ones?"

Carly shrugged her shoulders, but didn't respond verbally. She hoped that Darien's Cale and Dale discovery had put them on a path to *Pass GO* and collect the needed funds. She didn't see how any other approach could trump their proposal, but she relished the opportunity to hear new ideas, some of which might be offered by this group of students today.

At the end of the hall, they took one of the elevators to the third floor and headed toward the conference room along with their colleagues. Upon entering the ochre-colored room, Carly did a quick survey. The center-piece was a large oval table constructed of dark wood. Over a dozen chairs with tan leather seats surrounded the table, and a row of wooden folding chairs occupied the back and one side of the rectangular room. Pictures around the walls offered a full panorama of the White Sands Missile Range at sunset. By Carly's evaluation, the room was plush.

Miriam Graves greeted the incoming arrivals and instructed them to sit around the conference table. She smiled at Carly and Darien as they passed her. Carly wondered if the smile was an *A-Okay* signal or just a friendly greeting.

Looking rather solemn, gray-suited and gray-haired Dr. Sheldon Leonard stood at the head of the table. He was flanked by several professors, including Darien's advisor, Craig McLennan. The DARPA representative, Michael Overton, stood slightly apart from the group of academics. Carly studied Overton carefully. He was a tall square-jawed man with salt and pepper hair cut in an archaic flattop. Dressed in a blue suit and red tie, he projected an aura of competence and professionalism, maybe obstinacy, as well. Clearly, he was more than the usual government *suit* that showed up around the campus from time to time. He was the designated *point man* for a project which had President Horn's blessing. From her brief inspection of Overton, Carly anticipated he would eschew small talk and get straight to the point when he took the floor.

After the students were seated, Graves closed the door and joined the professors clumped together at the front of the room. Leonard motioned toward the chairs along the side wall and the professors sat down, leaving himself and Overton as the only people still standing.

"Good afternoon," Leonard said. "This is an exciting time for NM State. Our university has chosen to participate in the President's M13 Study. A few other universities, most of them larger than NM State, are involved in this study, as well; however, I believe our unique location and space-related history will serve to our advantage as this project proceeds. Our motto, *Be Bold, Shape the Future,* is not just an empty slogan. We live by it; therefore, I'm convinced that our mindset is in synch with President Horn's exhortation to explore new ideas."

Leonard nodded toward the students seated around the table. "Each of you is the beneficiary of scholarship funds for this study," he said. "As you know, this funding is being administered by DARPA. The DARPA liaison, Dr. Michael Overton, has been on campus for several days and has met with each professor who supervises graduate students working on this project. After having heard several very unique ideas, Dr. Overton requested the opportunity to meet the students who came up with them, so that's one purpose for having this meeting today. At this point, I will turn the floor over to Dr. Overton."

Overton replaced Leonard at the head of the table and gazed at the students with piercing steel-blue eyes. The students and professors sat in unmoving expectancy, waiting for Overton to begin. Carly sensed tension in the air. When Overton replaced Leonard, it appeared to symbolize that DARPA was taking control of the project. She wondered if a power shift had actually taken place or if her imagination was overactive. The next few minutes should tell.

"Thank you, Dr. Leonard," Overton said. He turned toward the students and continued, "Thank you for participating in the M13 Contact Study. I'm sure you're aware of the importance Mr. Horn places on this project. He went out on a limb to fund this unique approach which has many academics scoffing and refusing to participate. The President has charged me with the responsibility of overseeing the efforts of several universities, including New Mexico State. My orders are to see that this study succeeds. We're attacking the problem through a variety of approaches, both conventional and unconventional. For example, in addition to the astronomy-related subjects, DARPA is funding studies in psychology, cryptography, linguistics, anthropology, and exobiology. Other fields are being considered, as well. Mr. Horn believes this approach will produce a pool of creative young people who think differently.

"President Horn hopes to see some positive results soon; however, he certainly never expected the riddle to be solved by this time, just three months into the study. From what I've seen, several NM State students have conceived novel ideas and are in the early stages of exploring them."

At that point, Overton asked the students seated around the table to introduce themselves and make a brief statement regarding their involvement in the M13 Contact Study. He motioned toward the young woman at his right, signaling her to begin.

After each student had spoken briefly, Overton continued. "We'll proceed as follows. Within the next two weeks, each professor who is overseeing any aspect of this project will receive a DARPA evaluation of his/her team's project, possibly with suggestions for changes. For the time being, each of you should continue with your project as originally planned. In approximately three months, DARPA will repeat this review and determine which of the projects will continue to receive funding and which will be dropped. Are there any questions?"

A lanky young man, wearing a *Bookworm* tee shirt, raised his hand and asked, "What is the President's timeline on this study?"

"He hopes to see progress during his first term in office," Overton said, "and to have the study completed by the end of his second term."

"By *completed*, I assume that he means successfully decoding an incoming message?" the man said.

"That's correct," Overton said.

In a tentative voice, a frail blonde asked, "Will the current review affect our scholarships?"

"It won't affect any regular course work that you're taking," Overton said, "but if your work on the M13 Contact

Study reaches an impasse in the early stages, it could affect scholarships."

In silent unity, the students gazed at Overton. Carly recognized the DARPA agent's response as a *non-answer.* Puzzlement showed on the student's face who asked the question, but she didn't follow up, nor did anyone else.

After a brief silence, Overton asked, "Are there any more questions?"

The students did a quick *glance-around,* but no one spoke.

"My charge to you is this," Overton continued, "keep thinking outside the box. Develop novel ideas, and incorporate them into your research. I will return in about three months and review all work in progress on the M13 Contact Study." He looked toward Leonard and said, "Mr. President, is there anything else you'd like to add to my charge to the students?"

Leonard stood. "Remember, New Mexico State's motto speaks of shaping the future. At the moment, you are in the unique position to do just that. Don't let the opportunity slip through your fingers. Our time has come, and we must not let the moment pass." He looked toward Overton, gave a quick nod, and sat down.

"Thank you, Dr. Leonard," Overton said. "All students are dismissed except the Graves/McLennan team."

Carly glanced at Darien and his eyebrows shot up. They kept their seats while the other students got up and filed out of the room with question marks on their faces. Carly realized why Miriam Graves had greeted them with a smile and a nod as they entered the room. Their mirror image proposal had copped DARPA's backing, and Graves knew it before the meeting started. Carly had to resist the urge to wave a clenched fist in the air.

Graves beckoned toward Carly and Darien, and they came forward, as did Leonard and McLennan. The five of them converged on Overton, who remained standing near the head of the table. Graves said, "Dr. Overton, these are the students I discussed with you, Miss Hansen and Mr. Segura."

"Pleased to meet you," Overton said in a voice which had lost some of its sternness. He motioned toward the chairs. "Let's sit down."

Once seated, Overton's jawline relaxed a bit, making him seem less intimidating. "Congratulations," he said in Carly and Darien's direction. "DARPA has decided to fund your proposal for ESP tests on mirror image twins."

"Thank you," Carly and Darien said in unison. Since Overton had opened the conversation by referring to ESP, Carly was on the hot seat first.

Overton looked directly at Carly and said, "Miss Hansen, tell me how you came to believe that ESP is real."

Carly told her life story in five minutes, and Overton listened attentively without an interruption. At the end of her well-rehearsed talk, she invited questions.

"How many sets of twins do you propose testing?" Overton said.

"As many as we have to in order to find ESP," Carly said in a firm voice. "We want to test a hundred on the first attempt, and we prefer ages sixteen through eighteen years old."

"Why that particular age group?" Overton asked.

"So those who volunteer can have the opportunity to join the M13 Contact Study as students, if they want to," Carly said. "It's not likely we'll solve the problem on the first try, and twins in this age group might become the next ESP researchers."

"I appreciate your candor, Miss Hansen. Then what do you expect to learn from the first round of tests?"

"I think we'll discover something that confirms the validity of our approach."

"Thank you, Miss Hansen," the DARPA agent said in a tone indicating that he had no more questions for Carly. He looked at Darien and said, "And now, Mr. Segura, I have a couple of questions for you."

Darien nodded. "Go ahead."

"What led you into the field of astronomy?"

As Carly had done, Darien gave a five-minute story of his life. When he finished, Overton asked, "How do you plan to use ESP to decipher radio waves?"

"We're going to comingle brainwaves and radio waves in some way," Darien said. "We have some ideas but no concrete plan yet. We hope to have one soon."

"Do you know who Dr. Edward Pauling is?"

"Yes. I've read several of his papers and heard him speak."

"I've spoken to him about this approach," Overton said. "He thinks it has a chance to succeed, but most astrophysicists don't agree with him."

After the short Q & A session, Overton looked at Graves and said, "I like your team's plan for testing mirror image twins for ESP. As I said, DARPA will fund the test just as Miss Hansen described it, but before we fund the second step—attempting to use ESP to decipher the ET messages—they'll need to develop a more detailed plan and get DARPA's approval before putting it into effect."

"I understand," Graves said. "The team is working on that aspect of the project right now. We feel confident we can develop a novel approach which makes sense to all concerned."

"I hope so," Overton said, with a slight smile. "That would make all of our jobs easier, especially mine." He looked toward Carly and Darien and invited them to ask additional questions.

"How soon can we start recruiting twins?" Carly asked.

Instead of answering Carly directly, Overton looked at Leonard and said, "Dr. Leonard, DARPA has the personnel and know-how to help you set up a recruiting program. We will work with NM State to enlist the twins."

"That sounds good," Leonard said. "I'll provide you with a contact in our Publicity Department and tell her to expect your call."

From that point on, the discussion centered on the timing of the ESP tests. Leonard suggested running them on Saturday so they wouldn't interfere with regular Monday thru Friday activities. With Christmas less than a month away, and the December calendar almost full, January 20 was the earliest date that fit everybody's schedule. Overton and Leonard agreed on the date, and Carly breathed a sigh of relief.

CHAPTER 16

A few days after Michael Overton's visit to the campus, NM State's Publicity Department, with assistance from DARPA, launched an online promotional effort to enlist mirror image twins. Darien was impressed by the clever popups which invaded the internet but was surprised that the university had chosen to enlist the candidates via social media, rather than by searching NatGov's census records. After the campaign had been running a few days, one of Darien's friends, who worked for the university's Publicity Department, told him that DARPA had insisted on using the internet for the advertising campaign. As far as Darien could tell, the university had tagged, poked, invited, requested, texted, phished, tweeted and Instagrammed everybody in the United States, California, Canada and Mexico—a rather elaborate search to locate 100 sets of mirror image twins.

After ruminating a short while on the over-the-top recruitment program, Darien arrived at his usual conspiracy-theorist conclusion. Rex Horn was using the internet to thumb his nose at the RADS. Those opposed to Horn—and there were many—had presented their case to the public with help from Alphabet News, and President Horn had responded via social media. Tit for tat, as Darien saw it, a modus operandi likely to continue as long as Mr. Horn remained in office, and the RADS kept attempting to impeach him. Both sides had taken a no-compromise approach. A strange way to govern the most powerful country in the world. Apparently, no modern-day politician believed in compromise. All of them seemed determined to *win it all* or *lose it all* regardless of major casualties occurring on both sides of the battle line.

The enlistment program was launched in early December, and less than a week after the first ad hit the internet, Darien received a text from Miriam Graves informing him that the parents of more than 100 sets of twins had signed up their children for the test. The U.S. Census Bureau was in the process of examining their records to make sure they were mirror images, as claimed.

Today, Carly would join Darien for a brainstorming session. With her as his non-STEM research partner, he was trying to look at SETI afresh by concentrating on the *think outside the box* viewpoint that Rex Horn touted constantly. Although Carly had never taken a course in physics, her brief explanation of brainwaves indicated she would be a quick study when they delved into the electromagnetic spectrum.

Carly's skillful conversation with Michael Overton had impressed Darien. She'd showed good ability to think on her feet, probably better than he had. He hoped they could show some progress before the next DARPA review date, which would occur near the end of February if Overton stuck to his schedule.

As Darien was scrolling through a list of frequency charts on his desktop computer and printing hard copies of the ones he liked, he heard footsteps and looked up to see Carly approaching his corner niche.

"Hey, Darien," Carly said while still a few strides from his desk.

Darien returned the greeting and motioned toward the chair beside him. "Take a look at this electromagnetic frequency chart."

Carly sat down and leaned toward the monitor. "Okay," she said, after studying it for a moment. "I'm ready to talk about kilohertz, megahertz, gigahertz, or any other kind of hertz."

"Would you prefer to use *cycles per second* rather than *hertz*?" Darien said.

"No way," Carly said emphatically. "I've spent a lot of time learning the terms which precede the word *hertz* in these charts, and I'm going to use them every chance I get."

"Okay, use whatever designation you like, and I'll do the same," Darien said, aware that he had put his foot in his mouth by implying that Carly might have trouble with scientific terms. Obviously, that wasn't the case, and he anticipated that she would use the terms as often as possible today, just to prove she could.

"Now, take a look at this chart," he continued. "It starts with values from 3–300 hertz and goes up to some incredibly large numbers."

"What about the frequencies where brainwaves overlap audible sound?" Carly said, pointing at the chart. "Humans can hear frequencies from around 20–20,000 hertz. The brainwaves we're most interested in are in the range of 12–40 hertz. Maybe there's a way to glean some information from overlapping frequencies."

"That sounds good at first, but there's one big problem. The waves differ greatly in composition."

"Tell me more, STEM major."

"Brainwaves are electrical impulses," Darien said. "Sound waves are mechanical in nature and have to be transmitted through a medium such as air, solids, or liquids."

"If a tree falls in the forest and no one is there to hear it . . . etc., etc."

"A falling tree causes the air to vibrate at certain frequencies," Darien said, "and that's sound."

"Tell me a little more about radio waves."

"They're composed of photons—light—which can be transmitted through the near-vacuum of space."

Carly pointed at the monitor. "Here's why I prefer the hertz prefixes. Hydrogen's frequency is 1420 megahertz—over 1.4 billion cycles per second . . . that's incredibly fast."

"Take a look at visible light."

"Terahertz," Carly said, as if she'd used the term all her life. "Trillions of cycles per second."

"No overlap with brainwaves."

"Maybe there's some way to blend the different frequencies," Carly said. "Even though their composition is different. Let's kick it around and try to come up with some inventive ideas."

"I'm trying to formulate a scientific basis for blending them."

"That's where we differ," Carly said. "I've always wanted to study parapsychology—phenomena without an observable scientific basis."

"You may have gotten your wish."

"I'm making the bold assumption that we'll find people with ESP," Carly said. "Maybe they'll be able to decipher the FRBs as received."

"*FRBs,*" Darien said. "You really have learned to talk the language. You'd make a good astronomer."

"I'm better at analyzing eccentric people."

"Am I a good subject?"

"Definitely."

Darien caught Carly by the hand. She turned to face him, and their eyes met. They stared at each other. He'd never seen such beautiful eyes—large, blue, wide-set, and with an intensity that seemed to be peering into the depths of his soul. Her gaze was hypnotic, and for a moment, the research lab faded into the background. All he could think about was Carly and the warmth of her hand in his. Briefly, time stood still.

Carly squeezed his hand and pulled away.

Darien attempted to salvage the moment. "What are you doing for Christmas?"

"Hope and I are driving to Fort Worth to visit my grandmother."

Darien's heart sank. "How long are you going to stay?"

"Until after New Year's Day."

"*That long?*"

"That long."

CHAPTER 17

At mid-morning, Amazon-Southwest Flight 1130 departed William P. Hobby Airport with Garth in a window seat. The airport was near the Gulfgate neighborhood where he and Carly had grown up, but everything looked different from the air. The only easily recognizable structure was the gigantic tan cross near Sagemont Church. The cross was a well-known landmark, and on one occasion, Garth had participated in a math experiment to determine its height—170 feet. The experiment was an important milestone in Garth's life. Previous to it, he'd thought of math as a totally abstract subject. After seeing what could be done with it, he realized that it was a valuable tool. Suddenly, it became interesting.

Garth was looking forward to seeing Carly again but hadn't told her that he'd been assigned to the Mayflower Project and was moving to New Mexico for a while. After considerable thought, accompanied by misgivings, he'd decided to surprise her by showing up unannounced. She'd told him a lot about the study she was conducting, even mentioning that her research partner was a man named Darien Segura. The thought was disconcerting, even though Carly had been open about it.

He kept his eyes glued to the scenes unfolding below him as the airplane banked and circled directly over

Galveston Island, a slender strip of land nestled between Galveston Bay and the Gulf of Mexico. On the bay side of the island, the calm blue-green water was dotted with numerous boats, and on the gulf side, waves rolled onto the beach, dirtying the water several hundred yards from shore. Beyond the latte-colored water, fishing boats maneuvered along a line of seaweed floating in undulating green swells. Farther out, cargo ships powered their way toward the Port of Houston.

This was the Galveston Garth knew and loved. As a child, he'd enjoyed frequent day-trips to the island with his parents, often accompanied by other parents and their children. In spite of some obvious flaws, Galveston had two great features—it was near his home and had free beaches, both critical features for low-income families like his and Carly's.

The airplane reached cruising altitude, and the high-pitched whine of the engines decreased a few decibels as the pilot adjusted the throttle.

"Ladies and gentlemen," a voice boomed over the intercom, "this is Glenn Overton, your captain, speaking. Thank you for choosing Southwest Airlines. We are expecting a smooth flight, so relax and enjoy the ride. In a few minutes, I'll turn off the seatbelt sign, and you'll be free to move about the cabin."

The flight was about two-thirds full, a situation leaving the middle seat empty at Garth's right. The passenger in the aisle seat had spoken to Garth as they took their seats, but as soon as the airplane leveled off, he'd leaned his seat back as far as it would go and donned a sleep mask. So much for having a scintillating conversation with a fellow-traveler. He'd have to find something to occupy his time, maybe observe the other passengers for a while and then play a game on his iTab.

The pilot turned off the *Fasten Seat Belt* sign. Immediately, several passengers stood and stretched their arms and legs. A square-jawed man wearing a blue suit retrieved a laptop computer from the overhead storage bin. The suit made the man stand out from the sloppily-dressed passengers around him; so did the laptop, which was literally a super-computer in a world of ubiquitous iTabs. Garth studied the man, feeling that he'd seen him before, but he couldn't recall where or when.

Across the aisle from Garth, a pink-frocked baby screamed shrilly until her mother gave her a bottle of milk. A short line formed in front of the nearest restroom. When the aisle was nearly full, a flight attendant left the kitchen area and entered the fray, carrying a basket of snacks. She was an alluring young blonde wearing a navy blue uniform with a red scarf around her neck. So much for stories about flight attendants being frumpy middle-aged women with gray streaks in their hair. That was serious misinformation. Garth watched the woman hand out packages of peanuts and pretzels. When she reached the blue-suited man's seat, she smiled and they struck up a conversation. After a short verbal exchange, the attendant stepped back and motioned toward the cockpit. With computer in hand, the man got up and worked his way through the aisle traffic to the front of the plane. A moment later the cockpit door opened. The man went inside and closed the door behind him.

Garth watched the cabin door, anticipating that the man would pop out and return to his seat in a few minutes. When he didn't, Garth lost interest, and his thoughts went back to Carly.

He and Carly had met in the third grade. Garth was somewhat lacking in social instincts, and at that point in Carly's life, she was shy. They both needed friends, and their idiosyncratic personalities drew them together. Since they lived on the same block, it was a convenient friendship, and they grew up playing together, sometimes just the two of them, and at other times, with a small group of neighborhood friends. Garth had a sister and a brother; however, both were more than a dozen years older than he was, so for all practical purposes, his parents had raised him as an only child. He knew Carly better than he knew his own siblings. He and Carly had texted each other several times a day since she left Houston, and he knew her schedule in exact detail. Today, when he got to Alamogordo, she would be studying in the library. He wondered how she would react when he walked in.

Garth ducked his head and looked out of the window again, but clouds completely obscured the view below. To pass the time, he retrieved his iTab from his carry-on bag and loaded his favorite internet game, *Global Cooling on*

Mercury. With flying fingers, he maneuvered his spacecraft in orbit around Mercury, staying on the night side to avoid being incinerated by the sun. A cloud of garbage jettisoned into space from Earth swirled slowly around Mercury. He had to get force fields in place to prevent further shading of the planet, or it would freeze like a popsicle. His fingers danced frantically on the screen but with minimal results. Mercury's temperature declined sharply, forming an inverted *hockey stick graph* onscreen. Oh, no! That graph was the kiss of death. The planet was freezing. Game over.

As Mercury turned into a snowball, a sobering thought hit Garth. He hadn't brought a present for Carly. He mentally kicked himself for not buying something before leaving Houston. Since both of them were from poor families, they only bought presents for each other on special occasions, meaning birthdays and Christmas, plus a card from Amazon-Dollar General on Valentine's Day. But the current situation didn't fit their long-established routine. The reunion in Alamogordo would qualify as an additional special occasion, and a total surprise to Carly. She wouldn't have a present for him. Even so, it would be nice to have one for her.

He went to Amazon's website and began to browse the advertisements which popped up on their home page. The page showed a dozen product categories with pre-Christmas sale prices, a helpful feature since he wasn't sure what he was looking for. Reflexively, he clicked on jewelry, and a stunning display of rings, bracelets, and necklaces materialized onscreen. Hopefully, if he found something he liked, Amazon could drone-deliver it to the Mayflower Project by the time he arrived in the late afternoon.

Garth studied the collection for several minutes, barely blinking as his focus moved from one sparkling item to the next. All of them were beautiful but not quite right for the occasion. Looking for something special, he clicked on a tab labeled *Precious Stones,* and after a brief survey of the page, he selected the subheading *Diamonds.*

Engagement rings popped up.

He studied the fiery offerings for a moment after which shrugged and clicked the *Back* button, returning to the previously-viewed collection and returning to his comfort zone as well.

***

Carly sat alone in the library and gazed out of the window as the sun began to dip below the horizon. In the short time since her arrival in Alamogordo, sunset had become her favorite time of the day. She watched as waning sunlight turned the austere landscape into a sepia-tone panorama. The peaceful scene was relaxing. It was easy for Carly to study, even though a stream of students constantly passed her table as they trekked back and forth into the adjoining Starbucks. Long ago, she'd learned to tune out background chatter, viewing it as no more than *white noise.*

Unexpectedly, something broke Carly's concentration, and she looked toward the parking lot where a robo-bus had stopped to discharge a small group of passengers. A moment later, when the bus pulled away from the curb, Carly did a double take, wondering if the dim light was deceiving her eyes. One of the passengers looked exactly like Garth, but it couldn't be him. He was in Texas. He'd texted her from Houston earlier in the day and hadn't mentioned anything about coming to Alamogordo. Surely, he would have told her.

She squinted and stared until her first impression was confirmed. There was no doubt about it. Garth had just gotten off the bus carrying a small red bag. She watched as he entered the library and looked around until he spotted her. She stood and waited for him to approach her table. When they were face to face, he placed the bag on the table and put his arms around her. She returned his embrace, and they kissed.

Carly pulled away and said, "What are you doing here?"

"What kind of greeting is that?" Garth said. "Aren't you glad to see me?"

"Well . . . of course. But how did you . . . ?"

"Alpha Offshore sent me out here to work on the Mayflower Project as part of my internship."

"Why didn't you tell me?"

"I wanted to surprise you."

"Well . . . you certainly did. How long do you expect to stay?"

"As long as it takes. Probably until the end of the spring semester—maybe longer."

Mixed emotions flooded over Carly. The moment seemed surreal and out of synch. It was nice to see Garth again, but his unexpected appearance was a little disconcerting. It made her wonder if he was checking on her. One thing was sure—his presence would change her life considerably. Carly would be spending a lot of time working with Darien on the M13 Contact Study, and needed to be free to do so without feeling like Garth was peering over her shoulder all the time. She mulled over the situation, taking only a split second to conclude that she would schedule her time as she saw fit.

Garth interrupted Carly's introspection. "Let's sit down," he said, taking off his coat and hanging it over a chair.

"Where are you staying?"

He told her about his temporary quarters at the Project Mayflower site and then pushed the red bag toward her and said, "I brought you a present."

"Thank you," Carly said. "But you broke our gift-giving rules."

"Sometimes when a rule gets in the way, it's best to ignore it," Garth said with a shrug. "This is a special occasion. Rules don't apply."

"But I don't have a gift for you."

"I didn't expect you to . . . open it."

Carly took a blue jewelry box out of the bag, but before she could open it, Garth reached across the table, put his hand on the box and pinned it down. "Wait," he said, his voice rising. "Don't open it."

Carly looked up to see Garth staring at the gold nugget suspended from the chain around her neck. "What's wrong?" she asked.

"Where'd you get that?"

"I found it in Orogrande."

"You went into an abandoned mine?"

"No, of course not," Carly said, shaking her head vigorously. "I found it beside the highway where dirt from a mine had washed onto the right-of-way."

"Was this trip into the desert part of a school project?"

"No," Carly said, pausing briefly before continuing. "I went with the graduate student I told you about—Darien Segura."

Garth's face flushed. "You went on a date with that guy?"

"It wasn't a date," Carly said defensively.

"It sounds like one to me," Garth snapped.

"We went Dutch on sausage biscuits from McDonald's," Carly said. "How could that be a date?"

"I don't like it."

Carly gazed intently at Garth and said, "Darien and I have an understanding. You and I need to have one too."

"What is your understanding with . . . *him*?"

"That our relationship will remain businesslike—strictly related to our studies."

"I still don't like it," Garth said sullenly.

Carly resolved to settle the issue immediately, rather than discussing it every time she and Garth were together. "Garth," she said slowly, "long ago, I told you that I'd pursue parapsychology no matter where it led me. Well . . . it led me here. Now, to continue in the field, I have to work with others, including Darien Segura. That's the way it has to be, and I'm asking you to accept it gracefully. Can you do that?"

Still looking sullen, Garth mumbled, "Yeah, I guess so."

Carly caught Garth's hand. "I knew you'd understand."

"Open the box," Garth said, finally managing a faint smile, "and you'll see what upset me."

Suspecting what she would find, Carly opened the box to reveal a gold chain and pendant lying on a square of cotton. She took the necklace out of the box, and without unfastening the clasp, she slipped the chain over her head and the golden teardrop fell into place beside the nugget already hanging there.

"Thank you," Carly said. "It's beautiful."

CHAPTER 18

On New Year's Day, Darien—alone in his trailer—was trying to figure out something more productive to do than watch the Orange Bowl Parade. While visiting California, he'd watched Amazon-Macy's Thanksgiving Day Parade with Rachel, Juan, Marisol, and a few of their friends. He'd enjoyed the company, the conversation, and the food, but one lengthy parade a year was about right for him. Though he would skip today's parade, he definitely planned to watch the Orange Bowl game. It would decide the NCAA championship. The 2046 combatants were Alabama and Auburn, ranked Number 1 & 2, respectively. Las Vegas was showing Alabama as a slight favorite, but fans knew both teams had the firepower to win, and the winner might be determined on the last play of the game.

To some degree, he was glad to see the NCAA football season come to an end. He liked basketball a lot better and was already looking forward to the March Madness tournament. The perennial favorites had already claimed the top spots in the polls, with Duke holding Number 1. Darien generally rooted for Dr. McLennan's alma mater, Kansas, who had another power house this year, as they nearly always did.

Thanksgiving, Christmas, and New Year's Eve were considerably different from holidays past, starting with his trip to California. He'd enjoyed seeing his sister again and visiting the desert where she lived. He and Rachel had discussed, albeit briefly, the possibility of her returning to New Mexico, but at the moment, it didn't seem likely. Christmas was a complete enigma. Although he'd never celebrated Christmas with Carly, her going to Texas had dampened his holiday spirit. He'd eaten a traditional Christmas dinner with the Rhodes family—Dusty and April, their parents, a few other family members, and some close friends. Darien went through the motions by force of habit. And last night—New Year's Eve—he'd returned to the Rhodes' home for a small party, but as the ball dropped in Times Square, Carly was conspicuous by her absence. Darien was glad to ring out the old year and ring in the new, primarily because Carly would reappear early in January.

Kicking back in his rickety recliner, he picked up the TV remote and pointed it toward the TV. Eschewing the parades, he clicked on the news headlines and watched the banners scroll by for a few seconds. The hostilities continued unabated:

PARABELLUM DOSSIER INCRIMINATES HORN
HORN CHARGES RADS WITH PLANNING COUP
NEW RELIGION CLAIMS PLANET X IS HEAVEN

Darien clicked on the first headline ʸand the article appeared onscreen.

Washington—House Majority Leader Charles Sullivan gave a public statement Friday regarding the findings of a Select Committee investigation into electoral interference by the secret organization, Parabellum. org. Mr. Sullivan stated that several members of the Independent Party have indicated they will support impeachment proceedings against Mr. Horn if the dossier contains evidence that election laws were broken. Mr. Sullivan stated that the dossier contains such evidence; however, he seemed to extend an olive branch to President Horn by inviting him to appear informally before congress prior to releasing the document to the entire congress. At that point, the President called for a congressional probe into Mr. Sullivan's method of obtaining information. Lawyers for both sides claim they are ready to take this case all the way to the Supreme Court, if necessary.

Darien clicked on the second banner to see President Horn's response:

Washington—After Congressman Sullivan released his statement regarding the RADs investigation of Parabellum.org, President Horn called for a different kind of probe, saying it was time to "investigate the investigators." Mr. Horn stated that he is the victim of a coup attempt. He called for former President Keynes to testify before congress about using law enforcement entities to gather information on a presidential candi-

date (Horn), and illegally passing that information to RADS in high positions, particularly Charles Sullivan. Horn stated, "It's time for the RADS to be called to task for politicizing the DOJ and the FBI in a desperate attempt to hold power." He further stated that Sullivan's use of the illegally obtained information was a "crime" and an "act of terror." Horn said if he appears before congress, it will be of his own volition, not because of the recently-issued subpoena, which he has executive privilege to ignore.

As a conspiracy theorist, normally Darien would have enjoyed watching a political fight unfold, but not in this case. The timing couldn't be worse. He saw a strong possibility that President Horn would get embroiled in time-consuming legal hassles and pull back from the M13 Contact Study just when they were on the verge of making a significant step forward.

Still, even in the face of uncertainties, he was anxious for school to resume. He was convinced that, regardless of what DARPA did, he and Carly could figure out some way to move the project forward.

CHAPTER 19

With Miriam Graves and Craig McLennan trailing behind them, Carly and Darien exited NM State's robo-bus in front of the nearly-complete Pistol Pete Sports Complex on the main campus. The date was January 20, the Saturday selected for the much-anticipated ESP tests on mirror image twins. Carly's heart was racing with excitement and had done so during the entire trip from Alamogordo to Las Cruces. She was certain Darien felt the same way she did, even though he'd presented a fairly calm demeanor throughout the hour-long bus ride. Graves and McLennan also seemed remarkably calm. Perhaps the professors were in a *win-win* situation. If the ESP project succeeded, they would reap praise and honor. If it failed . . . well, it was a bizarre scheme dreamed up by a couple of overly-imaginative graduate students. The two PhDs wouldn't lose their jobs over it, but she and Darien could lose their scholarships. Carly, a proponent of positive thinking, sucked in a deep breath and evicted the unwelcomed negative thoughts which had crept into her psyche.

The air was crisp and frigid, 38 F, according to a news screen atop the Bank of America building. In spite of the cold weather, two groups of sign-carrying demonstrators, separated by a cadre of police officers, picketed in front of the building. One group occupied the sidewalk to the right of the entrance steps, and the other group claimed the left. Police commandeered the steps, and four unmarked black Suburbans lined the curb. Carly tried to see inside the menacing vehicles, but their heavily-tinted windows prevented her from doing so; nevertheless, she was certain they contained highly-trained NatGov Special Agents who were standing by in case the local police needed reinforcements.

As they stepped on the curb, two police officers came forward to escort them. On the left side of the steps, the posters consisted of jabs at the President:

REX HORN IS A SPACE ALIEN
EXILE HORN TO PLUTO

On the right side of the steps, pro-Horn demonstrators were lined up to display posters that countered those on the left:

PRESIDENT HORN'S ECONOMY IS BOOMING
VOTE FOR REX HORN IN 2048

One thing was obvious. The demonstrators weren't demonstrating *for-or-against* ESP tests; they were demonstrating *for-or-against* Rex Horn. No matter what the President did, half of the country supported it, and the other half opposed it. During the last few weeks, several polls showed Horn's popularity to be dropping sharply, so the constant anti-Horn diatribe seemed to be working.

Carly knew Darien's viewpoint—the politicians had divided the nation on purpose. She wasn't quite ready to buy into all of Darien's conspiracy theories, but some of them were beginning to make sense.

Carly studied the demonstrators as the police officers accompanied the researchers up the steps. Some of the sign-carriers looked familiar. She wondered if they were the same protestors who'd appeared at the monkey ESP tests last September. Maybe they were *demonstrators-for-hire*, a new kind of mercenary who would hire out to carry a sign for either side of an issue. With many sociopolitical pathologies infecting the country today, that would make a good business model. Maybe somebody was already doing it.

With Graves leading the way, the quartet entered the foyer and headed down the hallway to the gymnasium, the initial gathering place for the mirror image twins. The hallway connected to four spacious rooms which would be used as dressing rooms in the near future. Each room was set up to accommodate 25 sets of mirror image twins. In addition, the future office of the athletic director had been designated the *war room* for those running the tests.

As they walked along, one factor continued to bug Carly. DARPA, whose help in recruiting the twins had been invaluable, was still hovering over every phase of the project, including the ESP tests themselves. Today's tests would be transmitted live to Michael Overton's office in Washington. In addition to Overton's long-distance involvement, four DARPA technicians and eight interns were on site. The technicians had set up the equipment, and the interns would observe the testing process. While waiting for the tests to be run, the interns had served in every capacity from chaperone to chauffeur, even providing shuttle service between the university and nearby Fort Bliss, where the twins and their parents were housed in a complex known as the *BOQ—Bachelor Officers' Quarters*. DARPA had spared no expense, an indication of the importance Rex Horn placed on the M13 Contact Study. Carly couldn't help but connect the monetary outlay to the possibility that Mr. Horn anticipated quick results.

They entered the gymnasium and were greeted by new construction odors—fresh paint, plaster, glue, and pine sawdust. A throng of people milled about on the basketball court. Fascinated, Carly studied several of the twins near her. They appeared to be in their late teens or early twenties. At first glance, they looked like regular identical twins, but Carly knew a closer examination would reveal their mirror image features. Most of the twins were accompanied by parents or guardians. DARPA interns in bright yellow jackets mingled with the twins. A small portable stage equipped with a microphone was positioned at center court. In spite of her trepidation about DARPA's over-involvement, Carly was impressed by the layout of the facilities.

"Let's go to the stage," Graves said, "and I'll tell the parents to be seated." They worked their way through the noisy crowd, and once onstage, Graves took the microphone. With the volume set on high, she said, "Ladies and gentlemen, may I have your attention, please?"

The crowd noise continued.

Graves tapped the microphone, causing a loud thumping sound to reverberate through the room like a distant thunderclap. The mike-tapping did the trick, and the murmuring abated slowly until the gym was silent. Everyone in the room turned toward the stage.

"Good morning," Graves said. "Welcome to New Mexico State University."

Many in the audience echoed the greeting.

"Thank you, twins, for volunteering to participate in this extraordinary test," Graves said. "And thank you, parents and guardians, as well. At this time, I have a few instructions. Except for twins and DARPA personnel, I would like for everyone else to take a seat in the bleachers or, if you prefer, in the folding chairs in front of the bleachers. Please do it now and we'll proceed with the tests."

The crowd obeyed, and after the parents and guardians had withdrawn, Graves did a 360-degree survey of the twins encircling the stage. "Twins," she said. "I have a question. How many of you feel like you have an ESP link with your sibling?"

An affirmative roar went through the crowd—cheers, applause, and a few shrill whistles. After a moment, Graves held up a hand and the gym fell silent again.

"This test will last a little over two hours," Graves said. "We'll take a fifteen-minute break after the first hour, and when we finish the tests, lunch will be served in the university cafeteria down the street."

At that point, she introduced Carly, Darien and Craig McLennan and went on to explain how the test would be administered. Carly and Darien had set up a procedure for dividing the twins into groups numbered the same as the rooms, from 1 to 4. Four sets of twins had cancelled at the last minute, so ninety-six sets of twins would be tested. Carly, Darien, Graves, and McLennan had numbered themselves from 1 to 4, as well. Each would administer a round of tests in one room and then move to the next room until each had tested all four groups.

"Okay, volunteers," Graves continued. "You know which group you're in. So, follow your leader."

Carly stepped off the stage and started toward the exit with twenty-four sets of twins and two DARPA interns trailing behind her. They entered Room No. 1, which was set up similar to the lab used in the ESP pilot test. The receivers' table held consoles which resembled miniature voting booths shielded on each side for privacy. The operator's cubicle was positioned at one end of the long table with the transmitters' chairs arranged in rows behind the operator. The setup looked perfect to Carly.

When every twin was properly positioned, Carly explained that the test was based on the game, *Interplanetary Monopoly*, which would yield an average score of 50 with no ESP at all. She invited questions, and as expected, the questions were identical to those asked during the initial ESP test. Patiently, she answered the questions, after which she told the twins to don their helmet antennas and attempt to duplicate every move she made on the operators' console.

At the end of the first round, the average score for Carly's group was 51, barely higher than the average obtained on the original test in Alamogordo and certainly not high enough to get excited about. However, an anomaly stood out—one set of twins scored 55, suggesting a modicum of ESP.

At Carly's instructions, the transmitters and receivers changed places, and she repeated the tests. Again, the average score was 51, and the same set of twins scored 55, providing credence for the first test. The results were a paradox, leaving Carly pleased and disappointed at the same time—pleased because the tests supported the theory that ESP could be found in mirror image twins but sorely disappointed that the ESP detected was very low and occurred in only one pair of the twins she'd tested.

Following an urge to learn more about the highest-scoring twins, Carly clicked a tab next to their numerical designation, and their names popped up, Riley and Briley Smithers from Ruidoso, New Mexico. *Smithers? Ruidoso?* What a coincidence. She and Darien had discussed the Smithers family recently. Part of them had moved from Alamogordo to Ruidoso, and the rest to Houston. Moreover, the Smithers family that moved to Houston had given her Minnie, her rat terrier. The small-world scenario continued, but Carly had no idea what to make of it.

She checked the clock on her iTab. It was time for her to move to Room No. 2 and repeat the tests with her second group of twins.

The score for Group No. 2 with Carly as the operator was slightly lower than Group No. 1 had scored with the Smithers twins as members. It was time for a fifteen-minute break, so she headed toward the war room, leaving two interns behind to safe-guard the equipment and keep the young twins in check.

With her iTab clutched in taut fingers, Carly joined her three counterparts entering the war room. The mood in the room was fairly somber, suggesting that an interesting discussion was in the offing, but before Graves could launch into it, Carly asked Darien if he knew Riley and Briley Smithers.

"They moved away when we were toddlers," Darien said. "So, I don't really know them."

Knowing Graves was anxious to begin the next session, Carly didn't follow up, even though something in the data stuck out like a sore thumb. An *Alamogordo connection* was surfacing, something so bizarre it didn't make sense. The anomaly needed to be discussed thoroughly, but it seemed best to wait until all tests had been completed before going into it.

"Okay," Graves said, "let's compare our findings."

The results obtained by Carly and both professors tracked perfectly on the first two rounds of tests, including another score of 55 for the Smithers twins.

Darien's results, however, were vastly different. With him as operator, the average score for each of his two groups was 56, much higher than they'd scored with other operators. As they pored over the results, Carly's mind went into overdrive. Two factors were obvious. The Smithers twins had exhibited ESP, and apparently, so had Darien, even though he wasn't wearing a helmet. Though no one was sure what to make of the early tests, everyone in the war room joined in a lively discussion.

After several minutes, Graves glanced at her iTab clock and said, "We'd better start the next round."

"I think we should abandon the rotation," McLennan said, "and have Darien test the Smithers group, both with and without a helmet."

"I agree," Graves said. "I'll send the other three groups back to the gym, and we'll observe as Darien tests the Smithers group." She texted her instructions to the interns, and then the researchers went to Room No. 1 where the twins waiting there had evolved into the *Smithers' group*.

Carly and the professors watched as Darien called the room to order and repeated the tests. Without Darien wearing a helmet, the group scored slightly higher than either of the groups that he'd tested previously, the improvement coming from the Smithers twins. The results were nothing like Carly was hoping for, but even so, the Smithers had outperformed their peers just as before.

Carly held her breath as Darien donned a helmet antenna and repeated the tests.

The results were puzzling.

The only increase was in the Smithers' score, which jumped to 62, a significant increase but disappointing under the circumstances. She'd actually dared to believe that the Smithers twins would score near 100 with Darien wearing an antenna. She realized the idea was wishful thinking.

Before dismissing the group, they ran a couple of abbreviated tests with Carly and the professors wearing antennas. To no one's surprise, the tests revealed that Darien was the only one of the four researchers possessing ESP. Upon completion of the tests, Graves instructed the interns to usher the Smithers group back to the gym and hang out until lunch time.

Once back in the war room, the researchers huddled around a small table and looked at each other, perplexity showing on everyone's face.

"Okay," Graves said, "let's discuss our observations, then try to develop a plan for the next step. Carly, would you lead off?"

"The Smithers brothers are the only twins with any measurable ESP," Carly said. "Darien has it too. And he has more than the Smithers. The rest of us have none at all. That's what I observed."

"Darien, what did you see?" Graves said.

"I saw exactly the same that thing Carly did," Darien said. However, I don't think the Smithers' scores were high enough to consider bringing them into the M13 Contact

Study, even if we could. We need to put an asterisk by their names and move on."

"Craig?" Graves said.

"Carly and Darien mentioned everything that I saw," McLennan said. "As a side note, the Smithers' score was roughly 25% higher than those with no ESP at all."

"I don't have anything else to add to your summaries," Graves said, "but we need to work out a plan to push forward."

"DARPA is not going to be pleased with these results," McLennan said, shaking his head slowly.

"About ten percent of all twins are mirror image," Graves said. "We need to enlist another group and repeat the test."

"There are far too many mirror image twins in the country for us to test," McLennan said. "DARPA would have to get several other universities involved."

"I'd hate to see such a thing happen," Graves said. "Maybe it's selfish, but Carly and Darien came up with the idea. I'd like for it to remain a NM State project."

McLennan shrugged. "The idea of twins having ESP is not new and certainly is not patentable. We can't do anything about it if other universities take up the idea."

Dr. Graves pursed her lips thoughtfully, and her hesitation gave Carly the opportunity to take the floor. "I think we're in the best position to solve this mystery," she said. "There's some kind of *Alamogordo connection* in play which might give us an advantage over any other university."

Carly told the professors about her rat terrier's unusual behavior the night of her father's death. "Minnie was born in New Mexico," she continued. "She was the first Alamogordo connection. The monkeys were born here too. They were the second connection. The third—Riley and Briley Smithers, who moved from Alamogordo to Ruidoso several years ago. See what I mean?"

"An interesting concept," Graves said. "Dog, monkey, and human twins from the same area, all with ESP. Your theory sounds great, except for one thing. Darien has ESP, and he was born in Panama."

"He must fit in some way," Carly said.

"Regardless of whether or not Darien is some part of your Alamogordo connection idea," McLennan said, "he demonstrated an appreciable amount ESP. We need to test him further and find out more about his background."

Graves turned toward Darien and said, "We know you were adopted and have lived near Alamogordo since you were an infant. Is there anything else you can tell us?"

"You've just summarized everything I know about myself," Darien said.

"Is it possible that you have a twin?" Graves asked.

"According to my adoptive parents, the missionaries who found me heard some rumors to that effect."

"Did they investigate the rumors?"

Darien nodded. "Oh, yes. They tried several times, but couldn't get any cooperation from NatGov—or from the

Panamanian government either, for that matter—so they finally gave up."

Graves pursed her lips thoughtfully and said, "We need to find out more about you."

CHAPTER 20

As the war room fell quiet, everyone looked at Darien, and he knew a quantum shift had taken place in the minds of his three companions over the last hour. He was no longer merely a fellow observer; he was also being observed. Demonstrating the enigmatic property, ESP, had put him at center stage. Darien was just as surprised as his associates were. He'd always thought of himself as a logical and analytical thinker; whereas, he believed ESP—if it existed at all—would be found in intuitive and emotional types. That was a dubious idea that needed to be jettisoned immediately.

Mulling over his life, Darien remembered occasions when he and Rachel had seemed to read each other's minds, but he'd assumed that living in close quarters all their lives made them think alike. Maybe that was another wrong assumption as well. In fact, based on everything that happened today, all of his former ideas about ESP needed a serious reevaluation. Consequently, he was anxious to see what direction the conversation took when he and his three cohorts discussed his newly-discovered psi talent.

But before the conversation found any meaningful direction, a shrill ringtone emitted from the PA system, and the room's wall monitor came to life in a rainbow of swirling colors. The ringtone indicated that a *station to station* linkup had been activated from a location on the university campus. Darien and his companions stared at the monitor, waiting for it to reveal the originator of the link. Tension permeated the room. The monitor snapped into sharp focus and showed Dr. Sheldon Leonard seated behind his desk. Darien looked at Carly, and she raised her eyebrows inquisitively. He suspected what was coming—something related to DARPA, and it wouldn't be good. From day one, Michael Overton had hovered over the ESP tests so closely that Darien suspected he was under Rex Horn's orders to bail out quickly if the mirror image twins failed to exhibit psi phenomena. The just-completed tests could not be considered to be a smashing success, even by the most optimistic, and President Horn would likely consider them to be a complete failure. Maybe Rex Horn feared that he might not win a second term and was losing interest in anything which couldn't be completed during his first term.

"Good afternoon professors and graduate students," Leonard said in a somber tone which foreshadowed the discourse to follow. "Thank you for giving up part of your weekend to conduct this ESP study. Throughout the tests, Dr. Overton and I maintained a FaceTime link and watched as you conducted them. The tests were quite interesting but fell short of the anticipated results; therefore, it is my duty to inform you that DARPA is withdrawing support . . . "

A chorus of groans sounded throughout the war room, drowning out Leonard's last few words.

"Let me finish, please," Leonard said firmly. "As I was saying, DARPA is withdrawing support of the mirror-image twin studies, so you need to come up with an alternate plan to remain involved in the M13 Contact Study."

"Dr. Leonard," Graves said, "Mr. Horn encouraged everyone participating in this study to think outside the box, and I believe we've done just that. We've been working on this project less than four months. Surely, the President didn't think we could complete it in such a short time."

"Don't misunderstand me," Leonard said. "According to Dr. Overton, DARPA has no intention of shutting down the entire M13 Contact Study, just the search for ESP in twins. The study was expensive and didn't produce any worthwhile results."

"In my opinion, today's tests were worthwhile," Graves said firmly. "Surely, they were a step in the right direction. There are many more twins in the country that we could test."

"This type of test is very costly," Leonard said, "and could go on ad infinitum. Besides, today's results indicate that non-twins such as Mr. Segura are just as likely to possess ESP as mirror image twins. That was one reason DARPA pulled the plug on the twin study."

"Today's test proved that ESP exists in some mirror image twins," Carly said, "as well as in other people. Is it possible to carry on this type of test with university funding alone?"

"Not in the immediate future," Leonard said. "They're too costly for NM State to fund. We'll have to develop another approach."

"If DARPA is giving up on ESP, let's review the basics again and see where we might go from there," McLennan said. "Can we get NASA to release the exact files that led President Horn to refer to the radio waves as SOS, CEASE AND DESIST, and MAYDAY messages."

"I think that would be a good way to proceed," Leonard said. "I'll contact Dr. Overton immediately and request access to those files. In the meantime, continue looking for innovative approaches suitable for inclusion in the M13 study. We want to continue participating in this unique venture any way we can. Thank you for your time. Good afternoon."

The monitor faded to black, and the researchers left the war room. The robo-bus trip back to Alamogordo featured a quieter style of conversation than the ride which brought the ESP-seekers to the Las Cruces campus. The early morning dialogue had revolved around the next step to take after discovering ESP, now the talk was shifting to the development of a plan to study radio waves by methods not likely to include ESP. Although Carly showed no outward signs, Darien knew she was feeling some pangs of regret that she would have to resolve. He knew she would do it quickly and put her best effort into their work ahead, no matter which direction it led them. In the few months they'd worked together, he'd grown used to having Carly as a research partner and friend. He'd never met anyone like her.

As they explored ideas, the conversation eventually turned back to Darien's possession of ESP and the mood lightened.

"Tell us you haven't been reading our minds," Carly said. "We'd be embarrassed."

Darien smiled and shrugged. "You're not wearing antennas, so your thoughts are safe."

"Speaking of antennas," Graves said, "if everybody attending NM State wore one, we might discover ESP all around us, especially if Carly's Alamogordo connection has any validity."

"I still can't get that idea out of my mind," Carly said. "DARPA may not fund it, but they can't stop me from thinking about it."

As the bus neared the city limits of Alamogordo, Darien glanced out of the window just in time to see a public news screen flashing a pair of a startling headlines:

CONGRESS TO REVIEW MARS PROJECT
TERRAFORMING FUNDS IN JEOPARDY

"Look at that!" Darien said, pointing.

The bus zoomed past the screen so quickly that Darien's companions got only a fleeting glimpse of the stunning headlines, but everyone saw enough to conclude that Washington was operating in full chaos mode, the modus operandi which had become daily fare with Rex Horn as President. Darien's teammates lamented the turn of events concerning Project Mayflower, but he wasn't upset about it. Under normal conditions, he would have liked for the project to advance on schedule; however, that was not the case this time. He didn't care if it was delayed, at least long enough that Garth would be sent back to Galveston. He was fed up with tip-toeing around the Texan.

***

Later that evening, when Carly got back to her dorm room, she put on cozy flannel pajamas, made a cup of hot chocolate, and sat down at her cramped student desk. As she slowly sipped the chocolate, she visualized an extraterrestrial (*a little green man?*) on a distant planet adjusting dials on a transmitter and wondering *is anybody out there?*

We're here, ET, she thought. We'll answer as soon as we interpret your message.

Though it had been a long day, Carly decided to check the news headlines before going to bed. She activated the computer on her desk and touched the *Play TV* icon just as the local station was preempted by Washington, D.C. Carly perked up, expecting something unusual because the hour was late.

A computerized voice said, "Attention please. Stand by for a message from President Horn's Press Secretary. Attention . . . please stand by . . . "

Carly watched as the monitor morphed into a view of a small office somewhere on Capitol Hill. A trim woman with curly salt and pepper hair stood beside a desk with the American Flag behind her. The Press Secretary's name was Karen Haldon. Carly had heard her speak several times, usually from the Rose Garden but never at 10:30 p.m. This announcement would be a newsmaker.

"Good evening, my fellow Americans," Haldon said. "Thank you for tuning in. President Horn has instructed me to make a very brief announcement regarding the Parabellum.org dossier, which is in the news daily. As you have heard countless times, Mr. Horn's opponents claim the dossier contains evidence to prove that he violated election laws. Mr. Horn categorically denies all such allegations but has agreed to discuss these charges before an informal congressional hearing. Let me emphasize—this hearing will be informal. Although, congress insists that they have the authority to subpoena the President, Mr. Horn insists that he has the authority to ignore it. So in order to move ahead quickly, they have agreed to an informal format. Most members of congress are expected to attend. Both parties believe it is expedient to resolve this issue as soon as possible and will hold the hearing on the second of February.

"Late this afternoon, Mr. Horn made a change in his legal counsel by discharging his lead attorney and replacing him with Dr. Michael Overton. Dr. Overton was DARPA's point man on the M13 Contact Study, but has taken an indefinite leave of absence from that position in order to lead the President's legal team."

Haldon paused briefly and then added, "My fellow Americans, thank you for listening. God bless you, and God bless America. Good night."

CHAPTER 21

A s Carly and Garth stepped off the bus in front of the New Mexico Space Museum, she motioned toward the White Sands Missile Range and said, "Look at this incredible view."

"It's nice," Garth said, "but I like Galveston a lot better, even with its muddy water and seaweed."

Carly sighed in frustration. In the last few weeks, she'd showed Garth the White Sands National Park, Ground Zero, and some abandoned gold mines near Orogrande. Still, no matter where they went, Garth always compared it to Galveston, their *go-to* location for a day trip while growing up. And when not working at Mayflower, about all he did was hang around the university. She knew his intention was to spend as much time with her as possible, but he was on the verge of interfering with her studies. Garth had showed very little interest in learning about the desert, even though this was his first trip to the American Southwest. Carly realized that he had some growing up to do, a fact which hadn't been obvious before his move to New Mexico. Some of the problems in adapting to his new life-style had defaulted to Carly, and she was trying to help him as much as possible without becoming his baby sitter.

"Give the desert a chance," Carly said firmly. "You may be here for a while, so you'd better try to adjust."

Garth nodded. "You're right—you're always right."

Carly shook her head. "Not always, but I am this time." As they walked toward the small park surrounding the museum, Carly reflected on her shared timeline with Garth. Their first meeting, thirteen years ago, came at a time when both of them needed friends, and they'd bonded instantly. Upon reaching young adulthood, they looked back on their meeting in the third grade as the beginning of a series of childhood adventures which led to adult friendship, and eventually, to dating. They'd been dating for nearly six years, but as of late, their relationship had regressed. Carly knew Garth's major problem was due to her spending so much time with Darien on their joint research project. Since that part of Carly's life wasn't subject to change, Garth would have to get used to it. She'd already told him so, but he was having trouble accepting it.

Turning her attention back to showing Garth the park, Carly said, "This area around the museum is called the John R. Stapp Air and Space Park."

Garth perked up. "I know who John Stapp is," he said. "He set the land speed record on a rocket sled. He was called the fastest man alive."

"The sled's right over there," Carly said. "Stapp did a lot of other things too—not all of them related to science. He popularized the concept of Murphy's Law."

"Murphy's Law," Garth said, shaking his head slowly. He took Carly by the hand as they walked toward the sled. "*If anything can go wrong, it will.* Do you think Murphy was right?"

"About half of the time," Carly said, wondering if Garth meant to imply that the old adage described their relationship.

Though the weather was frigid, they examined the sled briefly and then moved to a rocket known as Little Joe II. At the base of the rocket, a plaque stated that it was 86 feet tall, the tallest rocket ever launched from the New Mexico desert site. Next, they examined the Daisy Decelerator, an air-powered sled system used to study the effects of acceleration, deceleration, and impact on the human body. As they hurried through the outdoor exhibits, Carly sensed a slight change in Garth's attitude. Due to his engineering background, she'd expected the unique gadgetry to grab his attention; clearly, it had done so. She was happy for him. Maybe he would stop talking about Galveston for a while.

They finished their hasty tour of Stapp Park and went into the ground floor of the Space Museum. At the entrance to the exhibits, they pulled up their student ID cards on their iTabs and showed them to the uniformed attendant. The man motioned for them to enter.

"Let's go to the Basin Overlook exhibit," Carly said.

"What's on display there?"

"The sunset over White Sands—it's spectacular."

"Elevator or ramp?"

"Elevator," Carly said. "We need to get to the Overlook ASAP."

Garth punched the *Up* button.

"The magic moment occurs exactly at sunset," Carly said as they entered the elevator. "About two minutes from now."

They joined a group of spectators standing in front of the Basin Overlook window. The evening was perfect for watching the sunset over the missile range, and the crowd was waiting expectantly. All eyes were fixed on the western horizon where the orange sun perched at the juncture of pale blue sky and white sand. A short distance above the horizon, the crescent moon waited its turn to descend into the desert, and near the moon, Venus glowed faintly.

As the sun dipped out of sight, a brilliant ray of green light appeared and shot upward like a flash of ground lightening. The ray lingered momentarily, flickered, and faded away. A chorus of *oohs* and *ahs* rippled through the small crowd, and for several seconds, everyone continued to stare at the horizon. The heavens, however, did not provide an encore.

"The show's over," someone said softly. In unison, the crowd turned and moved toward the exit, leaving Carly and Garth alone in the Basin Overlook gallery.

"That must be New Mexico's version of the northern lights," Garth said. "It was awesome."

"Would you like to go back to the ground floor and go through the exhibits from the beginning," Carly said.

"Whatever you want to do."

"Are you ready to go?"

Garth nodded. "I guess so."

CHAPTER 22

On February 2, Darien and Carly joined Craig McLennan and Miriam Graves in a small conference room in the science building annex. Both professors had lined up substitutes to take over their Friday teaching chores, and both the graduate students were skipping classes. McLennan had invited Darien and Carly to watch the House of Representatives' hearing on Parabellum.org. In addition, he'd arranged for their absences to be excused, which was a bonus, since they'd already planned to cut, whether excused or not.

Today's congressional hearing was receiving media coverage throughout the civilized world, and speculation regarding the outcome was running rampant in the U.S. According to numerous polls, half of the population thought the hearing would incriminate Rex Horn, and the other half thought it would exonerate him. Las Vegas agreed with the polls and set the odds at fifty-fifty that impeachment proceedings would begin within a month of the hearing.

Darien felt that today's hearing would affect everyone in the conference room, regardless of the outcome. He didn't see how there could be a clear-cut victory in the proceedings, even though Rex Horn had tweeted all week that the hearing would be *short and sweet*.

As they sat down at a small table, McLennan said, "I wonder why congress chose Ground Hog Day for this hearing?"

"The RADS want Rex Horn to see his shadow and crawl into a hole," Darien said with a chuckle. The analogy had been in his mind long before McLennan asked the *straight man* question.

McLennan picked up the TV controller and activated the monitor on the wall. The image of the House Chamber materialized. The Chamber had been remodeled several times over the years, with recent changes restoring the original Victorian look of 1857, when the House first met in the room. Over 450 armchairs were arranged in a semicircle facing the Speaker's rostrum, and an American flag hung on the wall behind the rostrum. The flag was flanked by fasces—bundles of wooden rods with projecting axe blades, an ancient symbol of power. A gallery for visitors and news media ringed the chamber on the upper level, and a crowd was gathering there. The lower room was nearly full, with many Representatives already in their seats.

President Horn was seated at an elongated pecan table between the semicircle of armchairs and the rostrum. Only one man sat at the table with the President—Michael Overton. A huge laptop computer lay on the table in front of Overton. Darien and his companions had expected a host of attorneys to be seated with the President, but apparently, Mr. Horn was putting his fate in the hands of one man, his distant cousin from Florida, Michael Overton, PhD and

JD. They watched as President Horn whispered to Overton. The President seemed to have a smirk on his face.

At 10:04 a.m., House Speaker Charles Sullivan took the podium in the center of the rostrum, and the RADS responded with a light ripple of applause. Sullivan pounded the podium loudly with a gavel. The applause and other background noise abated gradually until the room was silent.

"Good morning ladies and gentlemen," Sullivan began. "This informal meeting of the House of Representatives was requested by the Select Committee investigating the political activities of Parbellum.org, particularly as these activities relate to the last presidential election. They have completed their probe and are ready to present their findings. At this time, the meeting will come to order. A quorum being present, we will proceed.

"Welcome President Horn. Welcome Representatives. Before we begin, I would like to thank the President for attending this hearing. As you know, the House subpoenaed Mr. Horn, but he claimed executive privilege and ignored the subpoena. However, he has agreed to appear informally before this body, but not under oath. So we will move forward on that basis. I am looking forward to a productive discussion. To begin, I would like to introduce the five members of the Select Committee, and give each of them three minutes to make an opening statement."

"We're going to hear the same thing five times," Darien said. His cohorts nodded in agreement.

The first committee member to speak was an impassioned young Representative from New York, Bethany Depena, who was chair of the Select Committee. She began by stating that the committee had found ample evidence to prove that Rex Horn had committed election interference by colluding with Parabellum.org. She went on to state that Mr. Horn, while a presidential candidate, had received large donations from the secret organization; however, the identities of many individual donors still remained unknown because the funds had been laundered by several offshore banks controlled by Parabellum.org. Depena's charges had been repeated so many times by Alphabet News that it seemed like she was reading the evening news.

When the second committee member began to recite the same assemblage of talking points, Graves looked around the room and asked, "Well, what do you think?"

"This reminds me of a poker game," McLennan said, "but I can't figure out who's bluffing."

"Rex Horn isn't," Darien said. "He has a *tell.*"

"What's his tell?" McLennan said.

"A smirk," Darien said. "Apparently, he has an ace in the hole."

After each of the committee members had spoken, Sullivan leaned forward in his chair and said, "It's our goal to insure fairness in the election process by maintaining proper oversight of campaign financing, and I would like to thank the Select Committee for their diligence in that respect. The charges brought against the President serious, and the committee has gathered considerable evidence which will be presented during this hearing. Since this is an informal hearing, I think it proper to give the President the opportunity to speak at this time, if he wishes to do so. Mr. Horn, you may have the floor to make an opening statement, after which the committee would like to ask you some questions."

Rex Horn stared briefly at the committee members and then turned toward Sullivan and said, "Thank you, Mr. Chairman. I do not wish to make an opening statement, and I decline to answer any questions. I would like to point out that I am not under oath; therefore, I'm not *taking the fifth*, and would appreciate it if Alphabet News would report it that way. During the rest of this hearing, my attorney, Michael Overton, will speak for me. He will make a short opening statement, after which committee members may ask questions, and he will respond."

Upon finishing his statement, Rex Horn leaned back in his chair and stared straight ahead.

For a moment, the House Chamber was silent, after which all members of the Independent Party stood up and clapped while the RADS remained glued to their seats. The ratio was about fifty-fifty.

Sullivan picked up his gavel and struck the podium several times. When order was restored, he said, "This is an extraordinary situation, Mr. President. It was our understanding that you would answer questions from the committee."

Rex Horn continued his impersonation of Mount Rushmore.

"Mr. Chairman, the President has designated me to speak for him," Overton said in a powerful voice that commanded the room. "Ask your questions, and I'll answer them. If that's not acceptable to you and the committee, President Horn will exit the House Chamber immediately and this hearing will end."

The two men stared at each other until Sullivan said, "Proceed, counselor."

Overton picked up the aluminum laptop in front of him and held it in the air. "Ladies and gentlemen, this is Parabellum.org."

A discordant roar went throughout the room—cheers, hisses, boos, and applause.

After gaveling the cacophony to silence, Sullivan said, "You have the floor, Mr. Overton. We'd like to hear what you have to say."

"Thank you, Mr. Chairman," Overton continued. "The Parbellum.org which you have spent much time and money investigating is a computer program. It was developed by Simulacrum Inc. for a group of Florida businessmen who incorporated as Parabellum.org, the same name as the program. This laptop, which I never let out of my sight, is the central processing unit and primary memory for the entire computer program, the *mainframe*, so to speak. For obvious reasons, the program is not being stored in the cloud. Parabellum utilizes artificial intelligence to simulate election polls. It consists of a digital community of 10,000 AI citizens, each consisting of billions of electrical impulses on a computer chip. During beta testing, several AI citizens made large donations to a presidential candidate, as is often done in the real world. The transactions consisted of faux digital currency donated to a candidate who was digital as well."

Overton paused and placed the aluminum laptop on the table. He glared at the committee for several seconds and then slowly tapped the computer with an index finger and said, "*Parabellum dot org*. Ladies and gentlemen, this concludes my opening statement. Now I'll take your questions." When Overton finished speaking, he continued to look toward the Select Committee, all of whom seemed uncomfortable under his piercing glare.

"Do you have any questions for Mr. Overton?" Sullivan asked, his voice lacking the gravitas displayed by Overton.

Depena leaned toward her microphone. "Mr. Overton, would you please clarify something? Is Parabellum.org a computer program or a corporation?"

"Both."

Depena tapped her iTab briefly. "Regardless of its structure, we have records showing that Parabellum transferred large sums of money illegally."

"You've already stated as much," Overton said. "Do you have a question?"

"For example, here is a donation of ten million dollars from John Stone to R. Horn."

"What's your question?"

"Are you telling us that John Stone and R. Horn do not exist?"

"They exist as electrical impulses on this computer," Overton said, tapping the laptop again, "but not as real people."

"We contend that R. Horn is Rex Horn," Depena said hotly. "In addition, we've obtained records of numerous other illegal donations being made to his campaign, not just this one by Mr. Stone. There are many others."

"Produce the record of any transaction you care to discuss," Overton said, "and I'll show you the original ersatz document on this computer and the profile of the AI citizen who made the donation. If you like, I would be glad to display this information on the monitors around this room, so everyone in the chamber can see it."

Depena, now with flushed cheeks, tapped furiously at her iTab, stopping to study the screen from time to time. Momentarily, she looked up and said, "I still maintain that it was election fraud to use the name R. Horn to designate an AI presidential candidate."

"We strive for realism in our AI universe," Overton said.

Depena glared at Overton briefly, then looked toward Sullivan and said, "No more questions, Mr. Chairman."

"Would any other committee member care to question Mr. Overton?" Sullivan asked, his original enthusiasm now completely gone.

The committee members shifted their eyes back and forth between Overton and Chairman Sullivan, their body language signaling that they were ready to toss in the towel. Depena huddled briefly with her cohorts and then turned toward Congressman Sullivan and said, "We have no more questions, Mr. Chairman."

"Then this hearing is adjourned," Sullivan said, rapping the desk with his gavel. "Thank you, Mr. Overton. Thank you, Mr. President."

Darien kept his eyes glued on the monitor as the representatives filed out of the House Chamber. The congressional hearing had been a conspiracy theorist's dream, leaving Darien and his three companions stunned. Likely the RADS had broken the law, but obviously, that was exactly what Horn hoped they would do—take the bait. Overton had delivered a cleverly orchestrated kick in the groin.

Carly broke the silence. "It was short and sweet, as Rex Horn promised."

"I'm sure Michael Overton set this up a long time ago," McLennan said. "No doubt he deliberately left the data unprotected, knowing the RADS would hack into it while investigating the President."

"Who does Overton work for?" Graves asked. "DARPA? Simulacrum? Parabellum? President Horn? Himself?"

"All of the above," Darien said.

"Maybe we're AI citizens on Overton's laptop," Carly said.

"If so, shouldn't we be able to communicate with each other by ESP?" Darien said.

"I'm still trying to figure out why President Horn would concoct such an elaborate scheme," Graves said. "It looks like he'd have better things to do."

"Rex Horn sent the RADS on a wild goose chase to keep them occupied while he was doing something behind their backs," Darien said.

"And what might that be?" Carly asked.

"I think we'll find out soon," Darien said.

CHAPTER 23

On Friday morning, as snowflakes swirled around her, Carly dashed into the science building annex to meet Darien. In spite of DARPA's withdrawal from the ESP search, the last few days had produced several high points. Dr. Leonard had committed the university to remain involved in SETI research, even though most projects would receive no government funding. And, in spite of the fact that she'd completed only one astronomy course, Leonard had approved Miriam Graves' request to allow Carly to continue working with Darien. With the study shifting from brainwaves to radio waves, the professors switched roles. McLennan took over as project leader, and Graves continued as Carly's advisor. Since the new arrangement still maintained the link between astronomy and psychology, Carly saw it as a bold move by NM State's leadership.

At Dr. Leonard's request, DARPA had provided the password to a packet of M13 files processed for NASA by The SETI Institute. Carly was excited about the opportunity to study the files, even though she felt they'd gone back to square one with ESP reverting to back-burner status. She was still pondering the Alamogordo connection as it related to Darien. With him as the ESP mystery man, Carly felt sure the subject would resurface as they studied the radio waves. Maybe DARPA had waffled on the idea, but she hadn't and never would.

Accompanied by many fond memories of her first astronomy course, Carly entered the lab. It was here that she'd built a primitive sextant and calculated the distance to the sun and the movement of the moon. Near the end of the semester, the class had taken a brief look at fast radio bursts—*FRBs*, as she now called them. The course was a solid introduction to astronomy. She'd enjoyed it, and was looking forward to learning more about the field. The large wing of the L-shaped lab was furnished with black-topped tables, each serving as a desk for four students working as lab partners. One wall of the room held several monitors linked to a small radio telescope on the roof. This wing was utilized primarily by undergraduate students, while the small wing adjoining it, the Astronomy Research Lab, was restricted to professors and graduate students. The wings were divided by a wall and a locked door. This would be Carly's first time to enter the *stargazers' inner sanctum,* as she'd dubbed the room.

She approached the research lab as Darien was opening the door. He turned and waited for her. They hugged briefly and she stepped back. This fleeting hug had been their standard greeting for the past few weeks. The hasty embrace was drier than a desert handshake. Surely, it didn't violate any student/teacher guidelines. Still, if Garth knew it was happening, he would detest it. He was getting more and more upset about the amount of time Carly was spending with Darien. Having two men vying for her time was getting increasingly difficult to handle. Unfortunately, she saw no solution which would be satisfactory to everyone concerned.

They moved to a lab bench which held the command console, a tan cabinet running the length of the bench. The console held five monitors, each with a touchpad beneath it. Darien sat down in front of the display in the middle—the largest—called the *Control Station*. Carly took the lab stool to his right. Darien logged in as Carly examined the label beneath the screen in front of her and the one next to it. The first one read *Intensity vs Time* and the next one read *Intensity vs Frequency*. Carly was familiar with the terms, although the computers in the undergraduate lab weren't programmed for such specific use.

"Okay, Stargazer, let's see what we've got," Carly said. She was comfortable with Darien as the team leader. He'd shown the same attitude on the ESP study with her in the leadership role. She knew it was unusual for two high achievers like them to be able to switch roles seamlessly as the situation changed and felt like this character trait made them a formidable team, even though they'd yet to solve a single problem. Maybe they would do so today. She was beginning to feel it.

At NASA's web page, Darien navigated to the M13 Archives and clicked on a folder labeled *ET Archive, 2026–2045 #2*. A mini-screen popped up and requested a password. Darien entered the password obtained from DARPA, *si-vis-pacem,* and the folder opened.

"That's a pretty weak password," Carly said. "Any amateur hacker could break it with little effort. It's Latin for *if you want peace.*"

"I know," Darien said. "It's the phrase that precedes *Parabellum,* which means *prepare for war.*"

"Apparently, Rex Horn is still playing charades."

"NASA claims the files they released to us are unique because they were processed using The SETI Institute's recently-developed algorithms," Darien said.

"Why do you think NASA only gave us access to processed data?"

"They probably thought we wouldn't be able to handle the bogeys."

Carly raised her eyebrows. "What bogeys?"

"In addition to cosmic noise generated by the universe, SETI researchers deal with a sky full of constant interferences—things such as satellites, stealth aircraft, radar systems, various communication systems, high-tech pranksters . . . the list is endless. But it seems that NASA is convinced the new algorithms are effective in removing these interferences."

"Could you *un-process* the files?" Carly asked.

"What are you getting at?"

"It seems like they're sending us a prepared product, something like a can of vegetable soup. I was wondering if we could back up to the point where we could study the individual vegetables that went into the soup."

"Let's taste the soup first," Darien said, "and see where we go from there."

"But could you do it?"

"I could separate the signals that were produced by combining channels," Darien said, "but that shouldn't be necessary. All the signals NASA released are in the 1420-megahertz range."

"Are they *monochromatic*?" Carly said, emphasizing the term to show that she could speak the language.

With an approving nod, Darien said, "They're narrow band, but probably not totally monochromatic."

"There's the file we're looking for," Carly said, pointing toward the monitor. "*July 16, 2045*, which seems to be the one that caused Mr. Horn to go all in on the M13 Contact Study."

Darien linked the control station monitor to the one in front of Carly and touched the *Start* icon. The *Intensity vs Time* monitor came to life with a flickering green light that formed a set of pulsating waves originating on the left of the screen and flowing to the right. He repeated the linking process with the *Intensity vs Frequency* monitor and slid back his lab stool in order to get a better view of the monitor to Carly's right. As they watched, a sharp vertical spike rose to the top of the screen.

"That's a strong signal," Darien said. "However, an eyeball examination isn't going to turn up anything that The SETI Institute or NASA missed. If there was ever a time for creative thinking, this is it."

Carly stared at the waves moving across the screen. "How long is this first recording?"

"Based on the size of the file, I'd guess about an hour."

"Let's watch it all."

"What are you looking for?"

"I'm not sure," Carly said, "but will you humor me?"

"Of course."

For the next hour, they watched the waves continue their journey from left to right. Carly kept her eyes fixed on the screen, blinking only occasionally. Darien sat slightly behind her, just off her left shoulder. The waves were hypnotic. Over the entire hour, the frequency remained constant, each wave taking the same amount of time to move across the screen; however, the amplitude varied. Several short waves rolled by, followed by a tall wave, just like waves on the beach at Galveston. As a small child, Carly had heard that ocean waves came in well-defined patterns with every seventh wave being twice as high as the average, and every 700th wave—or maybe every 7000th—being three times as high. On her twelfth birthday, she'd counted hundreds of waves, only to discover that the magic attributed to number seven was nothing but folklore. Carly knew it wouldn't fit radio waves, either. Still, she thought she could see a hint of a pattern, even though the computer didn't flag it as a possible language.

After watching the entire file, Carly turned toward Darien and said, "A wild idea just hit me."

"Lay it on me," Darien said as he hit the *Pause* icon. "I'm ready to try something new, even a *wild idea*."

"Could you eliminate the 1420-megahertz band completely?"

"I can filter it out," Darien said with a nod, "but the recorded signals are all near that frequency, including the ones Mr. Horn called SOS messages. Many astronomers think it's the only logical choice."

"Do you think so?"

"Not necessarily."

"Then how about erasing the 1420-megahertz band and see if anything's left."

Darien shrugged. "Okay, let's give it a shot."

He instructed the computer to eliminate the frequency which astronomers had focused on since the infancy of SETI. A split second later, the wave-shaped lines disappeared, and the monitor flickered and went blank. Hardly blinking, they stared at the empty screen for five minutes.

"Well . . . so much for my wild idea," Carly said.

"Don't give up yet. I'll fast-forward through these recordings, and we'll see what happens." With the 1420-megahertz frequency filtered out, Darien set the computer on fast forward. Two minutes later, the playback ended without registering a single blip. Undaunted by the initial failure, Darien reset the computer to analyze the August 2045 file in the same manner. Again, the screen remained blank throughout the month-long period.

Ditto for the months September, October, November, and December.

"I wonder if The SETI Institute's new algorithm is so keyed to the 1420 band that it filters out some frequencies that might be worthwhile," Carly said.

"It might. We need an unprocessed file."

"We have a password," Carly said. "Let's see how far we can get with it."

Darien turned back to the control station and dragged the *ET Archive, 2026–2045 AD #2* to one side, revealing another folder directly beneath it. The folder had the same name, but ended with the suffix *#1*. He clicked on the folder, and it requested a password. As Carly held her breath, Darien entered *si-vis-pacem*. The folder vibrated rapidly, but didn't open. A dialogue box popped up again, repeating the request for a password. With no hesitation, he added *parabellum* to the password and the folder opened.

"Voila!" Carly said. "We're in."

"That was so easy it makes me suspicious."

"Me too."

"I'm guessing that #1 indicates these are the original FRBs," Darien said. "If so, there will be plenty of stray signals, so I'll have to set up cross-references to detect and identify all celestial interferences near M13. With twenty years of studying that particular star cluster, all bogeys near it should have been identified and cataloged. As before, I've set filters to block the 1420-megahertz band. That'll remove the bandwidths that most astrophysicists consider to be most significant, and we'll study the leftovers—if there are any." Darien touched the *Start* button and the monitor flickered as the recording began to play.

Immediately, a loud buzzer sounded and several points of pulsating light appeared onscreen. In each case, the computer identified the object as a known source of radio interference, and an alphanumeric label appeared beneath the object. With minimal talk, Carly and Darien kept their eyes fixed on the screen as bogey after bogey appeared and was identified by the computer.

Ten minutes later, Darien motioned toward the screen and said, "ET must have fallen asleep. We're getting nothing but bogeys."

"Can't you fast forward the recording?"

"Yes, but not at the rate that we ran the processed files," Darien said. "Identifying the interferences slows the computer down. Still, I think we should be able to view a 24-hour recording in a couple of hours." He increased the speed, and they continued to stare at the monitor, both leaning slightly forward.

"Would most astronomers laugh at us for taking this approach?" Carly asked.

"Probably. They don't advocate . . . "

Darien's voice broke off as a shrill beep sounded, indicating the detection of a signal from a non-cataloged source. A light flashed on the *Intensity vs Frequency* monitor in front of Carly, and they watched as a small smear the size of an infant's thumbprint scurried across the screen like a beetle. After that, the screen went blank again.

"What was that?" Carly said, her voice rising.

"It looked like a brief flash of low frequency waves," Darien said, as he adjusted the controls.

"Could this be a hidden message?"

Darien shrugged.

Carly pointed to the screen. "I still don't understand why the sender would hide his message in a high frequency band?"

"Low frequencies are far too weak to transmit over interstellar distances," Darien said. "They'd never reach Earth from another galaxy, and if they did, they couldn't be detected above the existing background noise."

"Do you think it's possible to transmit low frequency signals by using the 1420-megahertz band as a carrier?"

"Most astrophysicists would insist that such a concept violates several laws of physics," Darien said. "The only one I know who says otherwise is Dr. Edward Pauling, the retired professor who speaks a lot at local astronomy clubs."

"Do you agree with him?"

"I'm not sure."

"Maybe it has something to do with parapsychology."

"Maybe."

Carly put her hand on Darien's shoulder. "Are we thinking outside the box?"

"You are," Darien said, with a vigorous nod. "Filtering out the 1420 line was a good idea."

Five minutes later, Darien said, "I hope that blip wasn't a bogey which hasn't been cataloged."

"Let's give it some more time," Carly said. "I believe we're on to something big."

A few minutes later, her optimism was rewarded. Two small oval smears appeared. A chill went down Carly's spine, and she whispered, "Wow!"

"What do you think the next signal will be?" Darien said.

"I'm guessing three blips in a row."

"Me too."

They watched in silence until the next signal appeared five minutes later. As anticipated, three oval smears equidistance apart crawled across the screen. At that moment, student/teacher relationships were tossed aside. Darien and Carly laughed giddily and then jumped up and hugged. "I'm hereby deleting the word *Honorary* from your title," Darien said. "You're a full-fledged astronomer now."

"Thank you. I appreciate your confidence."

They sat down again. Carly watched anxiously for the next signal, wondering if it would continue the numerical sequence, or be something else entirely. Presently, the next signal appeared. It was identical in intensity to the previous smears, but stretched across the entire screen.

"What do you make of this?" Carly asked.

"I think the small smears indicate that this signal is from an intelligent being," Darien said. "ET is saying, *If you can count to three, stay tuned for the following message.* For years, astronomers have anticipated that extraterrestrial messages sent our way would contain prime numbers and other improbable numbers because such numbers don't occur in nature. Such signals would prove the sender was an intelligent being. Well, counting to three proves the same thing."

"And the long smear has to be the message."

"It was hidden in plain sight, so simple that everybody overlooked it."

"What now?" Carly asked.

"Let's play this whole video," Darien said, "filtered just like this short segment. That will tell us if the same signals are repeated over and over, or if it's a series of different signals."

"Why don't we treat ourselves to a Starbucks while the computer collects the data," Carly said.

"I have a better idea," Darien said. "Let's go to Sammie's."

"Didn't you have lunch?"

"Just cheese crackers and a Diet Coke. I'm starving."

"Okay, let's go."

With a jaunty spring in their walk, they left the building.

***

After a quick mid-afternoon snack, accompanied by considerable speculation about extraterrestrials and Chinese billionaires building spaceships, Carly and Darien returned to the astronomy lab. They sat down on adjoining stools, and Carly stared at the monitor anticipating that they were on the brink of a major discovery.

"I'm going to eliminate the area between signals, so we don't waste time staring at a blank screen," Darien said. He completed the procedure and added, "Okay, now we're going to see the condensed version of ET's phone calls."

The computer began to play the recording, which he had condensed to about ten minutes. Carly and Darien stared as the signals appeared onscreen. As they'd hoped, a clear pattern was obvious—one smear, two smears, and three smears in succession, followed by a long streak flowing across the screen. A minute later, a second set of signals joined the left-to-right march. Then, a third, fourth, and fifth set. As the playback ended, Darien and Carly stared at each other without speaking for a moment.

"I think that we just found what SETI researchers have been hunting for years," Darien said. "Unmistakable proof that intelligent beings have transmitted signals toward Earth."

"Is counting from one to three *unmistakable proof?*"

"It is to me. And along with the proof, I think we have the message itself."

"This is mind-boggling," Carly said. "We're in uncharted waters."

"Yes, we are," Darien said, "and we need to proceed with caution. These five sets of signals are probably identical, but I'll make sure they are before we do anything else." He signaled the computer, and a split-second later, it verified his assumption.

"It looks like ET had only one message," Carly said, "which he began transmitting repeatedly about 25,000 years ago."

"And we began receiving it twenty years ago. What an incredible time lapse."

"It must be important."

Darien pointed toward the screen. "Notice the frequencies—from 12—40 cycles per second."

"About like brainwaves."

"Are you coming back to the idea that ESP is the necessary ingredient to solve this riddle?"

"I never left it."

CHAPTER 24

On a cold and blustery Saturday morning, the day after discovering ET's message, Darien joined the early-breakfast crowd at McDonald's. As he waited for his order, he mulled over the amazing discovery. Since both McLennan and Graves were out of town for the weekend, he and Carly were the only ones who knew about it. They'd agreed not to mention their findings to anyone else before discussing it with their advisors. Darien knew that the professors would be inclined to pass the information along to DARPA, but as he saw it, the information belonged to NM State. He and Carly planned to make a strong case to that effect, and they believed they could decipher the message, if given time.

"Darien, your order is ready—number 132," a young Mescalero woman announced, smiling as he approached the counter.

"Thanks, Jessica," Darien said, picking up the tray which held his usual order, a Big Breakfast with Hotcakes, plus a large coffee. This meal had everything Darien needed for a frosty morning jump-start, ample carbohydrates, fats, protein, caffeine and salt.

As he was looking around for a place to sit, the front door opened. Amid a flurry of powdery snowflakes, April and Ashley scurried in with Dusty and Roger close on their heels. All four were bundled up in ski gear, but Darien knew they weren't about to hit the slopes any time soon. Both April and Ashley were seven months pregnant with twins—April with girls, Ashley with a boy and a girl. Darien waved to get their attention, and they returned his greeting. Giving hand signals for them to join him, Darien headed toward a booth that had just been vacated. As Dusty and Roger went to the order station, April and Ashley came to Darien's booth, hugged him, and sat down.

"Pretty raw morning for expectant mothers to be outside," Darien said.

"Regardless of the bad weather, we had to come," April said. "When we crave certain foods, there's no substitute."

"I woke up hungry for a breakfast burrito," Ashley said.

"How long do those cravings last?" Darien asked.

"Apparently nine months when you're pregnant with twins," Ashley said.

"Have you picked out names yet?" Darien said.

"We have several good ones," April said, "but no final selections."

"I suggested some great names to Dusty—May and June," Darien said. "How could you beat April, May, and June for three names in the same family?"

"We discussed that idea," April said. "Dusty likes it, but I think those names are a little old fashioned."

Dusty and Roger approached the booth carrying trays loaded with sausage biscuits, Egg McMuffins, breakfast tacos, and coffee. Before the men sat down, April and Ashley began to retrieve their selections. Darien was amazed at how much weight the two women had gained over the past couple of months. At Thanksgiving, their baby bumps were barely showing. Now both formerly-svelte women possessed massive abdomens and seemed incredibly happy with the sudden change in their lives. Darien realized his friends had entered a phase of life that he had yet to reach, and he was happy for them.

"Have you heard any new Planet X news?" Dusty asked, as he slid into the seat beside April.

"Are you talking about the tent city near San Diego?" Darien said.

"Yeah, that one," Dusty said.

"I haven't heard anything new," Darien said, "but that little community reminded me of a cult from the last century. It was called Heaven's Gate."

"I remember reading something about that group," Roger said. "Didn't they think a comet was going to pick them up?"

Sort of," Darien said. "Thirty-nine people committed mass suicide when Comet Hale-Bopp passed by. They believed that they would be transported to a space ship trailing the comet."

"They drank vodka laced with phenobarbital," Dusty said. "A mass suicide. We studied several cases like that in the academy."

"Is Hale-Bopp going to appear anytime soon?" Roger asked.

Darien shook his head. "No, not soon—a couple of thousand years, as I recall."

"California's law enforcement officers better keep a close eye on that group," Dusty said. "It already has about two hundred members. That would be a messy suicide."

"Stifle it, Dusty!" April said sharply, making a *zip-your-lip* gesture across her mouth. "Let's talk about something else while we're eating."

"Okay," Dusty said, with a shrug. "Pick a subject."

"How about baby names," April said.

For the next few minutes, the two couples discussed baby names they liked and others they didn't like. Darien listened, but didn't proffer any new suggestions, since April had already crossed his best selections off her list. While his four friends were talking, Darien became aware that the noise level in the restaurant was slowly dropping, and people were directing their attention to TV monitors positioned strategically around the room. Over the years, Darien had observed that very few people in McDonald's watched TV while eating, so he knew something unusual had seized the breakfast crowd's attention. Everyone looked toward the nearest TV as a news banner flashed repeatedly:

ASIAN BILLIONAIRES PURCHASE PARABELLUM

An Alphabet News reporter launched into a lively monologue punctuated with hand gestures, but the conversation in the room resumed quickly and blotted out her words.

"What next?" Darien said. He suspected there was a link between the Planet X advocates and Parabellum.org;

however, he couldn't imagine what it could be. The real universe was getting more bizarre than any conspiracy-theory universe he'd ever dreamed up.

***

When Darien got home that evening, he decided to do a little research on the Planet X cult in California. Seated in a tattered recliner covered with a blue chenille bedspread, Darien lay his iTab on his knees and began tapping at the screen. He did a quick survey of several blog sites purporting to be nonaligned news outlets. In a few minutes, he could tell that the pseudo-religious cult's theology was in its formative stages. They were registered as a California non-profit organization under the name of the *Planet X Disciples*, but hadn't included the word *Disciples* on their hand-painted city-limit sign. Moreover, at this point, the origin of the space ship which would transport them to their off-world destination was uncertain. The Mayflower was mentioned as a possibility, as well as a Mayflower duplicate supposedly being built in a secret location by Chinese billionaires.

The cult claimed to know the exact location of Planet X. Their claims were based on the Nebra Sky Disc, a 12-inch bronze plate discovered in 1999 by German treasure hunters. Darien was well familiar with the disc. It was the oldest known image of the cosmos, displaying images of the sun, moon, Mercury, Venus, Mars, Jupiter, and four constellations of the zodiac. The disc showed the sun in an eclipse, even though the moon was not in a position to cause it. By the anomalous eclipse, tenth planet advocates deduced that Planet X was causing the eclipse and also had caused the Earth to shift on its axis some 3800 years ago. According to their claims, the polar shift resulted in Planet X taking up a position in Earth's orbit on the opposite side of the sun where it couldn't be seen from Earth. The Tenth Planet Disciples believed that Planet X was a duplicate of the Garden of Eden, pristine and awaiting mankind's arrival, and they cited several verses of scripture to support their beliefs, primarily from the Prophet Daniel and The Revelation.

The claims were so full of mathematical and theological nonsense that it was comical. Darien was certain none of the tenth planet advocates that he knew believed the newly-formed cult's outlandish dogma. Thankfully, Roger and Dusty didn't. Finally, it had gotten too far out for them.

CHAPTER 25

On Monday morning, Darien woke up at 5:00 a.m., an hour before his alarm was set to go off. He'd tossed and turned all night, trying to understand how low frequency radio waves could be imbedded in the signals from M13. It really didn't make sense. Carly believed it was the result of ESP, but he was having trouble assimilating her idea because it seemed to violate several physical laws. Of course, that didn't bother Carly. The psi explanation was completely satisfactory to her—absolutely no math or physics required.

Badly needing a caffeine fix, Darien went to the kitchen and took a bag of coffee cartridges out of his nearly-empty refrigerator. There were only two cartridges left; moreover, his pantry was suffering from *Old Mother Hubbard* syndrome, so he would have to make a quick run to McDonald's for breakfast on his way to school. Maybe he would stop by Amazon-Kroger on the way home and pick up a few items. As the coffee maker began its comforting gurgle, he clicked on the wall TV. It sprang to life with multi-colored news banners filling the entire screen, except for the right side where mini-screens were stacking up like ABC blocks. In each small screen, an animated newscaster was urging viewers to turn to his/her broadcast. The head-line practically leaped off the screen:

GRAD STUDENTS DISCOVER MESSAGE
HIDDEN IN M13 SIGNALS

He clicked on the headline. A video materialized showing Alphabet News' studio in New York City with a man and two women, all smartly-dressed, sitting behind a glass-topped semicircular desk. Darien turned up the volume and listened intently as the man read the news:

"Yesterday a DARPA spokesperson confirmed that the agency has obtained files containing unusual radio waves from the M13 star cluster. According to DARPA, the signals were discovered by unidentified college students shortly after President Horn ordered NASA to provide access to recorded files of incoming signals.

"The radio waves are reported to be complex enough to suggest that they were produced by intelligent beings, possibly an extraterrestrial civilization in the distant galaxy. The message—if this is one—is preceded by signals that seem to repeat the numbers 1, 2, and 3. In spite of DARPA's optimism, several prominent astronomers insist this numerical sequence is too simple to prove the signals are authentic.

"Other concerns revolve around the methods used to process the incoming signals, particularly by filtering out the 1420-megahertz band which is known to be the most logical frequency for interstellar communication. After filtering, the signals remaining are in the 12 to 40-megahertz range, which corresponds to brainwaves. Most astronomers doubt that high frequencies could serve as a carrier for low frequencies, and several have cited physical laws to prove their point. On the other hand, a few astronomers claim they are developing equations that prove otherwise. Among those taking this viewpoint is Dr. Edward Pauling, who has theorized that the low frequency waves were imbedded in the high frequency bands at some point near our solar system, a theory that likely will excite Planet X advocates. In spite of the uncertainty concerning these files, DARPA has invited everyone to download them for study. A spokesperson for the RADS stated that many of her constituents believe that this DARPA announcement is another nefarious ploy by Mr. Horn, and they are considering an investigation into his actions. Stay tuned to Alphabet News for updates on this story and others as they develop."

Darien was astonished by the broadcast. He and Carly had made the discovery about forty-eight hours earlier, and it was already a major news story. He realized that DARPA had attached cookies to the files released to NM State, thereby giving them access to the computers used to process the files. Moreover, by using a weak password, they'd invited access to other similar files—deliberately, in Darien's opinion. He and Carly, along with the university, had been duped.

At mid-morning, Darien and Carly met in the astronomy research lab. As soon as they were seated at the control station, Darien instructed the computer to search all available data bases for radio signals similar to their recent findings. As suspected, no library contained low-frequency signals thought to originate in outer space. It was obvious why. Such signals were too weak to reach Earth from another star system, and no one had searched for them embedded in a strong signal. And if not for Carly, Darien wouldn't have done so either.

"Our find is unique," Darien said. "*Outside the box*, as you would say."

"So . . . how are we going to proceed?"

"Let's amplify them and play them as music."

"Music?"

"*Static*, really," Darien said, as he signaled the computer.

For the next hour, they listened to the recording. As the last ten minutes crept by, Darien leaned back and watched Carly as she listened. She sat with eyes closed, concentration lines on her brow, attempting to sync her brain waves with the signals from M13. Darien didn't expect Carly to hear anything other than what he'd heard—one thump, two thumps, and three thumps, followed by a low rumble lasting a couple of seconds. And, as expected, the audible playback was an exact duplicate of what they'd seen visually on the *Time vs Intensity* monitor and gave no additional clues whatsoever.

When the audible recording ended, Carly said, "We need to come up with another wild idea."

Darien thought a moment and said, "I have one. Let's give ESP another shot by putting on helmet antennas and listening to this recording again."

"Are you finally conceding that ESP factors into this?" Carly said, with a smug smile.

Darien nodded. "Right now, it seems possible."

"I love it."

Ten minutes later, after retrieving a pair of helmets from a nearby store room, they were seated at the console again.

"Remember," Carly said, pulling the helmet over her auburn hair, "I didn't show any ESP ability during the mirror image tests."

"I know," Darien said, "but we're not taking anything for granted." He adjusted his helmet and programmed the computer to replay three sets of the recorded signals. If three sets didn't show anything, they'd have to try something else, but at this point, he had no idea what *something else* would be.

"Close your eyes," Carly said. "That'll help you concentrate."

Darien signaled the computer to start the playback, and as per Carly's instructions, he closed his eyes. As the first audible thump sounded, a flash of red light illuminated his eyelids from within. At two thumps, two orange flashes appeared, and at three thumps, he saw three yellow flashes. Before the long rumble sounded, he suspected what he would see, and his suspicions were confirmed. The rumble produced a rainbow of colors on the interior of his eyelids. After a few seconds, the rainbow disintegrated into multi-colored fragments dancing on the interior of his eyelids. As he watched transfixed, the fragments clumped together to form a vague spherical pattern—maybe a moon or a planet but nothing clearly distinguishable. A chill touched his spine as the video began to repeat the same sequence of colors and patterns. No doubt, this was an ESP signal, even if it did defy the laws of physics.

"Wow!" Darien said, as the recording ended. "That was incredible."

"What did you see?" Carly said, looking puzzled.

"Didn't you see anything?"

"No . . . nothing."

Darien described the polychromatic vision he'd seen on the interior of his eyelids. "I'll link my helmet to one of the monitors. Maybe you can see what I saw," he said. He completed a Bluetooth linkup to an auxiliary monitor and signaled the control station computer to replay the recording simultaneously in audible mode and on the *Time vs Intensity* monitor.

They stared at the small monitor as the recording started. Momentarily, an audible thump occurred and a smear crawled across the *Time vs Intensity* monitor.

The auxiliary monitor remained blank.

Darien muttered under his breath.

"Close your eyes," Carly said.

Darien complied. As soon as he did, a multi-colored fog swirled across the monitor.

"That's it!" Carly shrieked. "A picture."

During the next few minutes, they discovered two important facts. First—the colors appeared when Darien closed his eyes and disappeared when he opened them.

Second—the blurred images on the monitor were identical to those Darien saw on the interior of his eyelids. Finally, they were making progress.

"We've got to find another person with ESP to link up with you," Carly said, "and see if that will bring these blurred images into sharper focus."

"Several of my friends had lab this afternoon," Darien said. "They're beginning to leave the building right now. Let's draft a few of them to see if they can link up with me."

Over the next ten minutes, Darien cajoled six friends into taking a brief ESP test. Thirty minutes later, the tests ended with disappointing results. None of the six volunteers had detectable amounts of ESP. The elusive psi phenomenon had eluded them again.

"Other than me, the Smithers twins are the only people we've found with ESP," Darien said, shaking his head, as the last volunteer left the lab. "And their ability is too meager to be of any use."

"We have to find someone else with your kind of ability," Carly said emphatically. "I think the only way we're going to do that is by tracking down your twin in Panama."

"I'd certainly love to return to the place where I was born," Darien said. "Still, the idea of me having a twin is only a rumor."

"Rumor or not, I'm convinced that it's true, and I'm trying to fit it into my *Alamogordo connection* theory."

"What have you come up with?"

"The theory isn't well-formed yet," Carly said. "I'm still working on it. Except for you, all the ESP we've found originated in Alamogordo. That includes dogs, monkeys, and people."

"My being born in Panama fouls up your theory."

"There has to be a connection between Panama and Alamogordo that we're missing," Carly said. "Do you think we could talk the university into funding a trip to the Darien Province?"

"Maybe we can. Let's give it our best shot."

CHAPTER 26

On Saturday morning, Darien sat at the student desk in his trailer, drinking coffee and trying to figure out what to do next. It hadn't been a very productive week. He and Carly had proposed a trip to Panama to search for Darien's twin, a long shot for sure, but one that seemed well worth taking. McLennan and Graves had run the proposal up the flag pole, but nobody saluted. The request was denied immediately due to lack of funds. Dr. Leonard had commended Darien and Carly on their creativity and promised to explore the possibility of funding the trip during the fall semester. *Explore the possibility seven months from now?* That was an uncertainty coupled with an eternity. They needed to do something now.

Darien idly watched news banners scrolling across the bottom of his desktop monitor. The news was boringly repetitive, consisting primarily of anti-Horn editorializing by Alphabet News and their affiliates. It had been that way since Rex Horn took office, and Darien expected it to continue until Horn was gone. The RADS would never get over the fact that Horn had defeated their heir apparent and upset the status quo of their carefully contrived *two-parties-in-one* system.

As he was draining the last drop of coffee from his cup and thinking about making a McDonald's breakfast run, his iTab chimed and a text popped up, *Facetime call from Michael Overton.*

Darien's heart almost leaped out of his chest. He collected his thoughts and uttered a minimalistic, "Hello," as he touched the screen to accept the call.

"Good morning, Mr. Segura," Overton said in a cheery *I'm-your-friend* voice as his image materialized onscreen. "I'm calling to see if you would consider taking a brief assignment with DARPA?"

Knowing from recent experience that caution was in order, Darien paused several seconds before asking, "What kind of assignment?"

"Would you like to take a trip to Panama?"

"Maybe," Darien said. "What are you proposing?" He struggled to keep a poker face, knowing that Overton was accustomed to playing no-limit Texas Hold'em with millions of NatGov dollars, while he himself had played nothing except penny ante.

"I'll get right to the point," Overton said. "After considerable searching into your background, DARPA has found convincing evidence that you're a twin. Moreover, there's a good possibility that your sibling is still living in Panama. We need your help in locating him."

"Before we go any further," Darien said, "tell me what you've discovered about the first few weeks of my life. I want to know everything that you know."

"Actually, it's very little, and part of it is conjecture," Overton said. "The story began over twenty-three years ago when a meteorite landed near Alamogordo. It was similar to the strike last year, except in addition to creating a dust cloud, it hit a power relay station and knocked it out of service for two days. The night after it struck, one of the local motels rented a room to a young couple. With no electricity to conduct the normal digital transaction, the couple paid their bill in cash under the name of Mr. and Mrs. John Stone, apparently an alias. Even though they used a fake name, they listed their address as Yaviza, Panama, which is the end of the Pan American Highway, as you probably know. We think they went to the Darien Gap to join a group of rebels fomenting an uprising at that time. This presents the distinct possibility that you were conceived in Alamogordo and born in Panama."

"What happened to my parents?" Darien asked, as a million thoughts raced through his mind.

"We don't know for sure, but it's likely they were killed in the uprising. Nearly all of the rebels were. A missionary organization known as *Ethnos360* brought you back to the states and put you up for adoption. That's about all we know, but if you have any other questions, I'll try to answer them."

Overton paused, giving Darien a few seconds to mull over the bizarre narrative. A startling thought struck him— as incredible as it seemed, Carly's Alamogordo connection theory was gaining traction.

"We need your help," Overton repeated firmly.

"How do you plan to proceed?" Darien asked, his heart racing.

"We're planning an expedition to the Darien Province," Overton said. "We'll take helmet antennas and other test equipment. If we locate your twin there, we'll run tests on the spot to determine if he can link up with you. If he's not there, we'll have to come up with another plan. At this point, the Panama search is a *no-go* without your help."

"How many people do you plan to take?" Darien asked. "And who are they?"

"Three or four DARPA agents, plus you."

"Have you contacted NM State about this?"

"No," Overton said, his friendly demeanor fading noticeably. "They have nothing to offer. This whole thing hinges on your psi talent. Moreover, it's your duty to help your country. You'll be rewarded well for your time and effort. Can we count on you?"

"I'll go to Panama only if my research associates can go with me," Darien said.

"Who are you talking about?"

"You've met them—Craig McLennan, Miriam Graves, and Carly Hansen."

"They can't contribute anything," Overton said, his tone defensive.

"I think they can."

"It's your duty as a loyal American citizen to help your government."

"My first loyalty is to my teammates," Darien said, now feeling calmer. Even on the small screen, he could see frustration showing on Overton's face. Clearly, the DARPA agent was accustomed to getting his way.

"They're not needed," Overton insisted.

"They go, or I don't," Darien said, tantamount to an *all-in* bet in his poker analogy. And unlike a real poker game, Overton couldn't fold. He'd have to call the bet.

"Would you like for President Horn to contact you?" Overton asked.

"That wouldn't change my mind."

After a brief staredown, Overton said, "You drive a hard bargain, Mr. Segura."

"All I'm asking is for fair treatment for my teammates."

"There's little chance for this project to succeed without your help," Overton said.

"I realize that," Darien said. "That's why I'm *driving a hard bargain*, as you just said."

Overton stared at Darien, and Darien returned the stare. "Okay, Mr. Segura, we'll do it your way. How do you suggest that we proceed?"

"I'd like for you to arrange this expedition through NM State with Dr. McLennan as the leader."

Overton's decisiveness returned. "I'll do it Monday morning. Thank you for your time, Mr. Segura."

As soon as Overton signed off, Darien called Carly and they talked for an hour. At the end of their conversation, he thought about how his life had changed since

Carly's arrival at the university, even though she spent a lot of her spare time with Garth. Darien was looking forward to taking the Panama trip with her. It would give them the chance to be together without Garth lurking in the background. And after the trip . . . .

Even while planning a bold move for Carly's affection, Darien knew a note of caution was in order. He still hadn't forgotten how quickly he'd fallen for Madison when she moved to New Mexico, nor would he forget the pain caused by her sudden return to New York. Six months ago, Carly had suddenly come into his life, and he didn't want to walk blindly onto a *Madison redux*. Still, the way he felt at the moment, the risk was well worth taking.

When Monday arrived, Darien was on pins and needles all morning, trying to imagine what was going on behind the scenes. At 1:00 p.m., McLennan called and relayed the good news. Michael Overton had done exactly what he promised Darien that he would do. He'd contacted Dr. Sheldon Leonard and offered DARPA funding for the Panama expedition, a deal which Leonard snapped up instantly. The trip would take place in March.

The next three weeks were a blur of activity.

Preparation for the trip began with inoculations for cholera, yellow fever, tetanus, typhoid, and even rabies—a disease known to infect bats. All travel documents arrived without a hitch, probably due to a nudge from Overton. Darien and Carly got their first passports, and everyone obtained visas and special permits allowing non-locals to enter Darien Province. In addition, they notified the Panama Border Patrol—*Servicio National De Fronteras*—of their plans to stay near the Panama-Columbia border.

Several changes occurred after Darien's successful rebuff of Michael Overton. Oddly, the first change related to the use of academic titles. At the initial planning session, the professors demanded that Darien and Carly call them Craig and Miriam—no academic titles allowed. In like manner, the professors would address Darien and Carly by their first names, not *Mr. Segura* and *Miss Hansen*. At first the change seemed quite odd, but after a week, it was perfectly normal. The quartet of *outside-the-box* researchers began to refer to themselves as *the team*.

While waiting for the departure date to arrive, they studied volumes of information about the Darien Province, concentrating primarily on geography, history, and local customs. The province had a long history of drug running, kidnapping, weapons smuggling, and guerilla activity. Their home base would be in Yaviza, which Wikipedia described as *an isolated backwater village once known as a haven for smugglers, prostitutes, and fugitives*. From all accounts, their destination had been wilder than New Mexico during Billy the Kid's heyday but had settled down after Panama instituted a variety of strict rules for traveling in the Darien National Park and nearby areas.

Over twenty years ago, Panama and Columbia had barred aircraft from landing within ten miles of the border dividing the two countries. This restriction was initiated to prevent drug traffickers from moving rapidly from place to place in helicopters or other small aircraft. The rule had successfully squelched the start-up of new drug cartels, which at one time had virtually ruled the Darien Province. Unfortunately, the rule had also made it difficult to get to isolated villages in the province.

Since many of the residents of the Darien Province were indigenous, and Spanish was not their native language, NM State hired a language professor from the University of Panama, Annabel Martinez, to meet them at the airport and accompany them throughout the trip. Dr. Martinez's credentials were impressive. She was a licensed Panamanian tour guide, as well as a jungle survival expert and linguist. Her doctoral thesis was *Languages and Idioms of the Darien Province*. She could speak a dozen languages including Embera-Wounaan and Cuna, both common languages of the Darien region.

At the end of the first week, they packed everything needed for the trip in an oversized foot locker and shipped it to Tocumen Airport in Panama, where a team of Ethnos360 missionaries picked it up. After clearing customs with the shipment, the missionaries took it to their home in Meteti, a small village thirty miles north of Yaviza.

The team discussed every aspect of the search for Darien's twin, including the possibility that he was no longer in the Darien Province after twenty-three years. Still, the trail started there, so it seemed to be a good place to start. If the twin had grown up in the area, his height would make him a foot taller than the average Embera or Cuna, something the locals might remember. On the other hand, his height wouldn't be much help in Panama City. If the trail led there, the search could get complicated and take a lot of time.

After three weeks of preparation, the team was ready.

CHAPTER 27

The wheels dropped into place with a thump as the airplane began its descent toward Tocumen Airport. From her window seat, Carly gazed at the verdant jungles of Panama. On the north side of the narrow isthmus, the Caribbean displayed its emerald glory in the afternoon sun, as did the Gulf of Panama to the south. In the distance, the horizon was blurred by clouds, but even so, the view made Carly feel like an astronaut orbiting the Earth.

From the middle seat, Miriam leaned to the left and peered around Carly's head as Darien tried to do the same from his aisle seat. Craig, officially the leader of the expedition, sat across the aisle from Darien. Official or not, a major portion of the leadership role had defaulted to Darien when he went *mano a mano* with Overton. The DARPA representative had agreed to keep the government completely in the background while helping in every way he could. In order to get this concession, McLennan had agreed to update Overton regularly during the trip and provide him a copy of the final report. Clearly, this venture was vitally important to Overton, an indication of its importance to President Horn, as well.

Carly turned toward Darien and said, "It's hard to believe we both have a Panama connection through our ancestors."

"Alamogordo connections, Panama connections—you're always looking for connections."

"That's what psychologists do."

"The Panamanians may not welcome you when they discover that you're the great granddaughter of Henry Morgan, the pirate."

"You left out several *greats*, probably so many they won't see the connection."

"We both had some eclectic ancestors," Darien said. "Pirates . . . soldiers of fortune. Who knows what else?"

"Everybody has some, if they go back far enough,"

Carly said. She pointed to the jungle below and added, "You were fortunate to grow up in Alamogordo rather than down there."

The Darien Province was a rugged stretch of land between the southern border of Panama and the northern border of Columbia. Known as the *Darien Gap*, it was the gap between Central and South America. In addition, it was the last gap in the Pan-American Highway. At one time, it was thought that the highway would eventually run from Alaska to Tierra del Fuego, but such a prospect was unlikely now. It was opposed by environmentalists, who knew that such a highway would change the region forever—and most likely, not for the good. Conversely, proponents of the highway continued to point out that it would improve the development of desperately poor areas. Both sides presented valid arguments, but neither had been able to persuade the other.

Wheeled vehicles had first crossed the area in 1972 when the British Trans-America Expedition successfully traversed the area in one hundred days. *One hundred days* was the magic number in this region of the world because the dry season was approximately three months long. Crossing the Darien Gap in a wheeled vehicle during the rainy season would still be incredibly difficult today. Since it was mid-March, they had plenty of time to complete their mission.

The plane touched down at Tocumen with barely a bump. A few minutes later, the airplane docked at a terminal gate, and the captain turned off the seat-belt sign. Most of the passengers stood and began to rummage around for their carry-on bags and other belongings. The missionaries in Meteti had confirmed receipt of the pre-shipped items, so the team was travelling with carry-on luggage only, hoping to be first in line at customs.

The exit door opened, and a blast of humid hot air invaded the cabin. An electronic voice said, "*Bienvenidos a Panamá, la encrucijada del mundo*—Welcome to Panama, the crossroads of the world."

"So . . . how's your Spanish?" Carly asked as they eased into the aisle.

"*No muy bien,*" Darien said with a shrug as they walked toward the main terminal.

Carly, carrying a bag in each hand, nodded toward the walls. "Look at these murals," she said. "They're giving us a history lesson on how the canal was built."

"I'd like to go to the old city and visit the Church of the Golden Alter," Darien said. "It's a famous historical site."

"I know all about it," Carly said. "The Panamanians smeared mud over the golden alter to hide it from my ancestor when he sacked Old Panama."

When they reached customs, the college professors selected one line, while Carly and Darien selected a parallel one. The process went quickly, and five minutes later, everyone had cleared customs. They completed the process using only their iTabs but had paper copies of the documents in their carry-on bags. They'd been told they might need them in Yaviza where the electricity went out frequently.

When the team reached the main terminal, Carly was the first to spot their contact, a trim, late thirty-something woman wearing tan slacks and a white blouse. She was carrying a placard reading *NM State Team*. Carly touched Darien on the shoulder and pointed toward their translator/guide/survival expert. They gathered around her and introduced themselves.

"I'm Annabel Martinez, your guide," the woman said. "Follow me to the ground transportation area. A bus is waiting to take us to a private hanger on the other side of the runway. Once there, we'll catch our charter flight to Yaviza."

Carly noticed that Annabel identified herself as a guide, rather than a translator or jungle survival expert. Employing a licensed Panamanian guide was the first step in visiting the Darien National Park. No one was allowed to enter without one, regardless of what languages they spoke or how much they knew about the jungle. The days of lone campers or hikers came to an end about the time Darien was born. Panama had clamped down on visitors so much that most groups visiting the area were attached to universities or other research organizations. Recently a medical team had discovered a new antibiotic-producing fungus in the depths of the rainforest. Appropriately, they named it *Darienicillin forte*.

The team fell in behind Annabel who led them to a green minivan in the passenger pickup area. The driver loaded the bags and everyone began to board. As she stepped into the vehicle, Carly replayed the last thirty days in her mind and conceded that kudos were due Michael Overton, regardless of the fact that he'd been difficult to deal with on occasion. Without leaving his office in Washington, Overton had orchestrated every phase of the journey, and so far, everything had been close to perfect.

The van joined the horn-honking melee near the airport. As they crept along, Annabel stood in the stairwell and said, "When we turn onto Via Tocumen, you'll see light manufacturing and high-tech companies, most of which have a counterpart in the United States. The canal keeps our two countries working together."

The excited passengers chatted and stared out of the windows as the van bumped along for a few minutes and turned onto a side street leading to a row of sheet metal buildings. The van stopped in front of a blue hanger where a twin-engine Cessna was waiting. Carly watched intently as the pilot went through his checklist. Compared to the commercial jet they'd arrived on, the Cessna looked like a dragonfly. Though neither Carly nor Darien had flown on a small plane before, they grabbed their bags and climbed into the Cessna without hesitation.

The plane was big enough for everyone to have a window seat, so they spread out and did so. Once in the air, the pilot set a course that intersected the Pan American Highway about halfway between Tocumen and Yaviza. Carly stared out of the window. The moment was surreal.

"Look on both sides of the highway just ahead," Annabel said. "You'll see where the rainforest has been destroyed by logging operations."

The clear-cut jungle scene unfolded below the Cessna. Some of the cleared land had been turned into small farms and cattle ranches, while other areas were being swallowed up by rapidly-growing vines and brush. Carly spotted a truck hauling a log so huge that the truck could haul only one log at a time.

"Yaviza is coming up on the left," Annabel said, as the plane begin its descent. "It's tucked inside a U-shaped bend in the Chucunaque River. Three sides of the town are on the river's edge."

Carly studied the small village. The most obvious feature was an abundance of rusty sheet metal rooftops. Buildings in various pastel colors were sprinkled among unpainted wood and cinder block structures. Yaviza was almost a perfect rectangle surrounded on all four sides by streets, with several other paved streets running parallel through the town. The Pan American Highway came to a dead end at the southwest corner of the village.

The Cessna touched down on the runway directly across the river from Yaviza. A National Guard bus waited for them at one end of the landing strip, and a border patrol Humvee flanked the bus. When the plane stopped, Annabel was the first to exit. As she did, the driver of the bus—a handsome young guardsman—reached for her duffle bag and said, "Hello, Dr. Martinez. Welcome back to Darien."

"Carlos!" Annabel said. "I'm glad they sent you." She introduced the NM State team, pronouncing every name with perfect diction.

"*Beinvenidos a Yaviza*, the end of the road," Carlos said, flashing a pleasant smile.

"We have to check in with SENAFRONT," Annabel said, as they transferred their luggage from the plane to the bus. "Then, we'll go to the hotel."

Everybody climbed on the bus, and a few minutes later, they reached the bridge crossing the river. A sizable guard house stood at the right of the bridge. The building was composed of sturdy concrete blocks and the flat roof was covered with multi-colored glass shards. A sign above the door read *SERVICIO NATIONAL DE FRONTERAS*, the phrase which had given rise to the acrostic, SENAFRONT. The military organization was Panama's permanent army, structured and organized to secure the border against enemy attack, and to assist other law enforcement agencies in maintaining law and order within the country when the need arose. SENAFRONT forces were trained and equipped by the United States, and currently, cooperation between the two countries was excellent.

A heavy-set black man dressed in camouflage fatigues, and carrying an AK-47, emerged from the guard house and approached the bus. Carlos opened the door. The armed man stepped inside, greeted Carlos and Annabel by name and carefully scrutinized the other four passengers. After his initial survey, he took an iTab out of his backpack and studied the documents identifying each person on the bus.

"*Todo esta bien,*" the officer said, nodding in Annabel's direction. "*Pueden ir adelante.*"

"*Gracias, Capitan Angola.*"

"*Que tengan cuidado,*" the officer added. "*Es peligroso aqui por los novatos.*"

Annabel turned toward the Americans and asked, "Did you understand the captain's last sentence?"

All four nodded, and Carly repeated the warning in English, "Be careful. It's dangerous here for novices."

Annabel and Captain Angola conducted a rapid-fire dialog in Spanish. Carly listened intently but understood less than half of what they said. Even so, she got the gist of the conversation. They were discussing the supplies held by the missionary team in Meteti. The initial plan was still intact. The NM State team and the missionaries would meet at the front gate of the SENAFRONT compound at 9:00 a.m. tomorrow. SENAFRONT would recheck the supplies and release them to the Americans.

As the bus pulled away from the guard house, Annabel said, "I'm sure you noticed that the captain's last name—Angola—is the name of a country. He's Afro-Panamanian, as are many residents of Darien. In fact, some call themselves Afro-Darienites. Their ancestors were brought to Panama as slaves in the 1500s and many of them took surnames from their country of origin."

In spite of the long day, Carly felt an adrenalin rush when the bus entered Yaviza and crossed the *Carretera Interamericana,* as the Pan American Highway was called in this part of the world. She examined everything in great detail as the bus crept along. The streets were fascinating. Apparently, they'd been built by constructing a wooden frame directly on top of the ground and filling it with concrete. The raised concrete served as a sidewalk, as well as a street, and people were ambling along in front of the bus. Carlos honked the horn and the pedestrians parted, allowing the bus to pass. Some of the pedestrians waived and shouted a friendly greeting, while others glared sullenly at the passing bus.

After making a few turns, Carlos guided the bus onto the unpaved gutter of the street and parked in front of a wooden building with a faded sign, *Yaviza Hotel,* above the door. The hotel sported a coat of pale green paint, and the buildings near it were painted in pastel blues and yellows. Carlos opened the door, and the odor of overripe bananas permeated the bus. With Darien leading the way, the passengers stepped out into the gutter littered with water bottles, styrofoam cups, and other debris. Carly heard shouting and turned to see four shirtless teenage boys racing toward them on rusty bicycles.

One of the boys extended a pack of Spearmint gum toward Carly. *"Chicle, Señorita?"* he said. *"Chicle de menta?"*

Annabel stepped in front of Carly and spoke softly to the boys in Spanish, calling the leader by name. After a brief dialog, she gave the youngster a few small coins, but declined the gum.

"Gracias, Profesora," the boy said. He turned to his companions, motioned, and they sped away.

"It's an entry fee," Annabel said with an amused smile. "Kind of like clearing customs or checking in with SENAFRONT. The chewing-gum peddlers won't bother you anymore as long as you're with me."

Carly was quite impressed with Annabel Martinez's proficiency. At the airport, she'd been instantly likable. Now, only a few hours later, she'd dealt with the national guard, SENAFRONT, and a gaggle of street peddlers—and called all of them by name.

"This is our hotel," Annabel said. "After we check in, we'll go to the *Wi-Fi Café-Cantina* down at the end the block. They're expecting us." She waved a hand and added, "This area around here is what you'd call *town center* in the states."

They lugged their bags into the hotel lobby and waited while Annabel went to the counter and rang the bell. "Angela," she called. "It's Annabel Martinez. We're here."

A plump Afro-Panamanian woman about fifty emerged from a tiny office behind the counter. "Hello Dr. Martinez," she said, smiling pleasantly. "Welcome back to Yaviza. Your suites are ready."

Everyone checked in; Angela handed each one a key and said, "The women are in Room 207, the men in Room 208. I put you on the second floor because it's a little cooler than the first floor."

"Thanks," Annabel said.

Angela escorted the weary travelers up a flight of stairs. As they were unlocking the doors, Annabel said, "Let's meet downstairs in thirty minutes and go to the café. Don't leave the hotel without Carlos and me."

As she entered the room that Angela had called a *suite*, Carly did a quick visual survey. She'd never been in a real hotel suite in her life but was pretty sure that Room 207 in the Yaviza Hotel didn't qualify as one. It was old and dingy with cracked walls and a musty smell. There was no air conditioner, but thankfully, it was a corner room with two large screened windows for cross ventilation. It had running water and electricity. Four bunkbeds formed a square in the center of the room, and an alcove near one of the beds held a single bathroom. A small white cabinet near the bathroom contained a supply of fresh towels and toilet paper. Carly's conclusion—the room wasn't exactly a suite, but it was okay. They hadn't expected to find a Ritz Carlton in Yaviza.

Each of the three women selected a bunk, leaving the one nearest the bathroom vacant. Carly sat down on the foot of her bunk, and it dipped six inches. Dropping to her knees, she looked under it and discovered that it was held up by cinder blocks which were about to tumble down. She aligned the blocks and ran a quick retest. It was fine.

Mosquitos buzzed around the room, and a giant cockroach sped across the floor like a toy racecar. Annabel tried to step on it, but missed, and it escaped through a crack in the wall. Carly and Miriam swatted at the mosquitos.

"Jungle survival school is now in session," Annabel said, and they all laughed.

CHAPTER 28

Feeling somewhat blue, Garth exited the Loop 54 robo-bus in front of the Vista at high noon on Sunday, not his usual day to be on campus. With Carly in Panama, Garth was on his own and needed to figure out a good way to pass the time. Carly had suggested that he explore the White Sands Missile Range, but he couldn't get excited about doing it by himself. Besides, it was too cold. He'd already taken a couple of shots at the gold mines in Orogrande but hadn't found a fleck of gold, so he'd crossed that destination off his daytrip planner, as well.

Upon arriving in New Mexico, Garth had memorized Carly's schedule in detail so he could synchronize his agenda with hers. He was off every Monday, the day that Carly was out of class from noon until 2:00 p.m. That was plenty of time for a leisurely lunch at Sammie's. The weekly lunch routine wasn't really about food. It was about occupying more of Carly's time which she might otherwise spend with Darien Segura, the *other man* as Garth saw him. Garth thought his *lunch-every-Monday* plan was clever and was trying to think up a similar approach to appropriate larger portions of Carly's time when she returned from Panama.

Garth wondered what was going on in the jungles of Panama. He imagined the worst—Carly and Segura huddling in a pup tent all night as tropical rains pounded the dark jungle. What a cozy arrangement Segura had weaseled himself into. Garth could accept the fact that Carly's studies made it necessary to spend time with Segura on the university campus, but now they were gallivanting through the jungle together. Things had gone from bad to worse.

It was easy for Garth to see why Segura enjoyed spending time with Carly. She had it all. On several occasions, Garth had overheard snippets of whispered comments about the beautiful newcomer from Texas. Her instant popularity among the college students had created a paradox. Garth was proud to have her by his side, but at the same time, he was wary of those giving her the once-over. He hadn't worried about such things while growing up. Back then, he and Carly were inseparable, so it never occurred to him that someday he'd have to compete for her time and attention. Now, he realized that he'd been naïve. The passage of time, along with career decisions, had changed their relationship, and he hadn't adjusted. The holding pattern they were in now wasn't working very well, and he fretted constantly about it.

As Garth saw it, Carly had moved through three distinctly different personalities while growing up. When they met in the third grade, she was in the *sweet-little-girl* phase—shy, but not stand-offish and always participated when others led the way. That phase ended abruptly when she reached twelve, became anorexic and assumed her second personality—the *non-participant-in-the-game-of-life* phase.

Garth suspected that the psychological eccentricities which triggered Carly's anorexia had served to catalyze her interest in psychology. Her third personality, the one she was in now, was the *conquer-the-world* phase. He was impressed by her competitiveness, but also intimidated by it.

Resigned to the prospect of dining alone, Garth turned up his collar and traipsed along the sidewalk toward Sammie's. He'd felt the need to get away from the Mayflower Project site for a few hours, and Sammie's was a much better place to eat lunch than the cafeteria at the construction site. The food was better and the price about the same. Moreover, for a small restaurant, Sammie's boasted an unusual assortment of guests. College students on a tight budget made up about ninety percent of Sammie's customers; however, the remaining ten percent presented a good people-watching opportunity. In his first half-dozen trips to the restaurant, Garth had seen an astronaut, an actress, a senator, and several men in black who were rumored to be power brokers promoting a secret space venture. Sammie's had several small rooms where the glitterati could dine privately if they wanted to. The presence of an occasional eclectic added a touch of mystique to an otherwise plain eatery in the desert town.

Garth entered Sammie's and was greeted by the aroma of frying bacon, causing him to salivate profusely. A few people loitered in the foyer. Several of them spoke as he entered. He returned the greetings and went to the front desk, where a diminutive teenage hostess told him to pick any table he liked. He headed toward the glassed-in patio where he and Carly usually ate. Shortly before reaching the patio, Garth passed a private dining room just as a waiter opened the door, allowing a brief glimpse inside.

He was taken aback by what he saw.

Four men, all of whom appeared to be Asian, were seated near one end of a long table. They were engaged in a lively conversation with a fifth man seated at the head of the table. The fifth man was Michael Overton. Garth had first seen Overton on the flight from Houston to El Paso but didn't know who he was at the time. Since that flight, Overton had visited Project Mayflower two or three times and had been the driving force in the M13 Contact Study. To add to the mystery, the pilot of the plane was Michael Overton's brother, a former astronaut, and the Overtons were President Horn's distant cousins. Garth conjured up a multitude of questions but no reasonable answers. This mystery had more tentacles than an octopus. He couldn't imagine what was going on, but one thing was certain—the blue-suited man with the huge laptop had his fingers in a lot of pies.

Garth had never seen the Asians in the room with Overton, and he assumed they weren't locals. He wondered what they were doing in Alamogordo. Maybe they were negotiating to buy the nearly-finished Mayflower spaceship, as rumors intimated. Pondering the situation, he entered the patio and chose a small table next to the glass wall.

"Hello, Tex," a voice chirped as Garth sat down.

Garth turned to see a slightly-plump, curly-haired blonde approaching his table. She wore a yellow uniform with a stiff white collar and was balancing a tray with several glasses of water on it.

"Hi, Roslyn," he said.

"Thanks for remembering my name, handsome," Roslyn said, flashing a broad smile. She placed a glass of water on the table and added, "I remember yours too. It's Garth . . . right?"

"Right," Garth said, realizing that Roslyn was on the prowl.

Roslyn sat the tray on a nearby table and turned toward Garth again. "In this job, I meet a lot of people," she said, "but have a hard time remembering their names."

"You got mine right."

"Some people use memory tricks. Do you know any?"

"I know one that helps sometimes," Garth said. "If I can link a person's name to the place they're from, I usually remember it. You're from Roswell, aren't you?"

Roslyn moved closer. "Yes, I am."

"Roslyn from Roswell," Garth said. "See how it works?"

"That's pretty cool. What other tricks do you know?"

"Order up, Roslyn," a loud voice called before Garth could respond. A skinny thirty-something man placed a tray of food on the counter, wiped his hands on a greasy apron, and went back into the kitchen.

Roslyn put her hand on Garth's shoulder. "Sit tight, handsome, and I'll be right back." She spun around and swished away.

Garth sipped his water and mulled over the situation while waiting for Roslyn to return. Obviously, the flirty blonde was anxious to talk, a situation which might provide the opening he needed. Maybe she would tell him how often Carly and Darien came into Sammie's together, and if she knew anything about Darien. He watched as Roslyn carried the tray of food to a silver-haired couple at the opposite side of the patio. As she was serving the senior citizens, Roslyn looked toward Garth several times and smiled. He surmised she would tell him everything that she knew.

Roslyn returned to Garth's table and asked, "Where were we?"

Garth didn't want to resume the discussion about remembering names, so he said, "Could I ask you a question?"

Coquettishly, Roslyn tilted her head. "I won't answer if it's too personal."

"It's not about you."

"That's too bad," Roslyn said, feigning a pout, "but go ahead anyway."

"Do you know Carly Hansen and Darien Segura?"

Roslyn nodded. "Sure, I do. They're students who come in here a couple of times a week."

"How long do they stay?"

"Not very long."

"An hour?"

"Not that long most of the time," Roslyn said. "They're always in a hurry to get back to some kind of science class.

Sometimes they take out their iTabs and study while they're eating."

"Are they chummy?"

"What do you mean by *chummy*?"

"Do they hold hands . . . hug . . . kiss . . . that sort of thing?"

"Not that I've noticed."

"What do you know about Darien?"

"He's handsome."

"I hadn't noticed that," Garth mumbled. He hated it when a woman told him another man was handsome. "Anything else?"

"I've heard other students say he's very smart, but why are you so interested in him?"

"Because Carly and I are going steady."

Roslyn's brows shot up. "Really?"

"Well . . . sort of."

"Does *sort of* mean that you're dating other girls?"

Garth shrugged but didn't reply.

"I broke up with my boyfriend last week," Roslyn said.

"I'll give you my phone number. If your girl takes off with that other handsome guy, give me a call . . . okay?"

"I'll take a BLT sandwich with French fries and a Dr. Pepper."

"Is that all?"

"All for the time being, I guess."

CHAPTER 29

Thirty minutes after checking in, Darien's team met in the lobby and left the hotel together. The sun was dipping below the horizon and the temperature had dropped a degree or two. They joined the locals on the raised street/sidewalk and started toward the Wi-Fi Café-Cantina. Foot-traffic in the street was picking up and young children were running to and fro. Several preteen boys kicked a soccer ball through a group of pedestrians walking in the gutter. Ahead, in a vacant lot next to the hotel, a pick-up game of basketball was in progress. One of the players was tall—about Darien's height—while the others were well under six feet. The thought, *twin brother*, flashed through Darien's mind until he realized that the tall player was Afro-Panamanian. So much for a quick solution.

As the team approached, the basketball players took a break and drifted toward the curb, curiosity evident in their demeanor. Darien's group paused, and the young men greeted Annabel by the title, *Profesora*. She returned the greetings in Spanish and engaged in brief conversations with several of them. Darien watched, fascinated. Annabel had credentials, confidence, and charisma, yet not a trace of arrogance. He realized that both he and Carly could learn something from Annabel Martinez—how to turn knowledge into wisdom.

"Hola, poste ligero," a short player said in Darien's direc-tion. "How about joining us. We need somebody to guard Yordan."

Darien's Spanish was good enough to know that *poste ligero* meant *light post.*

"I can't play today," he said. "Maybe later."

Yordan approached Darien and said, "Do you play basketball?"

"Every chance I get."

"Then join us sometime," Yordan said. "We play here nearly every evening. We really need another tall player. I can pick any one of these little guys and we can beat the other four every time."

Darien saw an opportunity to take the conversation beyond a discussion of basketball. "I'm Darien Segura," he said, extending his hand. "Could I ask you something?"

"I guess," Yordan said, shrugging.

"Did you grow up in Yaviza?"

Yordan nodded. "Uh-huh."

"Have you ever run into anybody around here as tall as we are? Somebody about our age."

Yordan shook his head. "Not any locals. Once a Harlem Globetrotter visited with some missionaries. But he's the only other tall person I've seen around here."

"Thanks, Yordan. I appreciate your help," Darien said, turning to go.

"Hey, *poste ligero,*" the short youth yelled. "Show us what you got."

Darien turned to see a basketball speeding his way. With reflexes acquired from years of playing the game, he plucked the ball from the air and estimated the distance to the basket. In a gymnasium, it would have been a *down town* shot, well outside the three-point line. Everyone watched as Darien dribbled the ball a few times and then launched a jump shot toward the basket. With a resounding thud, the ball hit high on the upper left corner of the backboard and ricocheted through the basket.

Both the researchers and the streetballers cheered loudly.

"That was the best shot I ever saw," Carly said.

"The worst," Darien said. "I was aiming directly at the basket." They laughed and resumed their trek toward the café.

"Does this place really have Wi-Fi like the name says?" Carly asked as they entered the nearly-empty Café-Cantina.

"Most of the time," Annabel said. "Hopefully, it's working now."

To no one's surprise, Annabel knew the manager of the café, a woman named Denise, who escorted them to a long table and took their drink orders. As they waited, Darien studied the room and reached the conclusion that it must have been constructed by the same carpenters who built the Yaviza Hotel. It was dull and drab. Still, on the positive side, it had a drink case near the entrance with plenty of soft drinks, including Diet Cokes. And the food smelled delicious. What more could they ask in a town that Carlos had dubbed *the end of the road?*

"Denise and Angela are sisters," Annabel said, as they sat down. "As if you couldn't tell by looking at them."

Darien had already noticed the strong resemblance between the two women. To him, they looked exactly alike. All of a sudden, people around him were beginning to resemble each other. Searching for twins had become an obsession.

"Do you know everybody in Yaviza?" Miriam asked in Annabel's direction.

"Nearly," Annabel said. "I taught English in the local school for several years."

Denise brought the drink orders to the table and returned to the kitchen. A few minutes later, she reappeared with a platter of fried plantains and a huge bowl of *arroz con pollo*, Panamanian style. The hungry travelers dug in. After the meal, they rated the chicken and rice. Everyone gave it five stars and said it was the best they'd ever tasted. Their first meal in Yaviza had exceeded expectations by a long shot.

"I have a suggestion," Annabel said. "Let's go to the SENAFRONT compound at 8:30 in the morning. Maybe we can get a chance to speak to the post commander while waiting for the missionaries to arrive."

"Do you think SENAFRONT will have any records of abandoned babies?" Craig asked.

"Probably not unless the abandonment was linked to a violent act," Annabel said. "Their job is to protect the border and keep peace and order in the villages, but they might have some general information that's helpful."

"What information can we expect to get from the missionaries?" Craig asked.

"They'll have records of any babies that they picked up during the time frame in question," Annabel said. "The law requires it."

Denise came to the table and said, "Dr. Martinez, I'll be closing in half an hour."

"Okay . . . thanks," Annabel said. "We'll take advantage of your Wi-Fi until then."

Taking Annabel's cue, the four Americans fell silent and retrieved their iTabs.

Darien typed a short text—*We're here!* He attached several pictures of Yaviza to the text and sent it to Rachel and several of his best friends in Alamogordo. He watched as the other team members deftly thumbed their iTabs. He surmised that Craig was sending a report to Michael Overton, Miriam was updating some of her friends, and they both would inform their department heads that the mission was going well. As for Carly, he knew she was texting Garth. That was the only incident of the entire day that piqued him.

At 8:30 the following morning, they arrived at the SENAFRONT headquarters north of Yaviza. The facility was a bona fide military compound surrounded by high walls topped with razor wire and broken glass bottles, not a simple checkpoint like the one where they stopped yesterday. Carlos parked the bus in front of a portable office building beside the main entrance. A chunky uniformed man came out of the building and ambled toward the bus. Carlos opened the door and Annabel greeted the officer as he approached. They spoke a few rapid bursts of Spanish, and the officer took out his iTab and tapped at the screen. A moment later, he looked up at Annabel, nodded, and said something else in Spanish.

Annabel turned toward the passengers and said, "Major Ghana, the commander of this post, has invited us to come in for a short visit. I've known him for years, and he's a fascinating story teller."

They climbed out of the bus and went into the portable building. During the next thirty minutes, the loquacious major spieled a half-dozen anecdotes about babies being abandoned during the guerilla uprising in the Darien Province. The timeframe was right, at least according to the major's recollection. Unfortunately, SENAFRONT had no documents to back up the commander's anecdotes. The stories were interesting but of no real value related to the current search.

Darien heard a rattling sound and looked out of the window to see a rusty green Ford Ranger approaching the gate, indicating that the missionaries had arrived. One thing had become obvious to Darien; their best hope for information—maybe their only hope—was the Ethnos360 missionaries who had rescued him over twenty years ago. The next few minutes could make or break the search for his twin.

With polished diplomacy that required a couple of minutes, Annabel disengaged from the talkative Major

Ghana, and they went outside to join the missionaries. By the time they reached the pickup, a young SENAFRONT guard was rifling through the contents of the foot locker while it was still in the back of the pickup. The guard unzipped each of the four bags in the locker, even though all bore stickers showing they'd been checked by Panama Customs at Tocumen Airport.

Annabel stepped to the back of the pickup and said, *"Hola, Alfonso. Va todo bien?"*

The guard looked up and greeted Annabel by the title *maestra*. Darien assumed that Alfonso had been one of Annabel's English students in the Yaviza school, although he had yet to utter a word in English. The local custom was obvious, *start off in Spanish—then switch to English.* So far, everyone they'd met could speak both languages.

As if reading Darien's mind, Alfonso said, "Everything checks out. You can take it into town." His English was excellent. Other than having a deep voice, he sounded a lot like Annabel.

The missionaries, both about fifty years old, introduced themselves as Tim and Margaret Conroy. An odd feeling came over Darien as they shook hands. He could tell they felt it, as well. They kept glancing at him while greeting the rest of the team.

"How long have you lived in this area?" Darien asked.

"Twenty-five years," Tim said, continuing to stare at Darien.

"In that case, you must be the couple who found me," Darien said.

"When were you found?" Margaret asked.

"March 2023."

Tim tapped furiously at his iTab. "That was a strange year," he said. "The Columbian insurrection was coming to an end, and all kind of unusual things were happening. We rescued three babies that spring. Our records show that one of them was a male found on March 31. That has to be you."

"Without a doubt, that was me," Darien said, feeling an instant bond with the couple who'd saved his life. Tim and Margaret threw their arms around him and they hugged. A tear trickled down Margaret's cheek and Darien felt a lump in his throat.

"Did you find any other babies around that date?" Darien asked.

"No," Tim said. "We found two other babies about a month later, but both were girls."

Tim's revelation was a major shock to Darien.

"We know you're looking for your twin," Margaret said. "The DARPA agent told us."

Darien took a deep breath and asked, "Were there any other groups in this area, missionary or otherwise, that might have rescued an abandoned baby?"

"Not any legal ones," Tim said, "but it was known that baby smugglers were operating in the area at that time."

"Smugglers?" Darien said, feeling a chill touch his spine.

"Yes," Tim said. "We heard of an underground group calling itself *Hacerlo Ahora*—which means *do it now*—operating in this area in 2023. Apparently, they abhorred the mountain of red tape required to get an orphan from here to the Unites States legally, so they did it illegally."

"How?" Darien asked.

"According to the rumors," Tim said, "instead of taking the babies to Panama City for processing, they went east to the gulf and smuggled them into Miami."

"How did they get around the records required for adoption?" Darien said.

"They didn't keep any records linking the babies to Panama," Tim said. "Instead, they left them on the steps of a fire station with notes claiming they were born to poverty stricken unwed mothers living in Miami. The ruse worked as planned, and Florida officials accepted the false documentation, thus the babies were accepted as U.S. citizens and put up for adoption without the usual red tape."

Darien swallowed hard, ruminating over what he'd just heard. The rumor seemed possible—even probable. A chilling thought hit him. Maybe they were searching in the wrong location. His twin could be in Miami instead of the Darien Province. What a twist of fate that would be.

"Did you tell Dr. Overton, the DARPA agent, about this rumor?" Craig asked.

Tim shook his head. "No, we have absolutely no proof that it's true."

"I'll go back to the SENAFRONT office and ask Major Ghana if I can use their Wi-Fi to text Overton," Craig said. "If Miami records show that babies were abandoned on fire station steps in the spring of 2023, and later adopted, he might be able to find out who they are."

"I'll go with you," Annabel said.

"I thought adoption records were sealed," Miriam said.

"Probably not to Michael Overton," Darien said.

"Now we have two trails to follow," Carly said, glancing at Darien. "We'll find your twin yet. And when we do, the rest of the Alamogordo connection will come to light."

A few minutes later, Craig and Annabel rejoined the group. Tim placed his iTab on the tailgate of the Ranger and pulled up a map of the Darien Province. "I have Annabel's phone number," he said. "I'll text this to her and she can share it with you when you get back to the Wi-Fi Cafe. We've added notes not found on other maps."

"We also have a laminated paper map that you'll need as backup," Margaret said. "It's well annotated too." She handed the map to Annabel.

"I suggest we get every scrap of information that Tim and Margaret have," Annabel said. "Especially the exact location where they picked up Darien. We'll decide what to do after that."

"Darien was found near Columbia beside a tributary of the *Rio Paya*," Tim said, pointing to the location on his iTab. "The small stream has no official name, nor does the village at its headwaters. Columbians across the border from the village refer to it as *el pueblo escondido*, the hidden village. During the spring that Darien was born, several foreign women gave birth in this village while their husbands or boyfriends were fighting as mercenaries. No doubt, the men were killed and probably the women, as well."

"Someone in the village delivered several babies that spring," Margaret said.

"We have to locate that person," Annabel said.

Although there was something alluring about the idea of a jungle trek, Darien hoped that Michael Overton could find some useful information in Florida's adoption records.

When the discussion ended, the team took the bags out of the pickup, loaded them on the bus, and headed to the Wi-Fi Café. They arrived at the café at 11:00, much earlier than Denise was expecting them for lunch, but she seated them and agreed to prepare a quick meal of scrambled eggs and fried plantains.

Annabel spread out the laminated map on one end of the table and said, "The village at the head of the little stream is at least twelve miles farther than we can travel by water this time of year. We'll have to hike in carrying twenty-pound backpacks. Can everyone do that?"

Everyone except Craig immediately asserted that they were well able to make the trek. Darien was sure that he, Carly, and Carlos could do it. They were all in their early twenties and in good physical condition. Miriam was ex-military and superbly fit. Craig was the outlier— forty-two years old and slightly plump. They might have to leave him in a native village along the way.

Eventually, Craig said, "I can do it." His tone was not reassuring.

Denise brought their meal and they plunged in with gusto. As they were finishing, Craig's iTab buzzed, announcing an incoming text message from Michael Overton.

"I'll play it," Craig said, touching the *Text to Speech* icon. A smooth computerized voice read the message:

Dr. McLennan,

I did a quick search of Florida's adoption records for 2023. They show that three unidentified babies were abandoned at fire stations in Miami during the spring of that year. It is certainly possible they could have been smuggled in, as the rumors claim; however, all three were girls, so they could not be Mr. Segura's mirror image twin. I recommend that you continue your search in Panama as originally planned.

Regards, Michael Overton

"That tells us what we have to do," Annabel said. "I suggest that we stay right here and go over the plans for our jungle trip."

Everyone agreed. Annabel called Denise to the table and got her okay to use the café as a classroom for as long as she liked.

CHAPTER 30

With Denise's blessings, the team stayed at their table all afternoon discussing plans for their jungle trek. The café's Wi-Fi system went off-line, so Annabel pulled the map of the Darien Province out of her iTab bag and lay it on the table. Everyone watched in silence as she unfolded the map and refolded it to put Yaviza at the center of a small square.

"I know you've been studying about the jungle for a while," Annabel said, "so consider this discussion to be a review before your final exam, which will start the moment we leave Yaviza."

Carly glanced at Darien and raised her eyebrows. He flashed a thumbs up and smiled faintly.

"I've already worked out plans for our trip," Annabel said. "The first leg of the journey will be by water and the second by land. To begin, we'll travel by boat down the Chucunaque River until it intersects the Tuira River. Then we'll follow the Tuira upstream to the Paya River, which is very small. There's a village, also named Paya, not far from the intersection of the two rivers. That's as far as we can go by water, so we'll leave the boat at the village and hike the rest of the way. The missionaries' precise details strongly suggest that Darien was born in *Escondido*, a village so small that it's not shown on any map.

"The usual mode of water travel around here is the piragua—a dugout canoe, but we're going to rent an aluminum boat instead, along with a driver/river guide. Flat-bottomed aluminum boats ride higher in the water than piraguas, so we can get farther up river. The locals seldom use them because they can make a free piragua out of a log . . . any questions so far?"

"How many miles will we travel by boat before we have to get out and walk?" Miriam asked. "We studied several maps, but couldn't tell for sure."

"It's about twenty miles by water and twelve by land," Annabel said. "The first part of the water trip will be easy. We'll stop at a couple of villages along the Tuira. If we buy a few souvenirs or some food, they'll let us use their rest rooms. But, when we reach the Paya River . . . well, it's jungle survival from there on. The water will be shallow in places. Hopefully, with an aluminum boat, we won't have to push, although we'll have to get out a few times to lighten the load. The water portion of the trip will take us at least eight hours—maybe longer."

"How long will it take to hike twelve miles?" Craig asked.

"It's hot and humid, the trek is uphill, and the footing is uneven in places," Annabel said. "Moreover, the trail is seldom travelled, so there'll be some machete work to do. But if we press on, we should be able to do it in a day.

"In order to travel light, we'll take dehydrated food. Actually, we wouldn't have to carry any food at all, if we didn't want to. We could eat at villages or find food in the jungle. As for water, we'll have plenty on the boat, but when we start our jungle hike, we'll carry canteens. We'll refill them from the Paya river and treat the water with chlorine tablets. My objective is to keep our backpacks light."

"Thank you," Craig said. Everybody laughed.

"Now, I need to tell you about various life-forms that we might encounter in the jungle," Annabel said.

An abridged biology lesson followed. In a smooth and fluent style, Annabel went through a list of disease-causing microbes, most of which they'd been immunized against. Then she moved to stinging and biting insects—ants, wasps, flies, and mosquitos. Next, well-known arachnids—ticks, spiders, and scorpions. A bizarre fish—the electric eel. Some poisonous amphibians—frogs and toads. Menacing reptiles—snakes and caiman. And finally, dangerous mammals—panthers, wild hogs, and bats.

"Now, some specific instructions about a couple of these animals," Annabel continued. "If you get bitten by a snake, try to kill it with your machete or pin it down it so either Carlos or I can identify it. I keep a snakebite kit in my backpack with anti-venom for every poisonous snake in the area. We may not even see a snake, but our motto is the same as the Boy Scouts—*be prepared.*

"We've encountered wild hogs known as white-lipped peccaries. If we meet one on the trail, especially an old male, we'll give it a wide berth."

"Do you and Carlos carry firearms?" Darien asked.

"I don't, but Carlos does," Annabel said. "He carries a 38-caliber revolver. However, he won't shoot a wild hog or any other animal unless it's necessary to protect human life. On a couple of occasions, he's fired into the air to scare away peccaries."

"Will we have contact with the outside world?" Carly said.

"To a limited degree," Annabel said. "Our boat will have a radio, and I'll carry one on our jungle trek. We'll leave the boat and driver at the last village when we go on by foot, so we can contact him if necessary."

The dialogue waned and Annabel concluded, "We'll pack this evening so we can hit the trail early in the morning."

As they got up to leave, Carly replayed Annabel's biology discourse in her mind and visualized a hostile menagerie waiting for them at the city limits of Yaviza.

The following morning, after a quick breakfast at the Wi-Fi Café, the team returned to the hotel to pick up their backpacks. Carly grabbed her gear and dashed to the lobby. Her teammates filed down the stairs, all wearing camouflage pants with shirts in differing colors. In addition to a backpack, each had a canteen on one hip and a machete on the other. As per Annabel's instructions, everyone wore straw hats. Once assembled, the six-member cadre looked like a military detail ready to engage in jungle warfare.

A short walk brought them to a dock paralleling the Chucunague River. Aluminum boats of all sizes were moored to the dock. A wooden sign on a post bore the words, *Barcos de Aluminio*. Several men on the dock were working at boat-related chores. One of them saw Annabel, greeted her by name, and spoke to Carlos in Spanish. The two men went to a wooden locker on one end of the dock and took out life vests.

"This is Julio, our driver and river guide," Annabel said, as the men rejoined the group. "He knows every trickle of water between here and the Columbian border."

Julio handed out the life vests and showed everyone how to put them on correctly.

"That's your boat," he said, pointing. "Climb in." He grabbed the mooring rope and held the boat against a row of rubber tires hanging along the water line. Carlos stepped into the boat first and stood by in case one of the land-lubbers made a misstep. Nobody did. Catlike, Julio jumped into the boat, cast off the line, and the boat drifted into the muddy river.

As Julio started the motor, Carly examined the boat and its contents. The boat was about twenty feet long, and riding high in the water in spite of its load. The contents were minimalistic: a water container, cans of gasoline, a tool box, two oars, and a neatly-coiled rope attached to an anchor—enough, but no frills.

Julio fired up the engine and crept past several dugout canoes stacked high with plantains. Some of the dugouts were nearly twice as long as the aluminum boats passing them. Each dugout had a three-man crew, one at each end with a paddle or pole to navigate and one in the middle bailing water with a plastic bucket. The canoes were so deep in the water they appeared to be sinking. Motorized aluminum boats slowed as they passed the overloaded dugouts. Carly suspected that a river courtesy code was in effect—unwritten, but recognized by all.

"Large boats come from Panama City to buy bananas and other produce, such as sugar cane," Annabel explained. "Merchants are waiting at the mouth of the river to buy everything on these over-loaded piraguas."

About an hour after leaving Yaviza, they intersected the Tuira River and headed upstream past the town of El Real. Unlike the Chucanaque, the Tuira was clear enough to occasionally glimpse a school of silver minnows swimming beside the boat. Carly studied her teammates' demeanor. A considerable change had come over them since leaving the boat dock. At first, they'd hardly talked while absorbing the sights of a world that was new to them. Now, they were engaging in a lively discussion about everything they saw.

As they journeyed upstream, the river narrowed, and they entered a green tunnel formed by giant trees hung with trailing vines. Huge blue butterflies fluttered among the branches overhead. Upon reaching the shade, all three Panamanians pushed back their hats and let them dangle beneath their shoulders, held in place by cords around their necks. Carly took off her hat and stuffed it under the bench where she was sitting. Spreading her fingers on both hands, she fluffed her hair and then pulled a small towel from her hip pocket and mopped her brow. She did a quick look-around at her travelling companions. None of the

Hispanics were perspiring a significant amount, whereas every American had conspicuous wet patches on their shirts, front and back. Craig's shirt was almost soaked, and his face was rosy.

Shortly after mid-day, they arrived at Boca de Cupe, a village of open-sided huts with shaggy thatched roofs. Children lined the river bank, waiting for the boat to arrive. Julio tied the boat to a tree at the water's edge. Everyone demonstrated their newly acquired sea legs by stepping ashore without Carlos' assistance. A SENAFRONT officer approached the group and nonchalantly checked the Americans' passports while chatting in Spanish with Annabel, Carlos, and Julio. Carly could understand about half of what they said, just enough to realize that the villagers knew the Americans would pass by today, and had prepared extra food in the village cantina. It sounded like they'd said *pork fried rice,* but she knew a Chinese dish wouldn't likely be on the menu in Boca de Cupe.

Annabel turned to the group and said, "They've roasted a wild pig and prepared rice with peas. I assume you'd prefer that over the dehydrated food we're carrying."

The vote was unanimous, and everybody headed toward the open-air cantina with the group of village children trailing behind them.

"Don't drink the water here," Annabel said, "or anything else except canned or bottled soft drinks." She glanced at Darien and added, "Sometimes they have Cokes."

"How did they know we'd be here around lunch time?" Carly asked.

"Information travels fast along the rivers," Annabel said, "In this case, the SENAFRONT office in Yaviza notified other stations in the area."

Once inside the cantina, an elderly woman seated them at a table of rough-hewn lumber and began to serve the pork and rice combo on chipped pottery plates. A small metal bucket in the center of the table held stainless steel flatware.

"These eating utensils became available when the U.S. closed its bases in the Canal Zone," Annabel said.

Carly was surprised to discover stainless steel utensils being used in the jungle. She'd had visions of eating boiled boa constrictor out of coconut shells, but so far, dining in the jungle had been a snap, and the food was good. The only negative—the cantina was out of soft drinks. The drink choice defaulted to tepid water from canteens. Otherwise, Carly was well pleased with the meal. The team finished eating in less than thirty minutes, Annabel paid the bill, and they resumed their journey up the Tuira River.

Shortly upstream from Boca de Cupe, the boat entered a stretch of river that was swift and shallow. Julio raised the motor until the prop barely touched water, and the boat slowed to a crawl. Carlos picked up an oar and checked the depth of the water. The Americans fell silent, and looked at each other.

A loud thump sounded. The boat lurched and stopped abruptly.

"We hit a sunken log," Carlos said, grabbing the mooring line and leaping into knee-deep water. With the line held tautly, he let the boat drift backwards to calmer water and then pulled it to the edge of the river and tied it to a log on the bank. When the boat was secure, he checked the area around the log and nodded at Annabel.

"We need to get out while Julio checks the motor," Annabel said.

When everyone was safely ashore, Julio tipped the motor until the prop came out of the water. "We sheared a prop pin," he said in a matter-of-fact tone. "I'll have it fixed in no time." He set the toolbox on the seat near the motor and jumped into the water with Carlos. Craig and the women sat down on the log beside the river. Darien waded into the water and joined the other two men.

Julio reached into the toolbox and retrieved an ordinary nail. "This is what we use for shear pins," he said, holding it up. "They're cheap and we use lots of them."

Annabel came to the river's edge and said, "Julio, should we walk past the rapids?"

Julio nodded. "I think that would be best."

Annabel looked toward Darien and said, "Come join us."

Darien waded to the bank, and the group walked along the river. To their left, the lower layer of jungle growth resembled a gigantic untrimmed hedge lining the river bank. The verdant thicket was alive with tiny yellow birds, twittering as they flitted from limb to limb. Rustling leaves indicated that unseen animals were moving around on the ground. Warily keeping their eyes on the jungle, the Americans hugged the water's edge as they eased along between the river and the jungle.

A few minutes later, they reached calm water and the boat arrived to pick them up. This *walk-past-the-rapids* scenario occurred three more times before they reached the Paya River and turned upstream into water that was clearer, calmer, and deeper than the Tuira. Carly dipped her hand in the water. It was several degrees cooler than the Tuira, and the air seemed cooler, as well. A yard-long fish appeared on one side of the boat and dove underneath it, reappearing on the other side. The jungle growth seemed primeval, as if the boat had travelled back in time.

About an hour before dark, they came to a stretch of very shallow water, signaling the end of the line for the boat. Fortunately, the village of Paya was less than a hundred yards ahead. Julio raised the motor completely, and Carlos jumped in the water and towed the boat toward a group of villagers forming on the shore.

"This is a Cuna village," Annabel said. "One of only two in the Darien Province. It's a little different from the Choco village where we ate lunch."

The villagers lining the river bank were topless. Everybody—men, women, and children. Nobody was wearing a shirt or blouse. Carly glanced at the Panamanians and could see they were amused by the Americans reaction. The jungle trip was a learning experience for the gringos.

Annabel spoke with the village leaders in the Cuna language, after which she turned to the Americans and said,

"Believe it or not, they were expecting us and have cooked fish and coconut rice, typical Cuna dishes." This time, she didn't mention dried food from their backpacks, and with no hesitation, the newly-arrived visitors went to the cantina and sat down at a rustic log table. Two young Cuna women served the food on hand-carved wooden platters but didn't bring utensils of any kind. The Americans hesitated, and the Panamanians began to eat with their hands, as the two women waited nearby.

"It's finger food," Annabel said, smiling in amusement as she dipped into the rice with her fingers. "I hope you've washed your hands."

Carly looked across the table at Darien and said, "Keep your eyes on your food."

Darien smiled, but didn't reply. When the travelers finished eating, the villagers took them to a rickety vacant building near the town plaza and invited them to use it for the night. After evicting a family of lizards, and inspecting for snakes, Annabel demonstrated the correct way to hang hammocks, and to get in and out of them.

When the sun went down, Darien, Carlos, and Julio went to the river with several village men, took a bath, and changed into clean clothes. After they returned, the women took their turn. Everyone rinsed their dirty clothes and hung them up to dry. After a brief discussion of the day's activities, and an application of mosquito repellant, the tired Americans climbed into their hammocks early. The Panamanians were not far behind.

Carly lay in her hammock watching night life in the village. With no walls, she could see everything that was going on. Women were putting up mosquito netting for their children and working at other household chores. The men went to the village plaza and played dominoes until ten-thirty and then struck up a band consisting of five-gallon buckets, a bongo drum, and an off-key concertina. They played the same tune over and over. Carly surmised it must be the only one they knew.

With the cacophony making it impossible for Carly to fall asleep, her thoughts drifted into a comparison between Darien and Garth, the two men in her life. Both men had several traits in common—they were responsible, highly intelligent, and had a bright future. Yet in spite of those similarities, they weren't at all alike. At first, she had a hard time pinpointing the major difference. But after working with Darien for six months, she saw what made the two men poles apart—it was Darien's passion. He had passion for his friends, passion for his chosen profession, passion for the desert he loved—passion for life in general. On the other hand, Garth was so even-keeled that he often seemed subdued. His *comfort-zone* approach to life was wearing thin. She and Garth had been best friends forever, but she now realized that they'd never truly been soulmates. On the other hand, she shared Darien's strong passion for life and visualized a possible future where they might become soulmates. A few weeks ago, such thoughts would have been absolutely foreign to her. But now...

At midnight, the band stopped playing abruptly, the men went home, the village fell silent, and Carly finally went to sleep.

309

CHAPTER 31

About 5:00 a.m., the village of Paya came alive. Radios blared and the villagers began their daily routine, though dawn was barely breaking. The cantina didn't serve early breakfast, so the team ate instant oatmeal and raisins. After breakfast, they changed into their still-damp clothes from the previous day and put the dry clothes back into their backpacks. They broke camp while Julio went to the boat and double-checked the radios and other equipment.

Annabel reviewed her checklist and said, "Okay, let's go." Everyone except Julio fell in behind Annabel and started toward the river.

Out of the corner of his eye, Darien saw Craig stumble and fall to the ground. He rushed to him, fearing that he had been bitten by a snake.

"I'm alright," Craig said, looking up at his colleagues encircling him. "I stepped in a hole."

"Can you stand?" Annabel asked.

Craig stood gingerly and said, "It's okay," but flinched when he put weight on his right foot.

"Sit down and take off your boot," Annabel said.

Reluctantly, Craig complied.

"Take off your sock too," Annabel said. She knelt beside Craig and examined his ankle, which was already beginning to swell.

"It's okay," Craig said again.

"It's sprained," Annabel said. "I'll wrap it with an Ace bandage, but you'll have to stay here with Julio."

"I want to go," Craig said, his voice insistent.

"We can't start hiking through the jungle with an injured team member," Annabel said. She sat her backpack on the ground, took out a bandage, and began to wrap Craig's ankle as the other team members watched in silence.

"It's not bad," Craig said, standing gingerly. "I can make it." Darien held his breath, hoping that Annabel's ability to display confidence without arrogance would assuage Craig's protest.

"Anything related to jungle survival is my call," Annabel said firmly. "I can't take you with us."

After a brief staredown, Craig gave a resigned sigh and said, "You're right. Besides, the hike would've been tough for me before this happened. You'll make a lot better time without me."

Annabel patted Craig on the shoulder and said, "Thanks. You'll be perfectly safe here with Julio."

"Does he speak the Cuna language?" Craig asked

"A little," Annabel said, "and most of the Cuna villagers speak Spanish."

Minus one member, the team walked toward the small stream which they planned to follow to their destination. Once outside of the cleared space around Paya, the trail became uneven, and the jungle thickened. Carlos unsheathed his machete and took the lead, hacking at vines and giant leaves. Annabel, also with machete in hand, was next. At Annabel's instruction, Darien brought up the rear with Miriam directly in front of him, and Carly in the middle of the five-member caravan. Carlos kept up a steady pace, and they covered nearly three miles the first hour.

"Here's a good place to sit down for a short rest," Annabel said, pointing to the roots of a massive tree that had buckled and fallen across the river. "Watch out for ants and hornets."

Darien and Carly sat down on a moss-covered root that had popped up out of the ground and formed a comfortable bench. Their companions found similar places to sit. The temperature was around ninety degrees, and everyone was perspiring heavily. Five canteens appeared simultaneously.

"Drink plenty of water," Annabel said. "Then we'll refill our canteens from the river and treat them with chlorine tablets."

Five hours and three rest stops later, they came to a small grassy clearing beside the gurgling stream, and stopped for lunch. Everyone broke out dehydrated food, with beef jerky being Darien and Carly's choice. As they ate in near silence, Darien studied his companions. All were in top physical condition. He and Carly played basketball, Miriam worked out as if still in the military, and Annabel was superwoman. They were well able to keep pace with Carlos as he pressed forward.

"I feel sorry for Craig," Carly said.

"Me too," Darien said, "but he would have slowed us down, even before he got hurt. Maybe his injury was a blessing in disguise. We're making great time."

"At this pace, we'll reach our destination well before nightfall," Annabel said.

Annabel's prediction turned out to be true. Two more rest stops and considerable machete work later, the weary hikers arrived at Escondido an hour before sunset. Darien, feeling an indescribable mixture of emotions, studied the village where he was born. It was similar to Paya, but had more of a *lost-in-time* look about it. It was truly the end of the line, a cul-de-sac surrounded on three sides by steep hills and enormous vine-draped trees on the other side. Several open-sided huts near the stream were vacant and tumbling down, and the village seemed to be on its last legs. A flock of multi-colored parakeets appeared high over the village and circled around in a shifting kaleidoscopic pattern. They screeched loudly as the visitors approached. Immediately, a small group of villagers appeared and the parakeets fell silent. Apparently, the parakeets were Escondido's security system.

Annabel engaged in a rapid-fire conversation with several people who appeared to be village leaders. This time, the discourse was in Spanish and was punctuated by hand-waving, head-nodding, and pointing. While talking with Annabel, the villagers glanced at Darien repeatedly, making him a little uncomfortable. When the first round of dialog ended, Annabel turned toward the Americans and said, "Escondido was a hide-out for injured revolutionaries during the uprising, and several babies were born here at that time, just as the missionaries indicated."

"Did a midwife deliver the babies?" Darin asked.

"Not a midwife," Annabel said. "A *curandera*—a witch doctor."

Darien's eyes widened. "Is she still here?"

After speaking with the village leaders again, Annabel said, "She's still here but is very old and near death. She sleeps all the time."

"Can we see her?" Darien asked anxiously.

Annabel made another inquiry and then turned back to Darien and shook her head. "Not tonight," she said. "She's sleeping, and they won't wake her under any circumstances. They've invited us to use the abandoned houses near the river and will let us know when she wakes up tomorrow morning."

Darien let out a sigh.

The night was the longest that Darien could remember. He glanced at his watch again and again. It was moving in slow motion, if at all. Upon finally falling asleep, he dreamed that he was standing beside the curandera's bed as a priest gave her last rites. The priest was Michael Overton. The nightmare recurred every time he dozed off, and each time, he woke up sweating.

Eventually, it began to get lighter.

Escondido came alive with less fanfare than Paya but just as early. As Darien and his companions ate instant oatmeal by the light of a small LED lantern, he resolved to see the witch doctor early in the day, no matter what it took. He didn't want to break ranks with his team but knew the village leaders wouldn't let five strangers barge into the old woman's quarters together. Maybe Annabel could talk her way in with him as her companion. That seemed like a workable plan, and he suggested it.

"Let's try that first," Annabel said, nodding.

Everyone agreed. By the time they finished breakfast, it was light.

Annabel looked at Darien. "Ready?"

"Absolutely."

As Darien and Annabel started along a trail leading toward the main village, two men stepped out of the shadows and blocked their path. They began talking rapidly in Spanish. When Annabel answered, Darien realized the Spanish they were speaking was quite different from what he'd studied in school. Though he could understand almost nothing, he was impressed by Annabel's rhetorical style. Her voice was silky smooth, yet laced with overtones of strong persuasion. And it was working. The expression on the two men's faces changed slowly as she spoke.

"*Pasen,*" one of the men said, motioning. Darien knew the man had said *come in* or *come on*. Annabel had done it again.

Following the two men, they walked past several open-sided huts and came to a gravel walkway with lattice-work running along one side and over the top. The bamboo lattice was covered in fragrant white-flowered vines—a pergola in the middle of the jungle. The walkway led to a hut with three closed sides. Although Darien didn't know much about jungle village protocol, it was obvious that Escondido held their curandera in high esteem. He hadn't seen any other houses with one wall, much less three.

While one man stood guard outside the hut, the other led Darien and Annabel inside and pointed to a corpse-like figure lying supine on a low bed. *"La Señora Adivina,"* he said, after which he retreated to join his companion waiting outside. A young woman sat on a short stool beside the bed, slowly waving a palm branch back and forth above the elderly woman's head. A coconut shell containing a dark liquid set on a table near the bed, and a talisman collection hung on the wall above it.

The eager duo moved to the bedside of the comatose woman. Annabel spoke briefly with the woman holding the palm branch and then turned to Darien and said, "She says that Señora Adivina usually wakes up about this time in the morning, drinks her meal, and goes back to sleep."

Darien leaned over and studied Adivina's wrinkled face, fearing that she had died during the night. After a few anxious moments, she took a shallow breath and her eyelids moved almost imperceptibly. Seeing that she was still alive, Darien let out a sigh of relief. He had no doubt that he was looking at the woman who'd delivered him. DARPA's investigation and the missionaries' records aligned so well that no other scenario made sense. There was some fulfillment in finding her and possibly much more to be garnered when she woke up. Hopefully, she would remember the delivery of twin boys twenty-three years ago, a lot to hope for, yet Darien was optimistic.

Adivina opened her eyes slowly and looked around. After completing her survey of the room, her eyes came to rest on Darien and she stared steadily at him without blinking. Darien and Annabel waited breathlessly to see what the curandera would say upon seeing two strangers in her room.

With her eyes fixed on Darien, Adivina's pale thin lips moved for the first time. "Are you the one?" she whispered in English.

Darien was shocked to hear Adivina speak English, and doubly-shocked by the cryptic question indicating that she was expecting him. He was determined to get as much information as possible before the curandera went back to sleep or died before his eyes. This was a *now or never* moment.

Darien leaned closer to the frail woman. "What do you mean, Madam Adivina?"

"Years ago, I delivered twins right here in this room," Adivina said, her faltering voice barely audible. "Are you a twin?"

"I'm certain that I am."

"Then you're the chosen one," she said, gasping for breath.

"Chosen for what?"

"To lead our village."

"I don't understand."

"Due to the war, I had you moved to safety," Adivina said, straining to speak, "but I prophesied that you would return some day and become our leader."

"I didn't come here to be your leader," Darien said, shaking his head in disbelief. "I came looking for my twin brother. What happened to him?"

Adivina stared at Darien a moment before saying, "Your twin was a girl."

"What?"

"Your twin was a girl," Adivina repeated. "A very different kind of girl."

"How was she different?"

Straining intensely, Adivina raised her head and shoulders off the bed and pointed to her eyes. "One eye was light, the other was dark," she said. After speaking, she closed her eyes and fell back on the pillow. A few seconds later, she let out a gurgling sound, which Darien realized was a death rattle.

Briskly, Annabel stepped to the bedside and felt Adivina's pulse. "*Nada*," she said in the direction of Adivina's attendant. The woman made the sign of the cross, spoke a rapid phrase in Spanish, and joined the two men waiting outside.

Annabel turned to Darien and said, "She told me Adivina had prophesied that she would not die until the chosen one returned."

Icy fingers grabbed Darien's spine, not because he'd been called the *chosen one* and had witnessed the death of the woman who'd delivered him, but because her last sentence revealed a startling fact.

Rachel was his twin sister.

"Let's tell the others," Annabel said, turning away from the bed.

The team convened in the still-empty cantina and began to discuss the curandera's revelation.

"This is a fantastic discovery," Carly said after hearing Darien's stunning report. "It proves the Alamogordo connection is real. On the other hand, it seems to destroy the idea of ESP in mirror image twins."

"Maybe we weren't totally off base," Miriam said. "Do you know what *semi-identical* twins are?"

After a brief pause, Darien said, "I'm not sure."

"Me either," Carly said, shaking her head.

"Semi-identical twins are of the opposite sex," Miriam said. "They're the result of a highly-improbable anomaly in which one twin gets a Y chromosome from his father and nearly all other chromosomes from his mother. The Y results in him being a male. The female twin, of course, has only X chromosomes, mostly from her mother. They're incredibly rare. Less than a half-dozen pairs of twins have been documented as semi-identical over the last hundred years."

"Wow!" Carly said. "How'd you know that?"

"I was a biology major before switching to psychology," Miriam said. "Now . . . let's pack up and head for Yaviza. We got what we came for."

Less than forty-eight hours after their discovery in Escondido, they were back in the Wi-Fi Café in Yaviza, which seemed fairly plush compared to the places they'd eaten the past few days. Everyone had sweated off several pounds during the excursion, and they were loading up on Denise's tasty *arroz con pollo* and fried plantains. Darien was finishing his second Diet Coke and considering a third. The return trip had been easy, partly because most of it was downstream, but also because Annabel had taken a group of greenhorns and molded them into a fairly competent jungle survival team. All four of the Americans had fallen in love with Annabel and were urging her to apply for a professorship at NM State. They assured her that she would be a shoo-in. She said she'd think about it.

Thirty minutes earlier, when they entered the café, a texting frenzy had commenced. Darien texted Rachel and his three best friends. Carly texted Garth and Hope. Craig and Miriam texted their department heads. Craig texted a brief report to Michael Overton, but the *Delivered* tag did not appear below the message on his iTab. He glanced at the screen repeatedly while eating chicken and rice.

"I don't understand this," Craig said. "Every text I've sent to Overton previously was delivered immediately, although he didn't read some of them for several hours. This seems to indicate that his computer is off line. I can't imagine that."

Everyone offered a guess as to what was going on with DARPA. The opinions were all over the board. This time, however, the level of concern had dropped considerably. With the information they'd learned the past few days, NM State would be able to proceed without DARPA, if need be. Dr. Sheldon Leonard had indicated as much immediately after receiving copies of Craig and Miriam's texts. Leonard informed them that he would instruct NM State's HR Department to create a temporary job for Rachel in order to compensate her for her time.

A few minutes after texting Rachel, Darien's iTab gave a ringtone indicating that she was texting him. The text said:

Dear Twin Brother,

I'm preparing to leave California immediately and will be waiting for you in our trailer house when you get there. I just talked to April and Ashley and told them our bizarre semi-identical twin story. They both claim that they knew we were twins all along.

Love, Rachel

He showed Rachel's text to the team. Everyone was happy to shelve the mirror image twin concept and go to one much more rare, semi-identical twins. They were convinced they'd found the Holy Grail of ESP, and at long last, would decipher an extraterrestrial message.

CHAPTER 32

Three days after leaving Escondido, the team arrived at El Paso International Airport at 10:30 p.m. A four-hour delay in Mexico City had made it a long day, but everyone was in high spirits, including Craig, who was still limping from his sprained ankle. In order to travel with carry-on luggage only, they'd shipped most of their gear directly to Alamogordo from Panama City. As a result, they cleared customs quickly and headed for a Shipley's donut shop in the food court. After the long flight, they were craving sweets.

Since it was late, upon reaching the donut shop, they ordered coffee and pastries to go. With treats in one hand, and luggage in the other, they followed the *Ground Transportation* signs to the passenger pickup area. When they left the building, a blast of arctic air greeted them, accompanied by a flurry of sleet and snow, quite a chilling experience after more than a week in the jungle. Fortunately, a university robo-bus was waiting at the curb, and they got in quickly.

During the ride to Alamogordo, while enjoying coffee and donuts, they discussed various aspects of the anticipated ESP tests with Rachel and Darien linked by helmet antennas. At this point, the university was going it alone; DARPA had moved to the sidelines again. Michael Overton was unreachable. He hadn't answered any of Dr. Leonard's recent texts, emails, or phone calls; nor had he acknowledged receipt of Craig's final text from Yaviza. However, recent information out of Washington provided a clue as to why Overton had gone incommunicado. A drama of epic proportions was unfolding in the Capitol, and the DARPA agent had likely taken his station as Rex Horn's armor bearer.

The current NatGov chaos revolved around Project Mayflower. The space ship was now complete, but the estimated cost of terraforming Mars had skyrocketed so much that congress had voted not to fund it. The decision to withhold funding left NatGov with a gigantic spaceship in the New Mexico desert with no mission on the docket. Congress was discussing the possibility of selling Mayflower. Some of Rex Horn's base had defected, and nobody could begin to predict what would happen next. Coincidentally, the Mayflower controversy had pushed the M13 Contact Study to the back burner. It was hard to believe that SETI was no longer making headlines. For the first time in the history of the world, it now seemed possible that a 25,000-year old extraterrestrial message might be deciphered soon.

Even so, Washington had lost interest.

About an hour after leaving El Paso, the bus reached Alamogordo. Both Craig and Miriam got off at a small apartment complex near the campus, leaving Darien and Carly alone together for the first time in over a week. Knowing how much things had changed between him and Carly during the trip, Darien had looked forward to this moment for days. More importantly, he was sure that Carly realized her relationship with Garth was winding down. Maybe she would tell Garth tonight, maybe tomorrow. Whatever the case, Darien believed it would be soon. As the robo-bus approached the campus, he felt a strong urge to take Carly in his arms, but knowing it would create an awkward situation for her, he held back.

Darien and Carly looked at each other. Even in the dim light, her eyes were bright and expressive. Darien sensed that she wanted to say something difficult to put in words. He waited for her to speak. Instead, she leaned toward him and punched him on the shoulder with her fist, breaking the spell.

"Okay, *Chosen One*," she said. "What are we going to do next."

"About what?"

"About the project, of course."

"I was hoping you were talking about us—you and me."

"No," Carly said, shaking her head.

Moments later, they got off the bus at a stop near the library. Darien wasn't in the mood to retrieve his car from the parking lot and head for Orogrande. What a downer that would be. He vowed not to let the evening end so abruptly.

"I'll walk you to your dorm," Darien said as they picked up their bags and exited the bus.

Carly hesitated a split second and said, "Okay, but you'd better be a good boy."

Darien laughed softly but didn't reply.

They walked past the library and turned onto the dimly-lit sidewalk that led to the dorms. After a few steps, Darien shifted his bag to his right hand and looped his left arm around Carly's right. She bent her arm, also making a loop, and they walked arm in arm until they reached the front door of the dorm.

"I really enjoyed our jungle adventure together," Carly said, uncoupling her arm.

"Me too," Darien said. "It was the greatest adventure I've ever had."

When they stopped before the dorm entrance, Carly turned toward Darien, giving him the opportunity he'd anticipated for a long time. He caught her by both arms, drew her toward him and attempted to kiss her, but she turned her head and leaned back.

"Don't, Darien," she said, her eyes glistening in the pale light.

Darien released Carly. They looked at each other a moment, and Darien said, "Can I come in for a little while?"

"No, you can't."

"Why not?"

"Because it wouldn't be right."

Darien knew Carly's reluctance was based on her long-term loyalty to Garth. Even though that relationship was frayed to the breaking point, Carly would have to tell

Garth face to face before getting involved with anyone else. That's the way she was, and Darien knew it. He'd been foolish to think otherwise. He admired that kind of loyalty, but wished she would waive it tonight.

"Just for a few minutes," he said. "What could that hurt?"

"It might spoil everything."

"Everything?"

"Yes, everything."

Darien let out a long sigh and moved a step away from Carly. "Okay. Maybe you're right."

"Thank you, Darien. See you tomorrow," Carly said, turning toward the front door of the dorm.

"Good night, Carly."

CHAPTER 33

At nine o'clock the following morning, with Rachel as an added member, the team assembled in the Astronomy Research Lab. They'd already stopped by a biology lab where a quick DNA test confirmed what they already knew—Darien and Rachel were the rarest of twins, semi-identical. Still, a major question loomed. Did being unique twins really mean anything in the psychology universe? Or was that just wishful thinking? Soon they would find out, hopefully today.

Craig took the seat in front of the control station monitor, and the others sat down on lab stools in a semicircle behind him. Carly helped Rachel don her helmet-antenna, after which turned to Darien and held both hands high in the air, showing tightly-crossed fingers.

"Keep them crossed," Darien said. "A good-luck charm might help." He was thankful that Carly was acting completely normal after the *attempted-kiss* incident last night. He hoped he was acting normal, as well.

Pushing the memory of last night aside as best he could, Darien adjusted his helmet and Craig instructed the main computer to link the two helmets. A sharp pinging sound indicated a successful Bluetooth linkup, and Craig signaled the computer to start playing the recording which contained the repetitive counting pattern.

A few seconds later, the first audible thump sounded, and a brief flash of red light illuminated Darien's eyelids from within, as he'd anticipated. The orange and yellow flashes, followed by the rainbow of bright colors, were also identical to his original observations, as was the low rumbling sound following the thumps. He watched as the fragments of light clumped together to form vague patterns, but at that point, he sensed something wrong and opened his eyes. The monitor showed exactly what he'd just seen on the inside of his eyelids.

"Look!" Carly said. "It just got clearer."

Rachel opened her eyes, and the monitor went blank.

"What's going on?" Darien said.

"When you broke the link by opening your eyes, the images from Rachel got much clearer," Carly said.

"I was expecting just the opposite," Darien said.

"Likewise," Carly said, looking perplexed.

Darien turned toward Craig and Miriam to get their input. They confirmed that they'd seen the same thing Carly had. Following a brief round-table discussion, they decided to record Rachel and Darien's observations separately and then mix the two recordings, replaying them as one. The consensus of opinion was that this approach would be similar to producing a 3D movie by using two projectors simultaneously. Moreover, with individual recordings, they could play one at a constant speed and vary the speed of the other in order to synchronize them precisely. Craig programmed the computer to record separate inputs from each helmet, and instructed it to begin.

Ten minutes later, the second round of tests ended in failure.

The images—no matter how Craig juggled the playback speed—never got any clearer. Darien looked around and saw frustration on every face in the room, even Carly's. This was the first time he'd seen a hint of doubt in her eyes. He felt it too. They'd run the gamut on twins including identical, mirror image, and semi-identical—and had struck out three times in a row.

"Okay," Craig said, "let's put on our thinking caps. We're missing something."

Darien took off his helmet, rested it on his knee, and tapped it lightly. After pondering the situation a moment, he said, "I wonder if these things are linked in parallel or in series? And would that make a difference?"

"Good question," Craig said, turning to face Darien. "Let's find out." Darien examined the helmet closely and discovered an almost-invisible plate just above the left ear After failing to lift the plate with his fingernails, he gave it a hard push. It clicked and popped open to reveal a small control panel with several buttons and a lone toggle switch. The switch controlled the link-up choices—parallel or series.

"It's parallel, "Darien said. "I'll change it."

"That'll double the voltage," Craig said. "Maybe it will help."

Darien and Rachel put the helmets back on, and Craig replayed the recordings. The change was obvious immediately. The pictures were twice as bright, but blurred even worse than before. So much for parallel vs series.

Within the next few minutes, Darien and Craig came up with several mathematical gyrations to try—multiplying and dividing the M13 signals by pi, prime numbers, and other improbable numbers. Knowing that this approach was totally foreign to Carly and Rachel—maybe Miriam, as well—Darien explained the process as Craig programmed the computer to perform the operations. While talking, he sensed that Rachel and Miriam were satisfied with his short explanation, but Carly wasn't and was about to ask a question for which he didn't have a good answer.

As if on cue, Carly said, "Why manipulate signals already in the same frequency as brainwaves?"

Darien offered a vague response, "Possibly, it might shed some new light on the problem."

As it turned out, it didn't.

At four o'clock in the afternoon, with no new information gleaned for their efforts, the team was preparing to leave the lab, when a piercing *general alert* ringtone sounded over the university PA system.

"Attention please," a computerized voice said. "Please stand by for an important message from Karen Haldon, President Horn's Press Secretary. Attention . . . please stand by . . . "

Everyone turned to the console and watched the main monitor come to life with an image of Haldon standing beside a desk in the press room with the American Flag at her back. She took a deep breath and paused as the camera zoomed in.

"Good evening, my fellow Americans," Haldon said. "Thank you for tuning in. President Horn has instructed me to make a brief announcement regarding the Mayflower Project. As you already know, due to escalating costs, congress has cancelled further funding of the effort to terraform Mars. When that happened, NatGov was left with a newly-completed spaceship without a mission. Since this news hit the airwaves, several countries and privately-owned corporations have expressed a strong interest in purchasing Mayflower, and in effect, they conducted a bidding war. The bids are now at such a high level that NatGov can recover the entire cost and even make a profit on this venture. In a surprise move, President Horn agreed with the RADS that selling the Mayflower is in the best interest of our country."

Haldon paused, as if letting tension build for a dramatic finale. Everyone waited in silence, and Darien quickly deduced that China had won the bidding war.

Haldon cleared her throat and continued, "Mr. Horn is pleased to announce that NatGov has agreed to sell Mayflower to Parabellum.org."

"Parabellum!" Darien echoed, realizing that his conspiracy-theory link between the computer company and the Mayflower Project was solidifying.

"Why does an AI community need a spaceship?" Carly asked.

A variety of theories were proffered simultaneously. The Press Secretary faded to black, and as soon as her image disappeared, a blitz of news bulletins flooded the monitor. Banner-style headlines covered the entire screen, except for the right edge where a stack of mini-screens exploded into view. Every small screen showed an agitated newscaster vying for attention. Most stations showed pictures of the Mayflower in various stages of construction, and all Alphabet News affiliates showed videos of protesters carrying anti-Horn placards.

Craig switched back and forth between several TV channels in an attempt to get the perspective from stations controlled the by major political parties, as well as those which were non-affiliated. The broadcasts were essentially identical. Over the next half hour, one main fact emerged— the sale of Mayflower to Parabellum had been finalized only hours before Horn's Press Secretary announced it. Little else was known. After reporting that lone fact, all networks launched into a steady stream of speculation, editorializing, and rehashing, plus the promise of a more comprehensive report at six o'clock.

Darien and his cohorts decided to remain in the lab while waiting for the six o'clock news broadcast. Miriam ordered Chinese food, and they went back to work on the ESP mystery. Two more hours of testing and retesting failed to shed a single ray of light on the big question. Why were the combined images worse than a single image?

At 6:00 p.m., Alphabet News' Chief Washington Correspondent, preempted all local stations with updated information. Looking rather smug (*we've got Horn this time!*), the small grey-haired man gave his report:

"According to reliable sources, Chinese billionaires were the driving force behind both Project Mayflower and Parabellum.org a long time before Rex Horn took office. Parabellum's surreptitious activities attracted the attention of concerned public servants, and they quickly developed a dossier on the organization. Essentially, Parabellum ran interference to detract attention from the illegal activities being conducted by Rex Horn and his Asian accomplices. Our news sources in China report that Parabellum consists of two distinct parts; one, an AI community set up to deceive the public; the other, a massive undercover financial operation. While the AI community created a diversion, the financial branch remained underground and deployed their plan to buy the Mayflower spaceship after the terraforming cost escalated out of control, as they knew it would.

"Alphabet News has uncovered a connection between the Mayflower Project and Parabellum. Several Chinese billionaires involved in the purchase of Mayflower are major stockholders in corporations manufacturing the equipment needed for terraforming Mars; therefore, it is believed that they were part of a cost escalation scheme. When congress killed the project, Parabellum.org bought Mayflower to use in a search for Planet X, as they'd planned to do from the beginning. It has been reported that the Chinese have engaged former astronaut, Glenn Overton, to captain the Mayflower during this venture. Overton is Rex Horn's distant cousin and the brother of Michael Overton, the point man for the M13 Contact Study.

"It is also known that these Chinese billionaires had done business with Rex Horn's Florida empire long before he became President illegally. Reliable sources report that Republican and Democrat leaders are planning to conduct an investigation into the newly-discovered Parabellum-Mayflower connection and will use their findings to impeach Rex Horn in the near future."

The TV station went to a commercial break, and the research team sat in shock for a brief moment.

Darien broke the silence. "Forget about DARPA. The M13 study is entirely in our hands."

"We can do it," Carly said, her voice laced with strong determination.

CHAPTER 34

After the long day of fruitless lab work, Carly was getting ready for dinner with Garth. As she brushed her hair, she reflected on the events of the last few days, especially thinking about the moment when Darien had attempted to kiss her. She was almost sorry she didn't let him, especially since she was visualizing him in her future for a very long time. Still, it wouldn't have been right to Garth since their relationship was still ongoing, albeit just barely.

Coupled with the change in her feelings toward Darien, Carly realized how much her feelings for Garth had changed, as well. It wasn't that she'd fallen out of love with him. Instead, she gradually realized that she'd never loved him in the romantic sense. Moreover, if Garth would examine his emotions honestly, he might reach the same conclusion. True, they'd voiced their love for each other over the years. But what did the word *love* mean to them at the time? Looking back, it was nothing more than an expression of strong friendship. Friends often expressed their love for each other, and she and Garth had become best friends at a very early age, a time when they needed each other. It would be ridiculous to claim that it was love at first sight since they were only nine years old when they met. Carly realized something else—when she entered the competitive phase in her life, Garth began to defer to her on nearly everything, and she became his security blanket. The possibilities that she and Garth would ever marry had fallen to zero. She would tell him tonight.

She and Garth had texted back and forth a couple of times during the day, but due to his unusual schedule, they hadn't seen each other since her return from Panama. This morning, he reported for work at 6:00 a.m. and had gotten off at 6:00 p.m. Today was his last day on Project Mayflower; it was ready to be turned over to Parabellum.org. Garth would return to Galveston soon, and Carly was sure that he was assuming they would continue a long-distance relationship. *Assuming* was over for Carly, and so was the idea of a long-distance relationship. She wished she could tell him by text, but she couldn't send a cold-hearted *Dear John* letter to a good man like Garth. She owed him more than that for his loyalty and friendship over the years. She had to tell him face to face, no matter how difficult it was.

While trying to figure out a good way to say what had to be said, Carly's iTab pinged, and Garth's picture materialized onscreen. She touched the picture and a text reading *I'm here* appeared.

Immediately, Carly texted *I'll be there in a minute.* Dreading the next few minutes, she left her room and went down the hallway leading to the foyer. She turned a corner to see Garth waiting just inside the front door.

"Welcome back," Garth said, reaching toward Carly as she approached.

She stopped short, and Garth took a step toward her. Carly held up one hand and said, "There's something we need to talk about."

"Can we talk about it on the way to Sammie's?"

"Let's go in there," Carly said motioning toward a small sitting room adjoining the foyer. She walked into the room and turned to face Garth, who was a step behind her.

"What's so important that we have to talk about it this instant?" Garth asked, apprehension showing in his voice.

"Our relationship."

"What about it?"

"It isn't working," Carly said, "and I want to end it." Her throat was so tight she could barely speak.

"I don't understand," Garth said, not seeming to grasp the finality of Carly's statement. "I came out here because you're here."

"That makes it harder to say what I have to say," Carly said. "You're the best friend I've ever had, but I don't love you, and don't think you really love me."

"I've told you that I do," Garth said, looking puzzled.

"And you've said the same thing to me."

"We started saying those words when we were children and kept repeating them as we grew up."

"I meant it."

"Did you?" Carly said. "You never even asked me to go steady, much less marry you."

"I thought we had a mutual understanding."

"A mutual understanding is no way to plan for the future."

"Carly, you made all of the choices for us," Garth said, frustration evident in his tone. "You chose whether we went to the beach alone or with friends, what games we played, after school plans, weekend plans . . . everything. I always went along."

Carly realized that, without knowing it, Garth had stated the main problem with their relationship. *He always went along.* She was strong willed and passionate, and the man she married would need to possess those character traits as well. In spite of her competitive nature, Carly didn't expect to *make all of the choices* in her marriage. Instead, she wanted an equal partnership, something that could never happen with Garth.

"We can't continue this way," she said, shaking her head slowly.

"What are you saying?"

"I've already said it, Garth. I don't love you."

"But . . . " Garth began. He stopped and stared at Carly. She saw a tear form in the corner of his eye and felt one roll down her cheek.

"You'll be okay," Carly said, patting his shoulder.

"I'll be leaving for Galveston soon."

"I know."

After a brief pause, Garth said, "So this is goodbye?"

"Yes, it is."

"Will you text me occasionally?"

"Of course, I will. You're my BFF," Carly said, putting her arms around Garth. They hugged briefly, and then Carly turned and ran down the hall.

CHAPTER 35

Darien was awakened by clicking and whirring noises from the kitchen, an indication that Rachel was preparing breakfast—a healthy breakfast, as she would say. The day she moved into the trailer, Rachel stocked the refrigerator and pantry with a variety of organic, gluten free, non-GMO, antibiotic-free groceries. Her breakfast specialty was an egg-white omelet with a bit of smoked turkey bacon, oatmeal, almond milk, and decaffeinated coffee. Darien didn't have any objection to that kind of food. It was quite tasty; however, a couple of hours after eating it, he always felt hungry again. A healthy breakfast didn't have the staying power of sausage biscuits and strong coffee. Food preferences aside, he was happy that his sister was back in New Mexico. Maybe she would stay.

When Darien came into the dining area, Rachel was peering into the refrigerator. Dressed in matching pink pajamas, robe, and house shoes, she looked like a model for a sleepwear commercial. "I was going to get everything ready and let you sleep a while before cooking it," she said. "You needed a chance to catch up on your rest."

Rubbing sleep from his eyes, Darien sat down at the tiny breakfast table near the kitchen. "I'm fine," he said. "Besides, I couldn't sleep late. I'm meeting Carly at eight-thirty, and we're going to figure out what to try next."

"Let's have coffee before I finish making breakfast," Rachel said, as she poured two cups of dark steaming liquid. She placed the cups on the table, sat down across from Darien, and added almond milk to her cup. As Darien sipped his black coffee, he sensed Rachel's eyes on him and looked up to see a quizzical expression on her face.

"What's on your mind?" he asked.

"I just thought of something that could be important."

"Lay it on me."

"You're left-brained and I'm right brained. Would that make a difference?"

"That's the missing clue!" Darien said, almost dropping his cup. "It has to be."

"Do you really think so?"

"It makes sense to me."

"What do we do next?" Rachel asked.

Darien thought a few seconds and said, "We need to get our helmets modified to pick up signals from the right side of your brain and the left side of mine. That might filter out the interference that makes the images fuzzy. "

"Can we do it today?"

"We'll try," Darien said. "Craig should be able to get somebody in the physics department to make the changes. I'll text him right now."

At 2:00 p.m., the team gathered in the astronomy research lab. Darien and the three women were waiting when Craig entered the room carrying two newly-modified helmets in an Amazon-Kroger shopping bag. At Craig's request, a physics professor had lined one-half of each helmet with lead-apron material obtained from a local dentist. Since the material blocked X-rays, it would block brainwaves. Whether that would help or not remained to be seen.

Excitement filled the air, but was tempered by a measure of caution. Once again, Darien felt that success was imminent but remembered the times he'd felt the same way before, only to come up empty handed. He was not accustomed to repeated failures, nor was Carly. They had to solve this riddle to get the *failure monkey* off their backs.

Darien and Rachel picked up the helmets. Darien weighed the device in his hands and put it on. Rachel slipped the helmet over her short-cropped hair, as Carly stood by to help if need be. With Craig at the control station, the others took their positions directly behind him as they'd done before. Quiet fell over the room.

"I'm linking your helmets together," Craig said, as he signaled the computer.

"No matter what you see, don't open your eyes,"

Miriam said. "Craig will record everything, and we can replay it as many times as we want to."

"Starting the message," Craig said.

In the last two minutes, Darien's confidence had surged tremendously. With eyes closed tightly, he waited for the 1-2-3 countdown to form the first image on the inside of his eyelids. He anticipated that the first number would be a preview of something spectacular to follow.

When the first thump sounded, the interior of Darien's eyelids displayed an explosion of bright red light. A real explosion this time, not merely the blurred flash of light he'd observed previously. This image looked like a giant rocket exploding high overhead at a fireworks finale and casting flaming red streamers into the air. He watched as the streamers floated downward, slowly fading out of existence.

"Wow!" Darien said, concentrating to keep his eyes closed.

His teammates echoed his exclamation.

Just as Darien expected, Number 2 consisted of two orange rockets exploding simultaneously, and seconds later, Number 3 completed the fireworks finale with three yellow rockets. The countdown was over, and now if all went as expected, an extraterrestrial message would be seen by human beings for the first time in history.

Everyone in the room gasped when a scene began to materialize.

As Darien watched intently, multicolored points of barely-visible light appeared and coalesced into an ephemeral image of a planet that looked much like Earth as viewed from the Moon. The distant world displayed polar ice caps, pale blue oceans, white clouds, and land masses. Every visible feature was remarkably earthlike, except the land masses which formed an archipelago of large islands along the equator. The significance of the photo was undeniable. It proved that planets other than Earth were inhabited; moreover, it proved that the inhabitants were highly intelligent beings. Otherwise, they couldn't have taken a picture of their planet from space and transmitted it to Earth. If this picture was, indeed, from the M13 region, it had been transmitted more than 25,000 years ago, and a civilization so advanced back then would be beyond imagining today.

The planet faded to nothingness and was replaced by a dim photo of unfamiliar starry skies. Darien studied the stars, trying to assemble them into the constellations he'd studied nearly all of his life. His efforts were in vain. Apparently, this photo was sent to show how the heavens looked from the planet shown in the first picture. One thing was certain—that planet was a great distance from Earth. Darien couldn't make out a single constellation.

The scene changed, and a gasp went throughout the lab.

The third picture showed four people standing in front of a bush covered with golden leaves. The people were totally human in appearance and seemed to be posing for a photograph. Apparently, they were a family—a man and a woman, plus a boy and a girl in their early teens. All wore identical clothes—pale blue one-piece uniforms. With tan skin and brown hair, the four people were as much alike as the clothes they wore. Unblinking, Darien watched as the camera slowly zoomed in until it showed only four faces. He was astonished at what he saw.

Both the woman and the girl had one dark eye and one light eye.

The scene ended abruptly, and a dozen questions were asked simultaneously, with no one expecting to get a worthwhile answer. After a brief discussion, they decided to watch a few minutes of the second and third messages to see if they were identical to the first. They were, so Craig paused the recording, and the analysis began.

Everyone agreed that the first two pictures were meant to prove the existence of a habitable planet and show its location. As for the third picture, there was no consensus of opinion. Craig reversed the playback and stopped on the close-up of the four faces.

As Darien studied the picture, he deduced what the first comment would likely be and who would make it.

"The young people in this picture look a lot like Darien and Rachel," Carly said.

"Probably just like they looked eight or ten years ago," Miriam said.

"We're from Panama," Darien said. "Not this mystery planet."

"I wonder why they didn't send some pictures of roads, homes, and cities?" Rachel said. "That would have given us a little insight into their society and lifestyle."

"They omitted those things on purpose," Craig said, "but I don't have any idea why."

"It's difficult to analyze people who lived 25,000 years ago," Miriam said, "but I have a theory. I think the first two pictures showed scenes which would still be essentially the same today as when the pictures were taken. Likely, that wouldn't be the case for cities and homes, so the transmitter of this message didn't think such pictures would be of any value."

"How does the third picture fit into that theory?" Carly said. "The people—would they be the same or different?"

"A good question," Miriam said. "One that we can't answer, I'm afraid."

"Maybe they're pointing out a change that's about to occur in *Homo sapiens*," Darien said. "One that started happening on their own world 25,000 years ago."

"Are you saying we should expect an increase in the birth rate of mirror image and semi-identical twins?" Miriam said.

"Maybe Alamogordo will have an increase in a couple of weeks," Darien said, thinking of the Rhodes and Carson twins who were due soon. For the next forty-five minutes, the conversation centered on the family in the third picture. Everyone agreed that their discussion was pure speculation, and that it was not likely they'd ever figure out what the sender of the picture was trying to indicate.

Still, Darien thought his guess was as good as any. Maybe he and Rachel were early examples of a mutation in the human genome that would become commonplace in the future. But why would that kind of information be worth transmitting a distance of 25,000 light years? It was anybody's guess. Maybe it had something to do with ESP.

"This almost fits my Alamogordo connection theory," Carly said in Darien's direction, a twinkle lighting her eyes.

"Except for one thing," Darien said. "This picture was taken a long way from Alamogordo—a *really* long way."

Everyone laughed, ending the seriousness of the discussion.

"Okay," Craig said, "we may as well wrap it up for today. Early tomorrow, I'll send a report to our department heads and to Dr. Leonard. I'm sure Leonard will send a copy to DARPA, as he should. Dealing with Michael Overton was plenty frustrating; however, this project would have been impossible without his help."

Darien pondered the significance of the discovery, knowing that it would be in the headlines for weeks, perhaps months. The news would send shockwaves throughout the civilized world, particularly the scientific and religious communities—both might have to rethink some of their dogma. Rex Horn would get kudos for funding the M13 Contact Study after many had said it was a foolhardy project. No doubt, he would pat himself on the back, but that was okay. There was plenty of credit to go around. NM State would get its share, as would everyone who worked on the project. It would be a while before life returned to normal, if it ever did.

As everyone began to gather up their personal belongings in preparation to leave, Rachel leaned toward Darien. "I'll take the robo-bus back to Orogrande," she whispered. "Hang around here as long as you like."

"Thank you. I'll do that."

Rachel headed for the door with Miriam at her side. They were so synchronized that Darien knew they were carrying out a plan they'd devised earlier. He glanced at Craig, wondering if he was also part of the plan.

On cue, Craig took a step toward the door, looked back at Darien and said, "Be sure to lock the lab door when you leave."

The sound of footsteps in the hallway faded away. Darien turned and looked at Carly, who remained seated in front of the enigmatic picture. She smiled in a way that was different from any smile he'd seen on her lips previously. At that instant, he knew she'd broken up with Garth the night before. She would tell him, but it wasn't necessary. Her smile said it all. An odd feeling came over Darien. He'd just participated in one of the most amazing discoveries in history, but it didn't hold the long-term significance in his life that this moment did. Carly meant more to him than any science project ever could, and he would tell her so before the evening ended.

He approached Carly. She remained seated and looked up at him, her blue eyes wide and expressive. Although they'd met over six months ago beside her crashed car, this was another kind of *first meeting* for them. They looked at each other in silence for a brief moment.

"Darien Segura at your service," he said, just as he'd said at their first meeting.

"Thank you for rescuing me . . . *again*," Carly said, standing and extending her arms toward Darien. Time stood still as they clung to each other. Darien felt Carly's body tremble in his arms and knew this moment meant as much to her as it did to him. He relaxed his embrace just enough to find her lips, and they kissed again and again as a 25,000-year old picture stared at them.

350

THE END

ABOUT THE AUTHOR
DON JOHNSTON

I was born in East Texas a long time ago and grew up with a sister and a brother. Upon completing high school, I joined the U.S. Air Force and served three years as a jungle survival instructor in Panama. Following my military service, I enrolled in Stephen F. Austin State University and got married. After getting my degree in biology and chemistry, we moved to Houston where our only child, a son, was born.

During the early years of my career, I wrote numerous technical articles and reports but no fiction until recently. Upon retirement, I became interested in writing science fiction. My first sci-fi novel, *The Dar Lumbre Chronicles*, was published in 2018. It took me about two years to write *The Alamogordo Connection*. At that rate, you can look for the third one, *The Photosynthesis Gene* in 2022.

My wife of 53 years died of cancer in 2014, leaving me the patriarch of a small family—a son, a daughter-in-law, three grandchildren, and two great grandchildren. My family is my pride and joy.

I have been a member of Sugar Land Baptist Church for over 20 years and have led Bible study classes throughout that time.

UPDATE:
My next sci-fi novel, which is now in progress,
is called *By Means of Peace*
instead of *The Photosynthesis Gene.*